P9-CDI-632

mirage

mirage

SOMAIYA DAUD

FLATIRON
BOOKS
NEW YORK

This is a work of fiction. All of the characters, organizations, and events portrayed in this novel are either products of the author's imagination or are used fictitiously.

MIRAGE. Copyright © 2018 by Sumayyah Daud and Alloy Entertainment. All rights reserved. Printed in the United States of America. For information, address Flatiron Books, 175 Fifth Avenue, New York, N.Y. 10010.

www.flatironbooks.com

Designed by Anna Gorovoy

Endpapers, map, and illustrations by Rhys Davies

The Library of Congress Cataloging-in-Publication Data is available upon request.

ISBN 978-1-250-12642-9 (hardcover)
ISBN 978-1-250-31535-9 (international, sold outside the
U.S., subject to rights availability)
ISBN 978-1-250-31534-2 (signed edition)
ISBN 978-1-250-12644-3 (ebook)

Our books may be purchased in bulk for promotional, educational, or business use. Please contact your local bookseller or the Macmillan Corporate and Premium Sales Department at 1-800-221-7945, extension 5442, or by email at MacmillanSpecialMarkets@macmillan.com.

First Edition: August 2018
First International Edition: August 2018

10 9 8 7 6 5 4 3 2 1

12957891

To my mother, without whom this dream would never have been realized

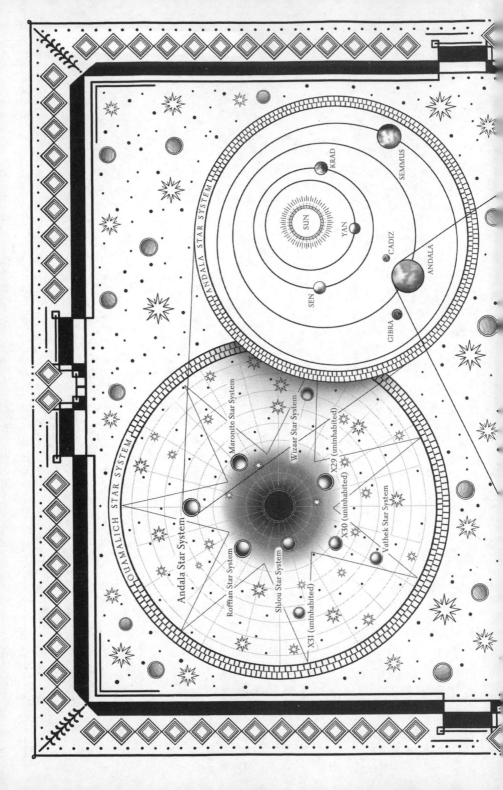

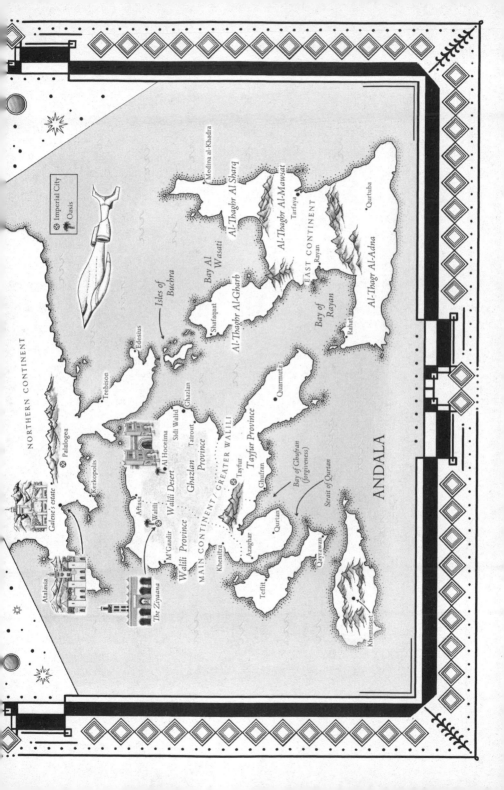

PROLOGUE

He is the only one of his family without the daan. They say this makes him ideal; no traditional markings on his face to identify him should he die. No way to trace him back to his family. He is young, not yet fifteen, too young for the daan ceremony. This is what she says to him when she comes to choose him.

That he is young and that he is skilled and that he is steady. This, she says, is all that matters.

He does not feel young. He feels hungry, the sort of hungry that gnaws at him day and night, until it is so much his companion he does not know how to live without it. He feels hard, because he knows how to take a beating, how to fall just so when a guard hits him with a baton. He feels angry, so angry, the sort of anger that does not need fuel.

He is invisible in a sea of invisible faces.

The crowd is silent, but then the crowds at these events are always silent. They are solemn. Too solemn. The nobles sit on velvet cushions behind gold rope, but those who stand, who look up at the podium waiting for her to appear, they are the poor. The hungry. The weak. They are here because they must be here.

The makhzen titter among themselves like jeweled birds, gowns glittering in the sunlight, scabbards flashing as men shift in the uncomfortable summer air. It is a wonder any of them are Andalaan; they all look Vathek now. They have accepted Vathek rule. They would not dress so, not if they were still Andalaan.

He thinks of his younger sister as he moves through the crowd. Dead for two summers now, her stomach bloated from hunger. His father, long gone, too weak to support them, to stay.

He has one sister left, and a brother besides, and his mother. All to be taken care of after this. She'd sworn. A husband for Dunya. A cottage away from the city for them all, with access to grain and a garden, and mayhap even livestock. Away from everything they know, but a chance for a new life.

His hands sweat. He has trained for this, he is ready, but he has never taken a life.

The blood never dies, he remembers. The blood never forgets.

This is for a higher purpose—one more important than his life, more important than any life. These things must be done, he thinks. In the name of Andala. In the name of freedom.

He marvels, as she climbs the steps to the dais, that one who looks so much like his kin is capable of causing such terror. He has heard the stories, knows that these things are often twisted through the telling. But his life, the lives of his siblings and neighbors, bear witness to some truth. The occupation is cruel. Its heirs crueler still.

The sun flashes against the silver metal of his blaster. He lifts it, aims, fires.

Twice.

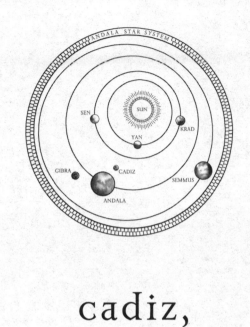

cadiz,
a moon of andala

MIZAAL GALAXY,
OUAMALICH SYSTEM

I

On a small moon orbiting a large planet, in a small farmhouse in a small village, there was a box, and in this box was a feather.

The box was old, its wood worn of any trace of design or paint. It smelled of saffron and cinnamon, sharp and sweet. Along with the feather there sat an old signet ring, a red bloom preserved in resin, and a strip of green velvet cloth, frayed around the edges.

I crept into my parents' room often when I was small, always to peek into the box. And its mystique only increased in my eyes when my mother began to hide it from me. The feather fascinated me. A five-year-old had no use for a ring or a flower or fabric. But the feather of a magical, extinct bird? Like all things from the old order, it called to me.

The feather was black, made up of a hundred dark, jewel

shades. When I held it up to the light it rippled with blues and greens and reds, like magic reacting to some unseen hand, roiling to the surface. It had belonged to a tesleet bird, my mother said, birds once thought to be messengers of Dihya.

When Dihya wanted to give you a sign He slipped the feather into your hand. When He wanted to command you to a calling, to take action, He sent the bird itself. It was a holy and high calling, and not to be taken lightly. War, pilgrimage, the fate of nations: this was what the tesleet called a person for.

My grandfather had received a tesleet, though my mother never talked about why or even who he was.

"A foolhardy man who died grieving all he did not accomplish," she'd said to me once.

I stared into the old box, my eyes unfocused, my gaze turned inward. The sun would set soon, and I didn't have time to waste by staring at an old feather. But it called to me as it had when I was a little girl, and my thumb swept over its curve, back and forth, without thinking.

There were no tesleet left on Cadiz or our mother planet, Andala. Like many things from my mother's childhood, they had left, or been spent, or were extinguished. All we had were relics, traces of what once was and would likely never be again.

I jumped when my mother cleared her throat in the doorway.

"Amani," was all she said, one eyebrow raised.

It was too late to hide the box, and I could not keep down the surge of guilt for having snooped in my parents' room just to bring it out again.

But my mother said nothing, only smiled and came forward, hand outstretched.

"Did . . . did your father give you the feather?" I asked at last, and handed the box over.

Her eyes widened a little. For a moment, I thought she wouldn't answer.

"No," she said softly, closing the box's lid. "I found it a little while after the bird had gone. In a moment of weakness in some shrubbery."

I rarely saw my mother look as she did now, soft and wistful, as if remembering a kinder time. She'd survived two wars: the civil war, and then the Vathek invasion and following occupation. She was hard, with a spine of steel, unbendable, unbindable, and unbreakable.

"What was your moment of weakness?" I asked. I wouldn't get a response. I never did.

But my mother surprised me and smiled. "I was running from love," she said. "Your father, to be specific. I saw in my own heart my father's capacity to lose himself in another person, and it frightened me."

My mouth dropped to her amusement. I knew my parents loved each other; it was obvious to anyone who watched them, despite their differences. But I'd never heard my mother say as much, and to hear her admit it of her own free will—

"What are you doing here, at any rate? You're meant to be getting ready for tonight."

I didn't know how to explain it, so I just shook my head and shrugged.

"I don't know. I just—I love it. I suppose I wanted to see it again."

She came forward and tilted my chin up. I was full grown, and my mother still towered over me by a full head. The backs of her fingers brushed over my cheek, tracing the lines where I would receive my daan—sharp geometric tattoos that would mark my first step into adulthood. I hoped they looked as hers did: stark and powerful, letting the whole world know who she was and where she was from in a single glance.

"I know this week has been difficult," she said at last. "More difficult than most. But it will pass, as they all do."

I bit my tongue rather than say what I thought. We shouldn't have to wait for them to pass. They should never be in the first place. We had suffered not only the burning of our fields this week, but the increased presence of the Vath.

But my mother surprised me into silence a second time, and set the box back in my hand.

"I think this should pass to you," she said, her voice soft again. "Hope is a younger girl's game, and you find more comfort in it than I do."

I opened then closed my mouth, wordless with shock.

"Really?" I said at last.

She smiled again. "Really," she repeated and kissed my forehead. "Perhaps Dihya will send you a second feather, and you shall have your own sign in these trying times."

My mother left me alone in her room, the box still clasped to my chest. After a moment I moved to hide the box away in my room, lest she come up the stairs and change her mind.

The sun was setting truly now, and I hurried to put it away, and find my things. Khadija would be waiting, and I hated to hear her skewer me for my tardiness. Outside, the village was quiet. Normally, around now, I could hear the quiet singing of field workers as they made their way back to the village, and the ringing of the end of day bell. The march of boots, the cries of sellers hawking their wares in our small village square, dogs and goats crying out; all those sounds were absent.

There were no fields left, not after the fire the Imperial Garda set last week. Rebels—or, more likely, starving thieves—had taken shelter in one of the gate houses. Rather than looking through each one, the Garda had set fire to the fields. We'd heard the rebels screaming from as far away as the village square. Now, with the fields gone, the village was counting down the weeks till winter, and the famine that was sure to follow.

What would I want my own feather, my own sign, for? In the wake of this—of life—I had no need for a sign. I wanted something else, something more tangible and immediate. I wanted the world.

The Vath were not settlers in our nebula—they'd lived on their planet, Vaxor, mostly peacefully and in accordance with galactic laws. But they'd poisoned their own atmosphere, and were forced to relocate to an orbiting moon. A stopgap measure, with an exploding population and a lack of resources. Some said it was inevitable that they chose to expand to other systems.

There were moments when I glimpsed the world as it was before the occupation of the Vath. When my mother or father spoke without thinking, or a village aunt said "when I was young," or a man sang an old song I'd never heard before. The bones of our old ways of life were there, barely traceable, and I wanted them back. I wanted all of us to remember what we'd been, how strong we were. And endurance was strength, to be sure, but even a rock wore away to nothing if asked to endure enough rain.

I could want until I was dead and nothing would come to pass. Wanting never solved anything.

I tucked the box away with a sigh, found my cloak and shoes, and made my way downstairs.

In the kitchen, I packed away the last of the food we were taking with us. We were celebrating my majority night. I and twelve other girls had finally come of age, and as was our way, the whole village would travel to one of the abandoned kasbahs. There, we would receive our daan and become adults in the eyes of the village, and follow with dinner and dancing to celebrate.

"Amani."

I turned to see Husnain, my brother, standing in the doorway. My parents had three children: Aziz, the eldest of us, more than ten years my senior. Myself, the youngest, and Husnain, fifteen months older than I was. I might have relied on Aziz for wisdom, but Husnain was one half of me, a twin despite the months between us. He had all the foolhardiness and fire of a second son, rarely tempered but for me.

"I brought something for you," he said when I sat down.

I grinned and held out my hands. "Give it to me."

"Close your eyes."

I did so, but kept my hands outstretched. A moment later a wide, thin object was folded into my hands. I peeked before he told me I could open my eyes and nearly dropped the sheaf of papers as if they were on fire.

"Amani!"

"Is that—?"

Almost a month ago we'd journeyed to Cadiza Prime, the capital city on our moon, to pick up supplies for the small farm my brothers and father kept on our tiny sliver of land. I'd wandered through the open market, and shoved in the back of a bookstall was an aging sheaf of papers—Massinite poetry. It was too expensive to even consider purchasing it, and besides, most religious poetry was outlawed. It had been used too often as a rallying point for the rebels during the occupation.

Massinia was the prophetess of our religion and though we all loved her, I loved her above all other things in our faith. Just as we had songs in her name, so too had an entire tradition of poetry sprung up venerating her life and accomplishments. I loved such poetry above all else, and hungered for it despite the risk of being caught with it. My hands shook as I reached for the collection.

"You took a huge risk—"

"Never you mind the risk," he said. "It belongs to you now, and that's all that matters."

I was afraid to grin or to touch them. Mine! I could hardly believe it. I'd never owned a collection of poetry before.

"Oh, for Dihya's sake," he laughed, and undid the twine around the pages before setting them in my hands. I would have to transcribe them to holosheets or put them in a database or some such. There was no telling if they'd survive the weather here, or if I would lose them or any number of things that could happen. And I would have to hide them, or risk them being confiscated by the magistrates.

Our souls will return home, we will return, the first poem read. *We will set our feet in the rose of the citadel.*

I closed my eyes, seeing the imagined citadel, no doubt now turned to dust. I could imagine the pain of the writer, could feel it like a bruise on my heart as my soul looked over its shoulder, leaving something treasured behind. I knew what it was like to trace a quickly fading memory in my mind, to watch it fade with every remembering until it was nothing but a feeling, a well-worn groove you could walk but not recall. The pain on the page was palpable—everyone had a citadel. The city of their birth, turned to rubble, family long gone, buried in an unmarked grave, all of it unreachable except through death.

And this, poetry like this, was all we had to preserve our stories, our music, our history.

"Thank you," I said at last, and threw my arms around him. "You have no idea—"

"I have some," he laughed, and kissed my forehead. "You are my favorite person in the the world, Amani. I'm glad to give you this. Dihya, are you crying?"

"No!" But I could feel the lump in my throat, ready to dissolve into tears at any minute. I'd been so afraid, so nervous about tonight. And in the end, it was a night of joy. I would step into adulthood not just with family and friends, but now with a treasure that would comfort me on nights too difficult to comprehend.

"Maybe now you'll write some of your own," he said, a little softer.

I snorted out a laugh. I was a poor poet, to be sure, and in a world where poetry didn't pay, I'd had no chance to improve.

"You're good," he insisted. "You should write more."

I flushed, hungry for praise. Husnain was the only person who'd ever read my poetry, but I knew he spoke out of the loyalty born between us and not out of any knowledge of what my skill looked like compared to true poets.

"In another world," I said, and clutched the poetry to my chest. *Our souls will return home, we will return.*

I looked up, and smiled at my brother, the other half of my heart. "But not this one. In this one, these poems are enough."

⤚ 2 ⤙

Most of our village had set out on the road before sunset, but Aziz, Husnain, and I set out later with a few other families. I'd tucked Husnain's gift in my pocket, reluctant to part with such a treasure so quickly.

"Amani, don't ruin the parchment before you even have a chance to read it," Husnain murmured, low enough that Aziz couldn't hear.

I glanced over at our eldest brother. Aziz had been born before the occupation. Of the three of us, he was the only one who remembered our lives before then, who'd known our parents outside the shadow. The years under the occupation had forged our brother into steel. He was wise, perhaps wise beyond his years, and reliable. While Husnain jumped before he looked, Aziz watched, relentlessly, as if in the end all the world would surrender its secrets to him. Including his unruly younger siblings.

"I won't," I promised Husnain, fighting a grin.

"I should have waited until after to give it to you," he said, but his grin matched mine.

Outside, the air was eerily silent but for the sound of Vathek probes whizzing overhead, their bright white beams scanning the ground. To our left was the orchard, scorched earth, the air above tinted red with the fumes of the extinguishing canisters the Vath had lobbed at it at the height of the fire.

A few weeks ago there had been three fields side by side—pomegranates and olives to the west, and a field of roses we grew to sell and make perfume facing the east. Now the west orchards looked like a graveyard with a hundred spindly, ashen arms reaching toward a red sky. The rose bushes and the trellises had gone, vaporized in the blaze of the fire. Smoke and red fumes from the extinguishing canisters still rose into the sky. Nothing would grow there now, not for years. I made myself look away. There was nothing to be gained by worrying at the bruise, nothing to be gained from wondering how we would feed ourselves this coming winter, or what we would do for work in the spring.

The fire had been set, they claimed, because of "rebels" in the area. But the only proof the Garda had that rebels sheltered among us was a phrase people said had been carved into the gatehouse.

The blood never dies. The blood never forgets.

It was a phrase from the Book of Dihya—most people believed it was a testament to our endurance and survival. But there were some who believed it meant Massinia might return—that her blood would call her back to the world in one form or another. Whichever meaning you took, rebels had been using it as a rallying cry, now more than ever.

Now the small village of shacks and houses on its outskirts, along with the gatehouses, were rubble. The people who'd lived there, those who'd survived, huddled together around a fire. I felt a pang of guilt looking at them—my family didn't have much, but our home was still intact, and we wouldn't go hungry as they would.

I reached into my bag, my hand settling on the bread I'd made that morning for the majority night celebrations. My mother and I had spent hours at the village oven, along with all the other girls celebrating their majority night, making enough bread for the whole village. We had so much—I could afford to spare a few loaves.

Aziz laid a hand on my shoulder and shook his head, as if he knew what I'd planned.

"They're being watched," he said, voice low. "The Garda believe the rebels hide among them."

I swallowed down my anger and looked away.

"It's difficult," he said and squeezed my shoulder. "But think of our parents, Amani. What would they do if you were dragged off for giving bread to a rebel?"

I glared at the ground. I knew he was right. He, more than I, knew the cost of being thought one of the rebels. At last, I drew my hand from my bag and let him guide me away, leaving the fields and the refugees behind.

Eventually we reached the old kasbah far beyond the limits of the village. The kasbah was an old building, now one rundown mansion among many rundown houses, overgrown with palm and fig trees. Once it might have belonged to a prosperous family, but was now the refuge of farmers and villagers on nights like this. Lights shined out of broken windows, and threads of music rose into the air, mixing with the sound of wind and wildlife. Suspended over the kasbah in the night sky was our mother planet, Andala, hanging like an overripe orange fruit. With such a sight it was easy to forget everything: our poverty, the rule of the Vath, the specter of loss that hovered over our parents every day.

We arrived with enough time to set up the courtyard and get dressed. All the girls who were coming of age tonight had private rooms in the kasbah for them to make use of before the festivities. The chatter of friends rose and fell as my mother helped me into the qaftan and jewelry.

I felt a frisson of nerves when I looked at myself in the mirror. My mother and I looked eerily alike. She was taller, but we had the same brown skin, the same sharp cheekbones and sharper chin. Her hair was as thick and curling as mine, and seemed to sprout from a too high point on her forehead just like me.

But there the similarities ended. My mother had survived too many horrors to count, and never spoke of them. But her strength was obvious to anyone who bothered to look. She was unshakeable, and I— I wasn't like my mother. I liked to think I was brave and filled with conviction, but I was untested. I'd suffered none of what she had, and to think of it made me shudder inside. How could I face adulthood, how could I expect to be a woman, when I couldn't even bring myself to imagine my mother's trials? How would I face my own?

"Becoming an adult is frightening," my mother said, as if she'd read my mind. "You are smart to be wary. It means you will approach things slowly, and hopefully with wisdom."

She urged me down into a seat in front of the mirror and got to work. There was not an abundance of jewelry to thread through my hair—we didn't have the money for that. But my parents' families had been botanists before the occupation, and my mother had managed to hold on to some of her own jewelry. Her sisters' jewelry, too, had passed to my mother after they were all killed.

This was all I had of our past—my mother's jewelry, and traditions like tonight. Soon, I would have my daan—a small inheritance, but a powerful one.

There was a chained circlet I had loved since I was a child, old and made of iron pieces shaped like doors, each hung with deep red stones. The majority night qaftan was my mother's, white with red embroidery all along the bodice and down the center.

My mother smiled at me again in the mirror as she secured a pair of earrings studded with red stones. "There," she said, and took hold of my chin to tilt my head a little. "You could be queen."

The courtyard where the festivities were being held had been strung with lights. It was an old building on the very outskirts of the moon's capital city. My spirit rose with the sound of music. The date palms were wound with bright, golden light, and caught on gold jewelry and embroidery on women's qaftans, and bent off metal teapots and tea glasses. There were low tables and cushions spread through the length of the courtyard, and the entire village had made it to the celebration tonight. At the north end was a small stage where a band played, their lead singer crooning an old Kushaila song.

The trees were full of lights, and there were lanterns bobbing merrily in the fountain in the center of the courtyard. It babbled, undercutting the chatter of the many families celebrating in the tight space. Eleven other girls and their mothers pressed into the entrance beside me, waiting. Eyes turned toward us until nearly all the room was staring. Husnain caught my eye and winked at me, and my nerves eased slightly. Next to me, my mother squeezed my hand.

All of a sudden, the drums stopped, and conversation tapered off. For a long minute, there was nothing but the sound of the water flowing in the fountain. Someone blew on a horn, a deep, sonorous note, and then the drums began again.

We stepped out, one by one, to the sound of our fathers calling our names.

"Amani, daughter of Moulouda and Tariq."

The purpose of the majority night wasn't celebration alone. Our true step into adulthood was receiving our daan. The thirteen of us sat on cushions in the middle of the courtyard and waited.

The tattoo artist was an elderly woman, her daan turned green with age and folded into the wrinkles of her face. But her hands were steady and I remained still, despite the sting of her needle. In the old days I would have bled and it would have taken weeks for the marks to heal—now I would only need a few hours before they settled permanently on my face.

A crown for Dihya and Massinia took shape, overlapping diamonds curving over my forehead. Sharp lines for my lineage—my grandfather had claimed descent from Massinia herself, and though neither I nor my mother believed him, her markings went on my left cheek. On my right were my parents' hopes for me—happiness, health, a good soul, a long life. I don't know how long I sat while the old woman worked, but at last she pulled back and smiled.

"Baraka," she murmured. Blessings.

And just like that, I slipped from childhood into adulthood.

My mother came to stand beside me, her face as stoic as ever, and squeezed my shoulder. Our daan were similar, almost mirror images of one another, and in that moment I hoped I could live up to them, live up to her. I lay my hand over hers and squeezed. With these marks I could face anything in the future. I hoped they would guide me toward joy and love instead of sorrow.

I followed the string of other girls and their mothers through the courtyard, weaving through the families watching, laughing, ululating in congratulations, to the banquet table at the north end. Those of us being celebrated tonight were to sit in the front of the banquet table with the elder women of our village and our mothers. My heart eased as I listened to them chatter. There was nowhere else on our small moon like these gatherings. Most of us were Kushaila, the oldest tribe group on Andala; my family was not the only one whose ancestors stretched back to the ter-raforming of our moon. The air rang with the sound of our mother tongue instead of Vathekaar, and our music and our laughter. For a moment I could imagine this was decades before the shadow of the Vath fell over our moon and conquered our planet and its system.

It was hard not to get swept away in the merriment, and when the songstress stepped down and a band took her place the tempo of music picked up. I loved the girls on either side of me—Khadija and Farah were my closest friends in the world. I'd grown up alongside Khadija. Our parents' farmed plots of land beside one another, our mothers had walked to the orchards to pick fruit before either of us were born, before the Vath had ever darkened our skies. We'd taken our first steps together, learned to read to-gether, and gone to school together. When it came time to register under the Vathek census, we'd gone to the capital city on Cadiz together.

It took no time at all for them both to grab my hands and pull me to my feet, and then we were off, dancing and laughing, sing-ing along with the music.

I don't know how long we danced, eventually joined by friends, laughing and chatting. The air was thick with incense smoke, the sharp sweet scent of cooked plums over lamb. The world seemed to glitter and waver as torchlight caught on sequins and false jewels. I know what we all must have looked like, had been a girl too young to partake only a year earlier. I had yearned to be part of the group, and now I was one of them: happy, crying out, fall-ing over one another while we giggled.

For a while, I forgot my worries. Rebels, famine, poverty—none of these things mattered tonight.

And then the doors to the kasbah slammed open and the music stopped.

3

It felt like long minutes, though it could not have been more than a few seconds, for my body to catch up. To notice the music gone, the laughter thinned, and joy replaced by fear.

When you are raised in a place like Cadiz, in a time like ours, you learned the signs. The absolute silence, followed by the soft, near imperceptible click of metal against stone. The soft whir of gears just loud enough to announce itself. The Vath rarely sent men to our homes. When they did—well. The cruelty of men knew few bounds. So there was some relief when the first body through the door was an Imperial droid, chrome and silver, its body etched in cruel, sharp designs.

Imperial droids weren't built to look human. They were always at least a foot taller than average, their skeletons built out of excelsior and adamant, glowing silver wherever they were. Their faces were blank except for the white line of light that passed for eyes, and their heads were framed by a fan of solid metal. The original designer chose to shape their torsos so that they resembled ribcages, without any of the flesh within or without so that the droid went from monster-like to full monster. They weren't shaped to be sent into war, but then you didn't need much more than two hundred pounds of metal to cow and brutalize civilians.

And the droids were very effective at that.

The violence Vathek men did was easily counterbalanced by a droid's calculations of life versus death. And to them, Andalaan life was always an acceptable loss.

The droids—there were eight altogether—had still not spoken. They gathered in the doorway, silent as death and just as unflinching.

I jumped when a hand wrapped around my arm, but it was only my brother, a grim look on his face.

"Aziz and our parents?" I asked, keeping my voice low.

"In the back," he said.

"All girls aged fourteen to twenty are to line up on the west wall," one of the droids announced. Its voice echoed as if a person inside it were speaking through a metal tube.

Ice crawled up my spine, but I stepped forward.

"Don't," Husnain said, tightening his grip.

"Don't be foolish," I hissed. "What if they scan the group and find I've lied? Better I go now and get it over with."

I understood Husnain's fear. We'd all heard the stories—the Vath appeared without warning when too many of us gathered in one place. They feared rebellion, and where groups of people met, or so the wisdom went, rebellion quickly followed. My father limped now because he'd attended such a gathering in his youth, and there were people from our village—among them my father's elder brother—who'd disappeared from such gatherings and never appeared again. I was too young to remember very much, but I knew the tightly wound fear that sat in your chest as the droids stormed a building. Knew the wail of a woman who knew she was about to become a widow.

Husnain looked ready to argue, his face screwed up in anger. "They can't do this."

The Vath never intruded on a majority night, something so clearly meant to celebrate the young in our villages when there were so few of us.

Or at least, they never had before.

"They are doing it," I reminded him, and tapped his hand. "Let me go and it will be done soon enough. I promise."

Husnain seemed to battle with himself for a moment, and then he released me. We were close because in so many ways we were alike. But here, we differed. I understood the world we lived in, the consequences of dissent. Husnain . . . he disliked bowing to anyone, and to the unjust most of all. He would risk his life in the name of an idea rather than live to fight another day.

The room divided silently, girls in the age range specified to the left, and everyone else to the right. The smoke had taken an oppressive turn, so that it was no longer the dream-like fog. Something thicker, like a funeral shroud.

Two of the droids came toward us and split us, one to the front of the line and another to the back. Khadija stood beside me, and we held hands, our fingers crushing each other's.

Her newly inked daan glistened on her cheeks and forehead in the firelight—she looked, I thought, more beautiful than she ever had before. After sharing so much of our lives together, it was right that we'd had our majority night at the same time. She gave my hand another squeeze, her face as clear of emotion as mine was. There was no training for how to face Vathek droids, but we all knew. No fear, no emotion, nothing that would focus their gaze on you.

Every few seconds there was a louder whir from both droids, and then a sharp beep before they moved on to the next girl. It was only when they were a few girls away from us that I realized what they were doing—a wide, green beam scanned a girl's face, and then the beep cleared her. They were trying to identify someone.

I heard Aziz's voice, warning me about the search for rebels, about appearing to aid those suspected. There were no rebels here—just a farming village that would starve in the coming months with our livelihood now smoldering. My gaze scanned the room. There was Adil the perfume maker with his lame foot. Ibn Hazm, the last member of a family prosperous before the war. Khadija's parents, farmers and fruit pickers. Everyone here knew the cost of sedition. No one here would risk it.

I remained still, my eyes fixed on a flickering torch as a droid stepped in front of me, leaned forward, and scanned my face.

The noise it made after was not the sharp beep, but a clang, like an alarm. It remained bent in front of me, frozen as if in confusion.

My heart raced—difference was never good. Different meant the Vath knocking down your door in the middle of the night.

I eyed the door they had come through, and then the back exit. I wouldn't make it if I ran, and likely I would cost friends their lives as they came after me.

"Take her," one of the droids said.

"No!" Husnain pushed his way through the crowd and came to stand beside me. "You can't have her."

Without warning, the droid raised a phaser from its hip and aimed it at his forehead. Droids never set their phasers to stun. It would have been easy to be frozen, to scream, to give in. But though Husnain was older than me, I had always taken care of him.

"Stop," I said, my voice firm, and stepped in front of him. "There is no cause for violence."

"You will come with us," the droid said, not lowering the phaser.

I buried shaking hands in the folds of my skirt and shook my head. "Tell me what you want with me. I have rights." Even as I spoke them, the words rang hollow. I didn't have rights, of course. I was a poor girl, from an oft-forgotten moon. And I was young, without any of the marks on my record that would have signaled me as loyal to the Vath.

"You will come with us willingly or by force," it said.

"I will not," I repeated. Too late I realized my foolishness. You did not stand up to the Vath, and you certainly didn't stand up to their droids, who would not be swayed by pleas or displays of emotion. I could feel the blood beat at the tips of my fingers, could almost hear the gears turning inside the droid as it turned its attention from me to Khadija.

There was no sound as the phaser went off, only the sudden weakening of Khadija's grip around my hand. Her fingers slipped from mine, and her body fell forward. Her knees hit the ground, and then she fell sideways, eyes open in shock.

She'd worn a white gown embroidered in green to the ceremony. Red bloomed on her shoulder like a flower, staining the green lines crisscrossing her arms. Her arms splayed out, crooked and doll-like, in a pose I'd never seen before. Her black hair was loose tonight and it fanned around her head, dark as midnight, complete as a death shroud in hiding her from me.

Now, I could not breathe. Now, my heart pounded too fast and my lungs shrunk and my body went numb.

The blood from her arm pooled beneath her.

Her mother screamed first and then chaos broke. I couldn't think, and I only moved because Husnain tugged me back and forced me into a run. He wasn't fast enough—no one had ever outrun the Vath.

A metal hand wrapped around my left arm, and I came to a jarring stop.

"No!" I screamed, but it was too late. The droid took hold of my brother's shoulder, and then threw him back nearly halfway across the courtyard. He landed against the fountain with a bloodcurdling sound, then fell to the floor, unmoving.

"Let me go!" I struggled against my captor, trying to make it to my brother as everyone else ran screaming, gathering children, trying to escape. I couldn't see the rest of my family. Only Husnain, lying motionless on his front, ignored by everyone else.

I screamed again, but the droids dragged me away even as I struggled, kicking and screaming, crying out my brother's name.

"Husnain!" My throat felt raw from screaming, but he didn't get up, and no one stopped to help him.

I was dragged up a ramp to a Vathek cruiser, and my last sight of home was the kasbah, lit by the spark of fire a droid had set just as the doors shut.

the ziyaana,
andala

4

I'd dreamed forever of leaving Cadiz, of visiting other star systems in our galaxy. But I'd never thought I would be taken against my will. I was dragged through the building, pulled onto a ship, silent and numb, then finally deposited in a holding cell.

My whole body hurt, and my vision was blurry with unshed tears. Below me was a glass floor, clouded and turning gray. But I could see where I was—and where I was going.

Cadiz was gone and left behind and Andala, our mother planet, grew minute by minute in my view. I wrapped my arms around myself, trying to contain the panic inside me. I prayed fervently that my family had survived the burning of the kasbah. I didn't understand—couldn't understand why they had taken me, or to what end.

I could not escape the image of Husnain lying motionless in the stampede, nor the sound his body made when it hit stone. Was he alright? Were my parents? Had Aziz gotten them out? And what of Khadija? The phaser's blast was aimed at her arm, not her chest; meant to threaten, not kill. But she had lost a lot of blood . . . My mind went round and round, from one thought to the next, trying to make sense of it, hoping for the best.

The Vath had gotten me, for whatever reason. My family and the village were safe.

They were safe.

At least, that was what I repeated to myself. I didn't know if I believed it.

Hours passed as I stared at the steadily approaching planet. At last, the ship slowed, and streams of cloud and mist engulfed my view. The floor melted back to its imposing steel gray color as the door hissed open. I stiffened, waiting for the Imperial droid to step through. Instead, an Andalaan girl waited in the doorway. She was dressed as I was, in a long qaftan, its sleeves tightened at the wrist, with a short sleeveless jacket. She drew a veil down from her red hair and freckled, brown face.

"Amani?"

I said nothing.

"I am Tala," she said. "You should follow me."

She led me from the ship into a courtyard that seemed to stretch on forever, filled with soft, pruned grass waving gently in the breeze. I gaped at the sights around me as Tala led me down an avenue of polished marble toward the garden's center. Arches striped in red and white lined the walkway, and their alabaster columns gleamed. Birdsong filled the air, and jewel-toned peacocks strutted across the pathway. The air was fragrant with the scent of incense and flowers, and warmer than I'd ever felt it on Cadiz.

I would have been a fool not to recognize the pavilions and mosaics that marked where we were: the Ziyaana, Andala's imperial palace. For centuries it had been home to our own royalty, Andalaan kings and queens. It was the last place to fall in the occupation. Now the palace played host to the Vathek king and his new court.

"Can you tell me what I'm doing here?" I asked, willing my voice not to shake.

"Come," she said instead of answering my question. "The king's stewardess, Nadine, is waiting in the east wing—she's to be your mistress. Have a care with her—she is one of the High Vath."

I swallowed. If one of the High Vath was involved in the assault on the kasbah, then my end would be grim. They made up the upper echelons of our conquerors, rarely seen away from our capital, and almost never alone. Their class was marked by pale silver hair, and it made them easy to pick out among their kind.

"And after?"

She said nothing.

She led me down a set of stairs, and through a collection of airy chambers. A breeze wafted through, lifting gauzy curtains, revealing dark wood trellises, cushioned alcoves, and carved pillars. But it was silent—gone was the sound of birdsong and flowing water.

Eventually, we came upon another courtyard. There was little grass, and what shrubbery was around was potted and foreign. A fountain murmured in the center, and just to its left was a table, high off the ground. The Andalaan comfort and luxury had finally given way to sanitized Vathek splendor. No life, no warmth—only stone and water.

A woman with gleaming silver hair, the trademark of the High Vath, sat behind the table, a stack of tablets on one end, and a holoreader in front of her. Her features were sharp—sharp cheek-bones, sharp nose, and a thin mouth that seemed ill suited to smiling.

"Your Ladyship," Tala said in Vathekaar. "I've brought the girl."

Her Ladyship, Nadine, said nothing, and continued to work.

Tala stood perfectly still, as though this were routine to her. Minutes and then tens of minutes, and then what felt like hours ticked by. I struggled to stay standing, my nerves fraying as time wore on, my thoughts cycling through the stories I'd heard in ever rising panic.

Near the end of the war, our moon had been a protectorate held by one of the High Vath. The mountains ringing our valley sheltered some of the last rebels, and the High Vath had hunted them down systematically, making examples of them. I wasn't born, but the scars of his tenure had remained. Adil's maimed foot. The empty village two miles south of us. The village to the west with its sole Kushaila inhabitant and her daughter, silver haired and blue eyed.

"Do you speak Vathekaar?"

I nearly jumped at the sound of Nadine's voice. My mouth opened and closed as I tried to bring myself back to the present. "Yes."

"Where did you learn?"

"School," I said at last.

"How old are you?"

"Eighteen."

"Do you speak any other languages?"

"Kushaila," I whispered.

It had been our moon's common tongue before the Vathek occupation. Here in the capital it had been the royal language. Now, if one were caught speaking it, they risked the ire of whatever Vath was in their path. If a droid or a member of the Garda caught you, your chances of being beaten and thrown into jail were high. Galactic law meant they couldn't outlaw an indigenous language outright, and all of Andala's various populations took pride in their mother tongues. But the Vath seemed determined to beat our language out of all of us, and the Kushaila in particular, no matter the cost.

Nadine snorted in derision.

"Do you have any skills?"

I heard Husnain's voice, telling me to practice poetry. Saw my father bent over the plants in his greenhouse as he taught me how to cross breeds. My mother's face, red and sweating in the kitchen as she taught me to make bread.

I couldn't close my eyes—I couldn't show weakness. So I took each memory, folded it over and over again, and put it away.

I shook my head. None that would matter to her.

Nadine folded her hands on the table and leaned back as though she didn't believe me. I could not say if she took pleasure in her questioning, in seeing me so openly afraid, but it certainly seemed that way. When I didn't offer an answer, she said nothing, and the silence stretched between us.

"I suppose it doesn't matter," she said, and stood. "We will find out one way or another. Cover her face, Tala. The seamstress is coming."

Tala rushed to secure a veil across my features, and soon a seamstress hurried into the courtyard and began measuring me. I was to live then. The idea brought me no relief. Why should I need new clothes? Who was to see me in them? Why must my face be covered?

What did they want with me?

"See what Agron's schedule is like in the coming days," Nadine instructed Tala. "The ball season is approaching—he may be booked for weeks."

"Yes, Your Ladyship." Tala's face remained impassive, and she refused to meet my eyes.

"You may go. I will send for you when I'm ready for you to collect her."

Tala did not look at me as she walked out, the seamstress following soon after.

I stood alone in the courtyard as Nadine worked through a series of tablets and passed them on to the droid behind her. It had been early morning when I was summoned, but time crawled forward as I waited to be dismissed.

I was not dismissed.

The minutes stretched into hours, and the shadows in the courtyard stretched with them. I knew patience, was used to the backbreaking work of picking fruits in the orchard, which we often did from sunup to sundown. But before long my back and feet began to ache. I hadn't slept or eaten since the majority night celebration had come to an abrupt end, and I felt dizzy, disoriented by the veil that shielded my face and narrowed my field of vision.

And then all at once it seemed that even the whirring of the droid stopped. Nadine set her stylus down, then straightened up. I straightened along with her just as footsteps, quick and precise, echoed in the courtyard.

Nadine rose from her seat and swept past me.

"You will remain here," she said, clipped and sharp, and then disappeared behind the shrubbery at the other end of the courtyard.

"As ever," I heard, "it is a pleasure, Your Highness."

My heart thundered in my chest. I could hear them murmuring with each other—Nadine and one of the royal household.

There weren't very many members. The Vathek king, King Mathis, had only had one child with his Andalaan bride: Princess Maram, who was rumored to be as cruel and Vathek as her father, despite being half Kushaila. King Mathis's queen had died of illness during the Purge—the systematic extermination of the Salihis, the most powerful Andalaan family, who had resisted the Vathek takeover.

"Kneel," Nadine said from behind me.

I sank to my knees clumsily.

"Well, your work is quite cut out for you, isn't it?" a second voice said. It was cultured and sharp, as though the speaker were used to cutting people down with it.

I could feel her eyes burning holes into the back of my skull, and then the sound of swaying skirts and jewelry chiming as she made her way in a large circle around me. The bottom of her skirt was a dark red, embroidered and shot through with black. Hanging from the gold belt around her waist were several long, thin chains that swayed and hit against one another as she came into view.

My eyes met hers, and I made a sound that was both a sob and a laugh. Looking at the girl in front of me was like looking into a mirror: it was my mouth on her face, the same dark eyes as mine, though they were lined in kohl. The same chin and cheeks—though hers were fuller, rounded with wealth.

No one on Cadiz had seen an image of the princess, not for a long time—her father had kept her hidden away on Luna-Vaxor, the Vathek homeworld, out of danger and out of view. But now I knew that standing in front of me was Maram vak Mathis, Her Royal Highness, High Princess of the Vath.

And she looked exactly like me.

5

The princess stepped closer to me, the move easy and graceful, pulled off my veil, then slipped a hand beneath my chin. She looked like the queen she would one day be, standing over me, one hand twisted lazily into the folds of her opulent gown. Sunlight glinted off her gold belt and the rings she wore. We were the same, I thought, and yet not. She wore more wealth than I'd thought to see in my entire life. And where I still retained the scent of a village girl, the princess smelled of sweet oils and incense. Her chambers were likely scented with bukhoor, her hair washed in sweet-smelling soaps, her qaftans folded away with satin-wrapped rose resin.

It was foolish of me to look her in the eye—she was a princess, after all. But each of us seemed to be riveted by the other, and the longer we stared the more painful her grip around my face became. I struggled not to twist out of her grasp.

The princess, I'd heard, had been raised on the Vathek home-world after her mother's death, among her father's relatives. She was every inch the Vathek scion, or so the stories went, cruel to family and friend alike. She'd willingly impoverished cousins who'd displeased her. And when she returned to Andala, one of her Andalaan ladies-in-waiting emerged two weeks later with her face disfigured as punishment for speaking out of turn. Her hatred of her mother's people and her legacy was legendary. She neither spoke nor read Kushaila, and she regularly derided its use whenever someone used it in her hearing.

Young as she was, and though half of her belonged to us, we expected her to continue her father's reign in just his way when she came to power.

"Why do you suppose you are here and not at home?" the princess asked softly.

"I am here because I was brought here, taken from my home," I said, letting some of my anger seep into my voice.

Her grip tightened painfully against my cheeks, and I sucked in a sharp breath.

"Don't play," she said. "I am not in the mood."

"I don't know why I am here," I told her, though it wasn't entirely true. I did know, or thought I did. My mind raced with thoughts of situations where they could use me—a disposable farmer's daughter—in place of the princess. I thought once more of the droids storming our kasbah, scanning the faces of every girl in the village who was coming of age. It was no stroke of luck that they'd taken me. They'd been searching for me—for a mirror image of Maram—all along, probably all over Cadiz and every other moon in our system.

"I don't know, Your Highness," she corrected, and shook my chin angrily. "Say it."

"I don't know, Your Highness," I repeated, trying to match her tone.

"What a darling mimic you are," she said. "One could almost forgive you for looking so much like me."

"I didn't choose to look like you," I said softly.

Her expression changed from banked anger to something uglier, crueler. The air stretched and thinned between us, until she released my chin. She moved quickly, like a viper, and backhanded me with her ringed hand. Pain was quick and hot; it radiated over my cheekbone and down my jaw, spreading like wildfire, amplified by the bitter taste of copper inside my mouth. I turned my head back slowly and gripped my skirts as tight as I could.

When our eyes met a ghost of a smile came and then left her face. She looked almost satisfied, and that more than her anger terrified me.

"Nor did I," she said at last, her voice even. "And yet here we are—a baseborn girl and a future queen. Now, answer my question."

"I don't know, Your Highness," I repeated.

She curled her lip.

"Her Highness," Nadine said, "has been blessed with a spare."

"I am not a spare," I gritted out.

Her satisfaction grew and transformed into triumph. My stomach sank as I realized I'd stepped into the trap she'd laid for me.

"The Vathek have a story about a man named Alexius who angered their god," Maram began, her mouth curving into a lazy smile. "He was strung up on a mountaintop and fed to birds of prey. Every day they pecked him until he died," she continued, and began to circle me. "And every night god healed his body so that these same birds could feast again with the rising of the sun."

I tried to keep my breathing even and my eyes fixed on a spot on the floor. Whatever she had planned, I would not cower. She couldn't make me.

Maram whistled, a high-pitched, thin sound and lifted her right arm. For the first time I noticed the long leather glove she wore. The sound of wings beat against the air, drawing closer and closer.

To her credit, Maram did not flinch or waver when the roc alighted on her arm. The bird was half her height at least, and when it spread its wings for balance, they spanned as long as she was tall. Its talons and beak were bone white, a stark contrast to the near midnight black of its plumage. It regarded me with one eye, as dark as its feathers, unblinking and fixed on me as if I were prey.

I swallowed.

"Nadine used to tell me stories," Maram said. She stroked a spot against its chest, and it warbled, an eerie sound from so frightening a creature. "The roc used to be large enough to carry grown men off to feed their nestlings."

When I met her eyes her smile widened. Fear beat in me, louder than my heart, and drowned everything out. I did not jump when she lifted her arm up and the roc launched itself back into the air, but it didn't matter. Keeping my composure would not stop what I knew was coming next.

"You will learn a great many things in the Ziyaana," she said. Her smile was sweet now, nearly congenial. There was a dimple in her left cheek. "Here is your first lesson: do not presume to speak back to me."

She whistled two short, sharp bursts. The roc cast its shadow from high above as it circled the ceiling, gave out an angry cry, and dove with its wings tucked against its sides.

I could not stop the scream of terror that tore itself out of my throat.

I had seen feral hawks and the like on Cadiz, watched them take down prey and feast with a detached fascination. I had never allied myself with the prey, had never imagined I'd be on the receiving end of claws and beak and terror. You could not be anything like prey and survive our village or our moon.

The roc was silent as its claws slammed and then dug into my shoulders. They clenched, digging into flesh and bone, before it lifted me off my feet and dragged me back several feet. It was not large enough to lift me more than few inches off the ground, but when the earth disappeared from beneath my feet I screamed louder than before.

What little composure I'd had broke when it dropped me on my knees. My majority night gown was soaked through with blood already, and I felt the thick, slow crawl of blood coming out of the wounds. I hunched over on the ground, sobbing.

You learned a different sort of fear when you grew up in a village like mine. Fear of hunger. Fear of Imperial droids. Fear of the low hum that came with Imperial probes. But that fear taught you endurance—you could let its unwavering presence wear you down, or you could learn to stand up despite it.

But there was nothing like this. I'd never experienced the bone-shaking terror that a roc might wing around for a second chance at my flesh. Nor the fear associated with the soft click of slippers on a courtyard floor.

I forced myself to meet her gaze when Maram came to stand over me. This time I could not understand her expression. It was disorienting to look up at her, at myself, and not understand what the different tells I understood on my own face so well meant on hers.

"What a dark, pathetic creature you are," she said at last.

Despite my wounds, I smiled. "Do you look in a mirror, Your Highness?"

She struck me again and before I could fall over caught me by the shoulder and squeezed. I cried out in pain and she squeezed tighter, looming over me, her face grim.

"You will not laugh in the days to come," she promised. I said nothing, but I hoped she saw my determination.

She released me and shoved me away with a sound of disgust. She made a gruesome picture now, with her blood-covered fingers and gown.

"The king," Nadine began, unconcerned with the pair of us, "values his daughter's life. And too often, of late, she has come under threat. She can rarely leave the Ziyaana for fear of rebel attacks." I held my tongue, though it seemed little wonder to me that she'd inspired such ire. "The advent of her eighteenth birthday and the confirmation of her inheritance will necessitate more public appearances. Our king has commanded that you will risk your life where she cannot. You will train, and you will become Her Royal Highness. You will speak like her, walk like her. You will even breathe as she does."

"If I do not?" I asked, trying to keep hold of my disgust.

"You will," Nadine said.

"Your very life depends on it," Maram added with a chilling smile.

I concentrated on walking, on placing one foot in front of the other, as a droid led me from the courtyard back to the side of the palace where I'd first arrived. We crossed no one, not even other droids. No one to see me, I realized. No one to see my resemblance to Her Highness.

Just when I felt I would collapse, the droid ushered me into a set of chambers where Tala waited, a small table in front of her and a cushioned bed just behind. She shot to her feet, her face ashy and colorless. Her eyes were wide, and her hands shook.

"Dihya," she breathed, and caught me around the waist as I swayed.

I cried out, pain radiating through my body. When she pulled her hand away, it was covered in blood.

She whispered a rapid prayer in Kushaila, and then helped me down to the bed.

"Thank you, Unit 62," she said to the droid.

"Yes, citizen." It whirred, and then strode away.

She worked slowly and meticulously, as I stared out at nothing. I had been bleeding for so long that the fabric stuck tight to my wounds. She sponged my shoulder carefully, until finally the dress could be pulled away so she could clean the wounds and wrap them with a glowing white cloth. The cloth was warm and stung, briefly, before sinking into the wounds as though it had never been there at all.

I knew it was not a kindness she did me. She was fixing me so that I could perform my duties, to return to Maram and be punished again. I flinched when her cool fingers touched my chin, and turned my face toward her. Our eyes met.

"It will take some time for the wounds to close," she said after washing my face. "You may bathe. The bandages will hold. But it would do you good to sleep on your stomach."

Her hands were covered in my blood. I watched her dip them into a bowl of murky water, watched the bowl grow darker. How many others had she ministered to in this way, I wondered. How many had it taken for her to learn to effect the cool, blank stare? The distance? Would I end up the same way?

"These are your quarters. You have full use of this suite and the courtyard beyond. But you are not to venture past the west gate, understand?"

Our eyes met for the second time. Some emotion slipped across her face and was gone.

"It is a hard lesson," she said, her voice dropping to a whisper. "But it is best learned early. There is no escape from what they want. Only survival."

❧ 6 ❧

Morning came to me in starts and whispers. I could hear a soft breeze weave its way through curtains, a door shaking, thin chains trembling. I did not hear the crows or roosters call at dawn, or the pawing of our old goat in her paddock. Nor could I hear my parents moving around downstairs, or my father give the soft call to prayer, a tradition he insisted we maintain despite the danger.

I couldn't bear to open my eyes or move. My whole body ached, and I was slow to rise out of the nightmare I'd experienced. But if I didn't rise soon, my mother would come and scold me and remind me that I had agreed to milk the cantankerous goat when we'd bought her. Worse, it was my duty to catch her when she escaped, which seemed likely given her silence so early in the morning.

"Momma," I groaned. My bed felt like air, and my whole body felt flushed from the warmth trapped beneath the covers.

"Momma," I said again and forced myself upright, then froze. It had been no nightmare.

The droid, my wounds, the princess—all real. I was in the capital city, Walili, within the royal palace, the Ziyaana.

My mind went blank with terror. I'd barely survived my first night. How would I fare the next night and the next and the next, never mind what would happen when I took my place as Maram's body double? I hunched over in my bed, fighting tears.

Someone had already been in my rooms and laid out tea and bread. Hanging on a hook by the entrance to the chambers was a cream-ivory qaftan. I imagined for the wealthy ladies of the Ziyaana it must have seemed plain—what little beadwork there was was constrained around the neck and the edges of the jacket's sleeves. But it was ornate and detailed, the beads flecked in gold and silver, and the cloth was light and rippled beneath my fingers like water. It was worth more than my family's farm, I was sure.

I washed and dressed, carefully avoiding my wounds, just in time for Tala to appear, silent as a ghost.

She was dressed in a qaftan similar to mine, though hers was black, the sleeves and lapels of her jacket embroidered in white. She wore a stiff velvet belt in the old style, over gown and jacket both.

"Come," she said, and gestured to a vanity and a set of cushions. "We have little time, and I must make you presentable."

I sat warily, and watched as she worked on my hair. She must have been a lady's maid to a daughter of one of the makhzen who worked in the lower echelons of the new government. Her fingers worked deftly as she oiled and parted my thick, tightly wound curls. I expected her to simply comb out the knots, but instead she wound gold and silver thread into the braids, before tying off the bulk of it into a long braid.

"Earrings," she commanded, "and a necklace. Here." She opened a small cabinet and a smaller jewelry box and picked out a pair of gold earrings with dark green stones, and a matching necklace. She set three rings in my hand without comment and waited while I slipped them onto my fingers.

"I think jewelry is the least of my worries," I said.

She had no reply to that.

Tala did not accompany me to Nadine's courtyard. Yesterday's droid—Unit 62—escorted me instead. I was not invited to stand after I knelt in greeting to her, and so I remained on my knees, eyes fixed on the cool stone floor. Nadine said nothing; she worked as she had yesterday, methodically and without distraction. It echoed yesterday's proceedings too well for me not to worry, but I kept my hands steady and my back straight.

The sharp taptaptap of heeled slippers on tile heralded the princess's arrival.

Maram swept in, a cloud of pink and black fabric rippling behind her. If anyone thought the pink might soften her features, make her seem sweeter or gentler, the black torque of beadwork undid it all. Her hair spilled over her shoulders, unadorned by gold or jewels, and there was a single, enormous bracelet set with a large black stone on her left wrist. She looked furious and wrathful. Her eyes were lined heavily with kohl, and when she turned her gaze to me I lowered mine and held back a shudder.

Her face was carefully blank, her footsteps precise, but her knuckles were white where she gripped her gown. She took a seat beside Nadine and gestured for me to stand.

"Your Highness," I murmured. She did not reply.

When I hazarded a look, she was staring at me, as though she found me as alien as I found her.

"You've cleaned her," she said at last and gestured me closer. When I knelt at her feet she gripped my chin, her manicured nails digging into my cheek. "The resemblance—"

I suppose with my hair combed back and draped in new and expensive fabric she could more clearly see the similarities between us.

Not similarities, I thought. We were nearly twins.

"What a barbaric practice," she said, and I flinched. "I thought we had outlawed such things."

"Among the nobility, we have," Nadine said. "But we have little care for what savages get up to." With shock, I realized she meant my daan.

Heat rose in my cheeks even as I struggled to keep my mouth shut. Her mother had borne such marks on her face proudly, as did her grandmother, the Dowager Sultana, who had survived the occupation but was now shut away from the world. They'd been outlawed among the makhzen, but they were a valued tribal custom, and not just among the Kushaila.

I wanted to ask her how she had come to hate half her lineage so. How had she become so fully and completely like her father?

"We will take care of her face, of course," Nadine added.

Nausea swam up through me, quick and fast. I knew what they intended.

"You can't," I said, and hated the waver in my voice.

Maram didn't respond, though her gaze didn't waver from the ink on my cheeks. She looked almost serene now, despite planning to take the one thing that was truly mine. My daan were everything—my family, my faith, my inheritance.

This was it, then: I was to be taken, reshaped in the image of my master, stripped of one of the only things that separated me from Maram. I knew so little of the Imperial princess—but I knew she was half Kushaila, and that her fiancé was Kushaila. Had she no love of them, or sympathy?

"I'm begging you," I whispered as her grip tightened around my face.

"Oh," she said, and in that single breath I heard the hard edge of her voice, her loathing. "You should never beg."

I wanted to scream, I wanted the whole palace to know what it was that she was doing to me. But then there was a pinch at the base of my throat. I looked down to see a tiny, spider-like machine scurrying down my skirt.

The last thing I saw was Maram, her face still carefully blank, one white-knuckled hand fisted in the folds of her gown, watching as I toppled over.

I slept, or thought I slept, and was plagued with nightmares. A great laser coming closer to my face. Insect-shaped droids creeping over me, cutting into bone. The raw hum of a small saw. Heat as they shaved down my cheekbones and rounded my jaw.

I floated into consciousness slowly. The closer I came to the surface, the darker the world seemed to feel. I was standing on the edge of terror, crying out in my mind, and perhaps in real life. No one came to comfort me. I remained suspended in a nightmare, until, finally, I woke up.

I stared at the ceiling, waiting for the interlocking stars in the wood paneling to come into focus. My body felt heavy as lead. The bed was piled high with covers, and the curtains that separated the room from the rest of the suite were drawn shut.

I struggled to sit up.

There was a moment of complete serenity in that disorientation. I could not remember how I'd gotten back to my room, what had passed in the time since my last lesson.

And then, I lifted my hands to my face, and felt bandages.

The sound that tore itself out of my throat was broken. I felt—I could not feel betrayed, and yet I did. I curled up in my bed, with my bandaged face pressed against my knees, and sobbed. Great heaving sobs that shook my whole body and rang out against the stone floors of my suite. I knew without checking that the new scar on my back was gone, the skin smoothed to match Maram's. I had lost a battle I'd never been equipped to fight. I'd been stripped of all things that were meant to be mine, that Dihya had blessed me with, and now— How could I keep myself, preserve myself, if I had none of myself left?

If all I had was Maram?

I thought of my mother's voice, of her brushing my hair, tucking my curls behind my ear. I thought of her hard at work, her thin face grim, as though she were prepared to wage her own little war in the kitchen. I had inherited far more of my father's whimsy, and less of my mother's strength. Now I wanted nothing more than for her to appear and hold me, to somehow pass some of her iron will on to me through her touch.

I wanted to see my family again. My mother and father, my brothers, the old women in my village whom I had called khaltou since I was small. I wanted to never dream of droids or the Ziyaana again. I wanted open skies and mountain air. I wanted to know my family was safe, that Khadija was unharmed, that Husnain lived. More than anything, I wanted to write my own story, free from Vathek intervention.

But there was no end to these days in sight. I would rise every day, a prisoner of the Ziyaana, at the mercy of Nadine and other

High Vath like her. And no matter what I did, how well I succeeded, the chances of my seeing my family again were low. Would
I ever be allowed to go back to Cadiz? Would I see my parents or
my brothers again? Would I even know if they were alive or not?

I wanted answers, but no one here would be able to give them
to me. My family, my fate, my home—they were all out of my
grasp for now. Perhaps forever.

I was drying my eyes when I saw it. Hanging from a wooden
room partition was my majority gown. It had been laundered and
repaired. Gone was the blood and dirt of that awful night, the
tears from running and being kidnapped. I raised a hand to touch
it and felt again that swell of grief, lodged beneath my breastbone.

And on a chair beneath it sat the sheaf of papers Husnain had
gifted to me on my majority night. Breath went out of me as I
stared at it, uncomprehending. I'd forgotten about it, forgotten
that brief moment of happiness. It had survived my trip to the
Ziyaana, my first encounter with Maram, and Tala's repair.

How?

My hands trembled as I undid the twine still holding them
together and pulled the pages out. A stiff piece of paper fell out,
sturdier than the parchment, with Husnain's writing on it.

May these words be suspended in your thoughts all your life.

Once more, my vision blurred with tears. I thought I'd lost
everything, every connection to my family and my past and the
people and things I loved. Husnain's handwriting was like a bea-
con after a long and dark night.

"Bright-feathered and cloaked it came to her, and inclined its
head," I recited in Kushaila. "And fixed to her crown a star, gold
as the sun. And it said, kneel for the Grace of the Most High."

I felt the words shoot through me like lightning. I loved the
stories of Massinia more than any other. She'd been the daughter

of a Tazalghit queen and as a child was kidnapped by slavers. Massinia had suffered under the weight of her bondage before finding a way to escape. They'd branded her and beat and claimed her. But she'd freed herself and Dihya had eventually delivered her, newly marked with His touch, to her mother and her family.

Later, the tesleet that first delivered her, Azoul, returned to her with the Word of Dihya which she transcribed first into her skin, and later into the Book. Her message united the Tazalghit tribes for the first time in their history.

In the courtyard, dim, false moonlight filtered in through the dome above, and the air was filled with a stream of orbs, glowing like a sea of dying stars. Every now and then one glowed brighter than all the others and emitted a soft, childlike hum. They filled this part of the palace, the only source of light at night. Coupled with the discovery of my brother's gift, they felt like a sign, like *hope*.

I prayed, fervently, for another sign, anything, to reveal my purpose in being here. I couldn't give up hope and I wouldn't. But I wanted to believe—had to believe—that there was a reason I was here, that there was meaning to this sudden change in fate.

The crown of Dihya had been stripped from me, my face changed, my body broken. But I was not a slave and I was not a spare. I was my mother's daughter, and I would survive and endure. I would find my way back home.

7

Nadine did not sit behind her desk today. Nor did she wait for me to unveil myself, but took it upon herself to tug at the face covering. I fixed my gaze to a spot over her shoulder while she turned my face this way and that.

"Well," she said at last. "You certainly look like her."

I said nothing.

"How biddable you now seem. Come," she said. "You may sit with me."

There were two chairs at the table, and a breakfast spread. I hesitated.

"My lady?" I said.

"You must learn to sit with your betters if you are to emulate Her Royal Highness," she said.

"Yes, my lady."

Her gaze was critical as I took my seat. "Do you understand the stakes of what you've been commanded to do? There is no room for error."

I watched her pour tea. "I do, my lady."

"We shall see," she said, then gestured at the food between us. "Eat."

I reached for a piece of bread, but before I touched it, Nadine rapped the back of my hands with a knife. I snatched my hand back in pain.

"I see we must begin from the first." She sneered. "You are not in a village. We do not eat with our hands."

"It's bread," I said helplessly.

"You will ask for things to be passed to you," she said. "If not, you will use a fork. Am I understood?"

"Yes, my lady."

"Again."

So the morning went. By the time the sun was up, my hands had dozens of purple bruises, and I'd eaten nowhere near my fill. Nadine did not care. She had the table cleared and walked to the center of the courtyard.

"Now," she said, sitting in her usual high-backed chair. "You shall walk to and fro on this walkway."

I stared from where I was sitting.

"Are you deaf, girl?"

I hastened to my feet. "No, my lady."

I'd taken three steps when something sharp snapped against my ankles. I stopped and closed my eyes, taking a deep breath.

"You are not a village girl," Nadine said when I opened my eyes. "You are no longer prey. I should see neither fear nor hesitation."

No longer prey, she said, as if I hadn't been exactly that from the moment of my arrival. "I don't understand."

"Walk with a straight back"—she snapped the thin whip at my back—"with your shoulders and head high"—another snap at my neck. "Again."

And again and again.

With my physical transformation complete, Nadine doubled down on my training. In the days that followed, I spent my mornings being tested by Nadine or being taught to dance by a droid, then retreated to my quarters in the afternoon to study. I spent hours frantically memorizing names and facts and histories. After lunch I met Nadine again for behavioral lessons. More often than not, Maram attended these sessions.

This morning, it appeared, I wasn't worth either of their attention. Perhaps Nadine was too impatient to deal with me and my painfully slow progress. In any case, I was being trained by nothing more than a droid.

"Let us begin," it said, "with the old families of the Ziyaana. Recite."

"There are five great houses who have resided in the Ziyaana for four hundred years," I began.

It rapped a hand against the wall. "No," it said. "As Her Highness. We have no interest in your knowledge; only in how well you can imitate."

I swallowed around an angry reply. I had been at these lessons for two weeks now, and I still could not affect the haughty tone the princess used, despite my life depending on it. Despite everything I felt no closer to being a stand-in for Maram. I lacked something that resided so deeply in the princess—her arrogance and pride rendered her voice as it was. I had none of that—and I didn't even know where to begin pretending that I did.

I straightened my shoulders, lifted my chin, and continued. The sun was high in the sky, and I could see the heat wavering in the air outside the palace dome. Most of the Ziyaana was taking its midday slumber.

"There are four houses," I began again. "Ziyad, of whom I am a direct descendant. Pledged to them are Agadaan, Ouij, and Fars. There are the Banu Salih, of whom my fiancé is the last. Pledged to them are Mellas and Azru."

The droid rapped against the wall again, a horrific tic-tic-tic that reminded me of spiders rushing their way across the floor.

"You have failed to meet her vocal register," it said.

"I don't know what that means," I snapped, finally giving in to anger.

A giggle rent its way through the air. It made my whole body stiffen in fear.

Maram carried her bejeweled slippers in one hand. Her dark hair spilled around her shoulders, a gorgeous torrent of curls threaded with gold. Today she wore a deep blue gown, and, like her hair, it too was threaded with gold. Between the two of us, I realized with a churn of envy, she was the more beautiful. Logically, I knew we were now identical. But round-cheeked, flushed with delight, the corner of her mouth turned up just so, she seemed leaps and bounds above me.

"I don't know why anyone should expect you to be successful," she said. "What does a lowly village girl know about being a royal princess?"

The droid, ever dutiful, stuck a finger against my neck and zapped me, a sharp electric shock to remind me to sink to my knees before her.

I kept my eyes on the ground—Maram's moods were as difficult to predict as desert storms. But I remembered my mother's stoic face, my disappeared crown of Dihya. Whatever Maram thought she could do to me, I could endure. I would endure and survive. I wouldn't let her break me. No matter how hard she tried.

When I looked up again, she was watching me with a curious look on her face. As if she found my existence as strange as I found hers. Our eyes met and a cold mask slipped over her features.

"Do not gawk, village girl," she said, voice soft. "It is unbecoming."

As the weeks passed and my training continued, my fear did not abate, but neither did my determination. My only hope for freedom lay in excelling in what they asked me to do—a failing village girl would incur their wrath. A successful one might be allowed enough freedom for a chance to escape. As the days passed, my will did to my voice what pride did for Maram: deepened it, made it ring with frigidity whenever I spoke. My vowels firmed, the ends of my sentences turned clipped, the words that might have been raised as questions were now enunciated as demands. I became so used to being shocked between my shoulder blades or rapped on my ankles that my back was constantly straight, my head high. Besides, it was easier to avoid Maram's gaze if my chin lifted just so, my line of sight falling just over her shoulder.

Together, these things made me into a better copy of her, and as some of the wounds inside me scarred over, I began to succeed.

Maram watched me with mute fascination as I sank to my

knees at the end of our daily meeting and flicked the folds of my gown so that they were spread out behind me like a bird's fanned tail. The droid stood beside her, its eyes hooded, whirring softly in warning.

"You're quite the little princess, aren't you?" she said. I remained silent. "Do I ever look so demure, Nadine?"

"Only before your father," the stewardess replied. "Which is to the good. I imagine she will not kneel for anyone else."

"Do you think she'll pass?"

"She should certainly hope so," Nadine said, and my fingers curled in the folds of my gown. "For her own sake."

There was a rustle of fabric, and then Maram's fingers under my chin, tilting my head up as she so often did. She wore an expression I'd seen more and more often on her face of late. Curious, contemplative, with an edge.

"I wonder which of us is more cursed," she said, soft enough that Nadine would not hear. "You for looking like me, or I for looking like my mother?"

Something strange turned in my chest. For a moment, I saw a younger, softer version of myself in her features. Lonely, sad— she probably had never had a friend.

The softness was gone just as quickly as it had made its appearance. She let me go, and made her way to the exit.

"I tire of watching you," she said, pausing near the door. "Do what you will with her, Nadine."

My gaze turned to Nadine after the doors slammed shut behind her. The roc had not moved from its perch, though it had puffed up in size and tucked its head down in preparation for sleep. Nadine made a sharp gesture with her hand, and a droid moved forward and caught the bird to return it to its roosting place.

For a moment we stared at each other.

"You've done quite well," Nadine said. I felt a shameful curl of pride in the pit of my stomach. "And not a moment too soon. We've chosen the Terminus ball, in two weeks' time, for your debut. The king will attend. You must impress him, you understand?"

I nodded. "Yes, my lady."

"You will be safe at the ball," she continued. "Dare I say, you may even enjoy it. But do your job well, and all will be pleased," she said at last. "You will observe court tomorrow, so that you will know Maram's circle by sight as well as name. For now, you're dismissed."

The following afternoon, Tala led me up a set of stairs to a screened balcony. There were a pair of gilt droids on either end of the screen, and a couch piled with cushions. She bade me sit and gestured to one of the droids. The screen cleared, its false wooden trellis fading away like smoke.

The garden below was at least the size of my parents' farm and seemed to me more like a paradise than a garden. Green grass was veined through with white stone pathways, shaded by pomegranate trees, heavy with red fruit. Here and there I could see the glittering reflection of fountains, and on its eastern end a stream wove its way through several small orchards. In the very center was an enormous gazebo.

I watched as Maram's attendants came in groups and waves.

Tala murmured their names in my ear, the final lesson before my final test at the ball. Their voices filtered into our small alcove—even the makhzen in the Ziyaana weren't free from Vathek surveillance, it seemed. They took their seats at the table inside the gazebo, arranging their gowns and cloaks like petals on wildflowers. Their hair was out, brushed to gleam in the morning light, and threaded with gold and silver and small jewels. They were from all over Andala; only two, as far as I could gather, were from the city of Walili.

I studied Maram as she made her way to the table, glad for my hiding place. Her features were haughtier than mine had ever been. Even after all my training, I could not understand her pride and disdain. What must it be like for her, to find the world constantly at her feet?

She walked at her own leisure, her gown trailing at least three feet behind her, followed by two Vathek girls and flanked by a young man. He was tall, with dark brown hair curled just beneath his ears, green eyes, and olive-toned skin that looked as if it would turn even darker beneath a desert sun. I would have thought him a prince of old, if it weren't for his face, which was clean-shaven in the tradition of the Vath and bore no daan.

"Who," I asked, "is that?"

"The amir, Idris ibn Salih."

I struggled to contain my surprise. The Banu Salih were the largest cousin tribe of the old Andalaan royal family, and the first tribe to oppose the Vathek invasion. In those days, their families had numbered near the thousands, and they'd thrown all their might behind the opposition. But no one survived against the Vath. The Banu Salih had held out until the Purge, until the queen—Maram's mother—begged her cousins to capitulate. As part of their surrender, Idris, the last surviving heir of the Banu Salih, had been pledged to Maram.

Now, he was her fiancé, permanently bound to the Vathek crown.

As breakfast continued below us, I couldn't stop myself from staring at him. He seemed so at ease with Maram, nudging her playfully, offering her food from his own plate, leaning down to whisper in her ear. I shivered. They seemed so close. I could not understand it.

"Layaan, you look far too happy so early in the morning," Maram said conversationally to one of the ladies of her court, and a girl raised her hand to cover her mouth. She had been smiling, I noted, though now she fought to hide it.

"I don't know what you mean, Your Highness."

Princess Maram raised a dark eyebrow. "You should know better than most," she said. "Every secret outs itself in the Ziyaana."

Whatever response the girl might have made was cut off by the sound of the enormous doors opening. For a moment, it seemed as though the courtiers were all frozen, staring at the woman who made her way through the doors. Then Idris shot to his feet, and ran at her with a cry. Her arms opened up, and even from across the garden, I could see the light in her eyes and her smile at the sight of him. He swept her up and spun her twice. The trail of her gown, a dark burgundy, whipped through the air behind her.

I turned to Tala to ask the woman's name, but Idris's voice cut me short. "May I present to you," Idris said, coming to stop in front of the princess, "the Lady Furat—"

"Of the Wattasi clan," Maram finished, her voice flat. "We are much acquainted, yes."

I shot a look at Tala, but her eyes were fixed on the scene in front of us. If Furat was of the Wattasis, then she was Maram's cousin—a member of the former queen, Maram's mother's, extended family. They were Zidane, not Kushaila, and had held strongholds in Qarmuta, to the south. Their alliance with the Ziyadis and Salihis hundreds of years ago had brought stability in a time of civil war. Morbid fascination jogged my memory; Furat was the last of the Wattasis. The king had executed her parents, and her elder brother. Like Idris, she was their last surviving heir. What had made him spare one small child at the start of the occupation? And why would she ever willingly return to the Ziyaana?

"Isn't—wasn't she in exile?" I whispered.

"Look," Tala replied. "Her daan are gone. Likely the price for being welcomed back."

A chill came over me—she had bargained away what I would have given anything to keep.

"What brings you back to court, cousin?" Princess Maram said.

Furat sank to her knees elegantly. "I come to serve," she said, her eyes on the ground. "As is my duty."

Maram pressed her lips together, eyes flashing. "We shall see."

After several days of such observation, I was called again by Nadine for testing. If I were to be successful, I would need to understand the complicated relationships Maram had formed with the rising makhzen—Andalaan nobility who were folded into the new world order—and High Vathek class. Maram stood with her in the courtyard today, her features hard.

On days like this it was easy to feel small. Maram's hair was threaded with gold chain, her mouth rouged, and her bejeweled slippers dazzled in the light. She was rarely serene, but today there was a calm in her, a surety. I knew what it was she felt, could feel it in her gaze. Today she was sure she was my better, that despite our looks, she was the future queen, not I. It was easy to feel small when she felt this way, but it was also easy to feel safe. When Maram was sure, everyone was safer.

"Let us see what she has learned, then. Can she name the members of my circle?" Maram said, not looking away from me.

"Ask her," Nadine said.

Maram said nothing, though she raised both her eyebrows as if to prompt me.

Her silence sparked annoyance in me, and I spoke almost before I thought. "Your Highness, there's Furat of the Wattasi clan, heiress to the Dowager Sultana's estate on the moon Gibra," I began.

She moved so quickly, I didn't see it coming. Today she'd worn no fewer than four rings, and they each made themselves known against my cheek as she backhanded me. Pain radiated through my face, and I tasted blood. My heart beat in my chest so fast I could scarcely draw breath.

Still, despite the pain, a grim satisfaction rose inside me at her response. I was the Andalaan, I was the Kushaila girl with Kushaila features. That she had been born with my face, my same brown skin and twisting dark hair and dark eyes—the same forehead and cheeks and mouth . . . It was the height of cruelty, remarkably unfair. If not for this link, I would never have been kidnapped out of my village. I might still be living with my family.

I didn't break my gaze with Maram.

"Why," Maram began, taking an angry hold of my face with one hand, "do you start with her?"

"I remembered her—" I started, and she struck me again on the other side of my face.

"Furat," she spat at me, "is a disinherited lesser cousin, with no holdings and no prospects. There is nothing to remember."

Her eyes were wide, her face flushed, and there was, I realized in a moment of disembodied horror, my blood on one of her rings. It was strange to feel calm flow over me like water. I was still frightened, I still understood that Maram could hurt me. But something inside of me had changed; I knew now that she could change my body but she had no power over my spirit. And more satisfying, I knew that she had a weakness—she was not so different than me. She was not untouchable.

"You should not let her bother you so," Nadine said, her voice even and calm. She meant Furat, not me, I realized; my presence was too insignificant to register. "She is, as you said, a disinherited lesser cousin."

"Why? Why does he allow her to live? Why does he allow her to live with my grandmother?" The weakness in her voice both satisfied and frightened me. I'd learned that it was in moments of weakness when Maram was her most cruel.

"There is misery for her in the absence of all she could have been and had," Nadine said, as though she were reminding her. "You should pity her, not fear her."

I realized, too late, that I would have been better served lowering my gaze. When Maram turned to look at me again, something still and eerie settled in her face.

"Are you enjoying this?" she asked me, her voice finally under control. "Do you like seeing the object of all your hate upset?"

She caught me by the throat, her rings pressing down so hard I could barely breathe. "Don't worry," she breathed into my ear. "You will understand soon enough."

She pushed me away, hard enough that I stumbled back and fell. When I had gathered myself again, she was already making her way to the exit, the train of her gown billowing out behind her.

9

Every morning the dome over my courtyard brightened to mimic the light of the rising sun. Shut away as I was deep in the Ziyaana, there were no windows, no glimpse of a real sun or breeze. Only the dome and its hollow sun and the humming orbs that came to fill the courtyard at night. I sat in the gazebo, a mantle around my shoulders, and cradled a glass of tea in my hands. Across the way a droid hummed softly as it pruned a tree. It had neither flowered nor borne fruit, and I wondered if the droid would decide the tree wasn't worth saving.

My mother said my brother had once had such a tree, a sapling he'd saved all through the occupation, intending to plant it when it was over and watch it flower to life. But like all our hopes and dreams at the end of the occupation, the sapling had withered and died.

"Amani!"

I jerked my mind back to the present and found Tala standing directly in my line of sight, hands on her hips.

"How long have you been standing there?"

"Some time," she said. "Be quick, if you please. We're on a schedule."

"Why?" I asked as I followed her to the bath chamber.

My days had grown predictable of late—the mornings were mine, but in the afternoons I spent much of my time observing Maram's court, and reviewing lists and notes, focusing on the information I had yet to learn. I was summoned usually in the evening to be tested on the day's learnings by Nadine, but Maram had lately not bothered with me.

Part of me wondered why, and if our last interaction had kept her away.

Good, I thought with some viciousness.

"They're giving you a final test before the ball," Tala said simply, and then, voice softening, "I'm sorry. I don't know anything more than that."

I stared at my reflection in the mirror as Tala moved around me, tightening the sash around my waist, arranging the folds of my gown. There was jewelry, too—a large bracelet for my right wrist, and several rings for my left hand.

My hands shook as I followed the droid out of the courtyard. So far my tests had been simple. But I was dressed as Maram today. There would be more at stake.

The droid led me toward the north wing of the Ziyaana, where Maram and the king had their quarters. All my training had been done in the abandoned east wing where my chambers lay—home,

I had learned, to the queen before she died, and deserted now, shuttered off.

This portion of the palace somehow surpassed the beauty of the old queen's wing. Gleaming stone walls were carved with arabesque arches and inlaid with bright blue and orange tiles. Many of the walkways opened up onto gardens and courtyards, and birdsong twined with the sound of babbling water. True sunlight streamed through glass ceilings. I was led through porticoes and lovers' alcoves, passed through clouds of perfume and air filled with the trill of music. Here I could imagine the Ziyaana of old.

At last, the droid opened up a door at the end of a hall onto a rotunda. The air was clear and crisp, bright with the sunlight that poured in from an opening in the dome. The floor was white and smooth, and my footsteps echoed, punctuated by the rush of fabric as my gown swept behind me. Just beneath the opening of the dome sat Maram, and just behind her stood Nadine and another droid.

Maram smirked as I sank to my knees before her dais. She was perfectly arranged in a gown identical to the one I wore, spread around her like a flower. She reached forward and tucked a soft, manicured hand under my chin.

"My," she said, examining me with a sharp eye. "I could almost believe you were beautiful."

She rose effortlessly, and gestured me up to the dais.

"Your Highness, how may I serve?" I murmured as I settled down and arranged my skirts. I sounded flippant, even to myself. Part of me felt as though a sliver of my soul had floated up into the ceiling and was watching an exchange between a pair of cruel twins. I marveled at my new ability to remain cool, even as Maram smiled.

"Show me that you can be me, village girl. Show me what you've learned." With those words, Maram stepped out of sight, behind a pillar. Nadine said nothing as the great doors opened to admit a bevy of servants.

The servants set up several wardrobes, a second dais, several mannequins, and a display of fabrics. They arranged themselves like a small souk just in front of the dais. I watched them, a bored expression on my features. Maram, I knew, barely consented to dress in the fusion of Kushaila and Vathek attire she often wore—a reminder she was the link between regimes, between cultures. Every fitting was a struggle.

I sighed, the picture of irritation, when the head seamstress dropped a spool of fabric and it rolled toward my dais. Her face paled visibly, and she froze, as if unsure if she should come forward to collect the mess or leave it as it was. She was old, and I imagined she had dropped the spool because of her shaking hands.

"Well," I snapped as Maram so often did, "are you running a zoo or do you expect me to pick it up?"

"N-no," she stammered. "I—I mean, yes, of course, Your Highness."

"I don't see why this is necessary," I said, looking at Nadine.

"The seamstress has new fabric she'd like you to approve for the winter gowns," Nadine replied, the corner of her mouth twitching.

My own mouth stayed in a grim line. I did not find the humor in the situation; what would happen if they discovered me to be a fraud?

"You set up a dais for me to merely approve fabric," I said, my voice cool.

"We also have a new gown for you," the head seamstress piped up, speaking out of turn.

My back stiffened, Maram's rage radiating out of me. I turned my gaze to the head seamstress and watched her turn pale. She was more than three times my age, older than Nadine even, and yet she sank to her knees before me, her knuckles white in the folds of her gown.

"How many seamstresses do we have?" I said without breaking my gaze.

"Several," Nadine replied.

"I never want to see this one again. I should have your tongue cut out for speaking out of turn. Happily for you, I am in a good mood today, and I don't wish it spoiled by blood on the floor."

"Y-your—"

I lifted an eyebrow and she choked on her own words and lowered her head.

For a moment, I understood. Was this what Maram always felt like—secure in her power? Secure in herself? Absolutely in control because she knew even the strongest, oldest tree would bend to her will on a whim?

It was heady and sickening all at once.

"Escort her away," I said, and the droid beside Nadine lurched forward.

The only sound for some minutes was the sound of the seamstress's heels skidding against the marble floors as the droid dragged her away.

"Where is the fabric?" I asked, after the doors had closed. My shoulders relaxed in a practiced move, the same sudden change to leisure I'd seen Maram make a hundred times.

A seamstress came forward, holding a roll of fabric, and knelt before me, bearing it up over her head. It was velvet, or something quite like it, rich and soft, rippling with shades of blue and black. I ran a steady hand over it, and for a moment had the cruel impulse to twist my hands in it and tear the whole thing away from the girl.

"I hardly think it's a flattering shade," I said at last. "And what would you make out of it?"

Silence.

"Was I not clear in my question?" I said after a heartbeat. "Or am I meant to drape it over myself like some sort of barbarian?"

"W-we hadn't—"

Maram's smirk emerged on my features without thought. "You took a portion of my morning to display to me a piece of fabric with no design in mind?"

The silence stretched, until the air in the room was tight as a drum.

"Get out."

The women scrambled to pack everything up, and did it admirably quickly before they rushed out into the hall. The doors clanged shut behind them. For a moment, their echo was the only sound.

Maram appeared beside me, stepping out from the shadows. She was grinning, a true, radiant smile that transformed her angry features into something beautiful—and happy.

"That was magnificent," she said, grabbing my arms. "I hardly thought you could do it. Isn't that right, Nadine?"

"Indeed," she drawled, amused. "One hardly thinks a village girl has it in her to berate first an old woman, and then all her subordinates."

Maram continued to beam at me, though she released the grip on my arms. I felt an answering smile rise, tentative and hopeful, and I struggled to contain it—why should I relish her praise?

"I'm quite pleased," she said.

Her pleasure seemed to make Nadine sharpen. "There are

days left before the ball where you will make your debut," she said to me. "Have you any idea where it is? For whom? For what?"

The voice that came out of me was not mine, but Maram's. "The festival is held yearly in the northern continent, in the mountainous country of Atalasia. It is a celebration of their first snowfall, and it imitates the Vathek custom of the wintermarch."

For the first time in our brief acquaintance, Nadine looked impressed.

"Very good," she said after a beat. "I suppose you're ready."

atalasia,
andala

❧ 10 ❧

In the center of the Ziyaana was a giant dome that doubled as a landing area for the palace's spacecraft. As far as the eye could see, the royal household stood in rank, prepared to leave for Atalasia and the Terminus ball. There were three air transports, luxury cruisers, lined up and gleaming in the early-morning sunlight. Those in the court's favor would ride in the royal transport. Everyone else would have to find their own way to Atalasia.

A guard stood at one end of the suite designated for me, arms folded across his chest, silent and watchful. Dressed as Maram, I had chosen to ride alone in her quarters rather than risk discovery before the ball even began. I used these precious few hours to review the invitation list for the ball, memorizing names and faces from the holoreader Nadine had provided.

All my hopes at success rested on my debut as Maram. She had stayed behind so that no one could chance on her while I was at the ball. *Succeed*, she'd commanded me before I left. I didn't want to entertain what the cost would be if I failed.

The transport traveled quickly, crossing the vast desert more rapidly than I could have imagined. Before I knew it we'd sailed over the sea separating the main continent from the northern climes, and the orange, sunburnt sky turned blue. I sat by a window with a round table in front of me, laden with bowls of fruit and a crystal decanter filled with a drink I didn't recognize.

The door at the far end of the train car hissed open, and I looked up to find Tala there.

"Are you ready, Your Highness?" she asked, but I heard the question she was really asking—was I ready for my masquerade?

Disembarking was fast and efficient. The Atalasian air had a bite to it that even I, who had grown up at the foot of Cadissian mountains, was not prepared for. I pulled my cloak tighter around my shoulders and looked up at the carved stone wall of the palace. It was a long, flat structure, a single story, with turrets rising out of the outer wall at regular intervals. The very tops of the walls were carved with sharp geometric shapes, and every now and then a large, heavy tapestry dropped over the wall. It was stationed on a hill, and behind it rose up the tallest peaks of the Atalasia mountains, snowcapped and intimidating.

I was put in a series of chambers meant to be Maram's, as opulent and luxurious as anything I'd seen in the Ziyaana. Dark wood and thick fabrics decorated the room. There was a gilded mirror set just above a vanity covered in glittering pieces of jewelry. And at the far end of the room a table bore a tea set, the pot made of precious excelsior, the glasses gilded and traced in gold. Hanging on the armoire was what I was meant to wear tonight.

I was to be the winter queen to Idris's waning autumn prince. It was a tradition cobbled from Vathek and Atalasian ways. Before the occupation, Atalasia had venerated a series of seasonal monarchs and the Vath had feasted under the eyes of a summer queen on their home world. Now that Andala was the capital of their empire, they had reversed the tradition to ingratiate themselves in the country that fell first on Andala.

I couldn't resist touching the gown. It looked heavy, silver with wide sleeves, buttoned up to the neck, the skirt shot through with bright white thread and studded with tiny, glittering rocks. They weren't diamonds, were they? Hung around the waist was something closer to the Kushaila waistband, which ran from just below the chest to low on the hips, made to wrap around more than once. And hanging from the shoulders was a sheer, gauzy cape that was feet longer than the skirt of the dress, studded with embroidered snowflakes.

I'd suffered and trained for this moment, and at last I would have my chance at success. A flutter of nervousness rose in my belly. I was confident of fooling her cousins and courtiers. I was less sure about fooling her fiancé. I'd seen them together— always close, like confidants. The dress wouldn't be enough to fool him.

I didn't think Maram really had friends, and if she were believed, her engagement to Idris was a matter of the state and nothing more. Nevertheless, I worried. What did he expect of Maram? And if she'd kept secrets about their relationship from me, how would I manage?

Why would she keep secrets? I thought.

Why did Maram ever do anything?

Tala made sure I ate before she helped me out of the gown I wore and sat me in front of the vanity to do my hair. She braided the ends and twisted them against the back of my head, then caught them in a silver net hung with ornaments shaped like small raindrops. She looped a chain across my forehead, from which a dark blue gem swung. I watched as the face already alien to me grew even more so.

"One last thing," she said, and lifted a pair of enormous earrings, flattened silver from which hung two smaller gems of the same color.

The end product, with the gown and its cape, was someone who looked as if she'd been born into wealth, someone beautiful, someone sure. I couldn't help remembering the last time someone had adorned me with beautiful jewelry—my mother, on my majority night—and felt a pang of guilt and longing deep inside my chest.

Tala smiled behind me and squeezed my shoulders. "You can do this," she said. "I have faith in you."

I nodded, and set my shoulders. Tonight, I would be Maram before the entire Vathek-Andalaan court.

I could not fail.

The Kushaila of Andala didn't really hold balls, not the way the Vathek did. We held large banquets that went far into the night, where we sang and played instruments and conversed. But Vathek balls involved dancing, and, despite my training, I was nervous. Dancing with a human was different from dancing with a droid.

Idris waited for me in the entryway. His dark hair was dusted with gold, and he wore a Vathek military uniform—black jacket and black trousers—with red trim. His only concession to Kushaila dress was the sash tied around his waist. It pained me to look at him, the leader of the bravest of Andala's houses, dressed as one of them. Turned into one of them.

He smiled when he saw me. "Your Highness," he said and held out a hand. "Ready?" I slipped a ringed hand into his, which he squeezed as if he sensed my nerves. My heart pounded a steady rhythm in my chest.

The doors yawned open before the two of us, revealing a balcony that led down to the ballroom floor, and beyond that, a dining area. It was decorated like a winter wonderland with an enormous ice sculpture at the very center of the room of a tesleet rising into the air, wings outspread. Tesleet were creatures of heat, made of fire with molten gold in their veins. Despite the incongruity, its presence comforted me.

"The High Princess of the Vath, Protectress of Andala and her Moons, Maram vak Mathis and her escort, Idris ibn Salih."

He held my hand tightly as we descended the stairs together. Everyone was dressed in varying shades of gold and silver and blue, and it seemed to me as if the entire cavernous room shimmered with their jewels and the ice and a nervous energy, as though they all expected some axe to fall tonight.

Idris led me immediately to the center of the floor for the inaugural dance we had to lead. Just as the instruments began to play he tugged me against his side and settled a hand on my waist.

"Ready?" he asked again, but this time with a lifted eyebrow, testing me. I didn't flinch when he leaned in close, and his mouth brushed against my ear. "This can't be harder than last year, can it?"

He was so close, and I could feel my face warming, which was not like Maram at all. He was far more beautiful in person. His eyes were ringed with thick lashes, and his face—stoic now— looked as if it had been carved out of antiquity. I swallowed my fluster and lifted my chin. A hint of a smile reemerged when I looked up, determined, and the arm around my waist tightened in support. His continued poise in the face of hundreds of court members watching us helped me to remain upright and steady.

We stepped easily into the waltz, one step and then another, the trail of my gown whispering against the marble floor. I could hear the music as if through a roar, and the titter of other dancers and members of court watching us. Idris's hand on my waist was ever present and warm, and every now and then he would lean in close and his hair would brush my cheek.

The dance ended with Idris bowed over my hand. The only sounds I could hear were of my earrings swaying and my heart pounding in my chest. The rest of the room came to me in flashes: people clapping; a mix of Andalaan and Vathek courtiers passing us by; Idris's frown, there and then gone in a second; and Nadine's watchful eyes from where she stood on a riser, observing me.

"Ah," Idris said, and settled a warm hand on my waist again. "Here comes your most ardent admirer." His hair brushed against my cheek and for a moment I could not help staring, he was so close.

"Your Highness," someone said from behind me. Remember why you are here, I told myself, and turned around. Maram's smile was reserved for a precious handful of her cousins, and she'd been sure to educate me on just how much of her goodwill was spread through court so that I wouldn't accidentally compliment one of her disliked peers.

"Corypheus," I murmured as the Vathek man bowed over my hand. It was not difficult to imitate the barely veiled disdain Maram had expressed toward him. I was hard pressed not to wipe my hand on my skirts when he released me at last. "You remember my fiancé, His Grace of the Banu Salih."

"Yes, of course," he said and straightened. It seemed Maram's lip curl was a trait shared by all her distant kin. "The Upstart."

I bristled, but held my tongue when Idris tightened his grip around me.

"How are your holdings faring, Cor?" Idris asked.

The vak Aphelion family held the oldest excelsior mine on Vaxor, the planet around which their own terraformed moon orbited. But its source was thinning after many centuries of mining. They were close to their end if the king continued to ignore their emptying coffers.

Corypheus, for his part, looked furious. Two red spots flamed to life on his cheeks. I said nothing because Maram would have said nothing. She enjoyed watching Corypheus twist in the wind. He'd had hopes, she told me, that his family could finagle an engagement out of the king. But nothing had come, and he'd become increasingly desperate.

At last, he turned his eyes back toward me. "May I have a dance, Your Highness?"

There was some satisfaction in letting Maram's smirk settle on my face.

"You may not," I said.

The bright spots on his cheeks grew brighter in embarrassment, a sight, I thought, Husnain would have enjoyed seeing. All the Vath we'd seen in our village had evidenced a terrifying emotionlessness. To see one so worked up—and at my doing—would have felt like a small, irrational victory.

"Shall we?" I added, turning to Idris, and closed the door on the image of my brother's face.

Idris tucked my hand into his elbow, his grin barely contained. "Of course. We owe the vak Castels felicitations for their marriage."

I felt as though I were walking on air as we made our way around Corypheus and to another cluster of young nobles. Theo, the vak Castel scion, held out his hands for me, a welcoming smile on his face.

"Cousin," I said, and let him pull me close and kiss my cheeks in the Kushaila way, one on my left cheek and two on my right. Theo was seldom on Andala, but he and Maram had spent a great deal of time together on Luna-Vaxor. A younger son, he'd been as at the mercy of their large horde of relatives as she had.

I let Idris take the lead, interrupting only to murmur pleasantries with as much of Maram's distaste as I could manage. Few of Maram's Vathek cousins had love for her, though as far as I could tell, they were good at pretending. At one point during the conversation, I looked up to Idris to gauge how I was doing. His smile was warm and open, indulgent, and he brushed a stray curl of hair behind my ear. His fingers stayed there for a moment before he linked our hands.

I said nothing, but my heart beat a fast rhythm. Idris was a practiced actor, that much was obvious. But Maram and Idris's engagement was a matter of the state, not the heart. He didn't love her—did he? Did he know her well enough to know an impostor?

I tugged my hand out of his without comment and tucked it into the crook of his arm. He said nothing; his conversation with Theo didn't miss a beat.

"Another dance?" Idris asked, though it sounded closer to a command than a suggestion. He was already stepping close when I looked up at him. He was very tall, I realized suddenly, more than a head taller than me, with broad shoulders that dwarfed my frame.

I had not realized how much I had missed looking into faces I understood, faces that looked like my kin. Some of Maram's attendants were Andalaan, but in my new day-to-day life, I was surrounded by droids and Nadine. Save for Tala and the few times I'd listened in on Maram's small court, I'd been deprived of this—of the comfort of familiarity. Though I knew, viscerally, that there was nothing transparent about him, there was something instantly calming in his features.

Be careful, I reminded myself. There were few within and without the Ziyaana who knew Maram better than Idris. He was engaged to her, and not a dissident but a lord in the Vathek court. He looked like my kin—he was not. He was just as Vathek as the rest.

"Yes," I murmured, and held myself carefully as he wrapped an arm around my waist and linked our hands with the other.

As we moved through the steps to the complicated dance, I barely heard our conversation, so focused was I on the movement. Any missed step could reveal me. Idris's hands burned like fire where he touched me, constant reminders that the slightest error would be noticed. But the weeks of lessons didn't fail me. My body knew its way through the dance, even as my mind whirled.

"Food?" Idris asked, peering down as the dance drew to its end.

At last, I let myself smile. "Please."

II

Idris tucked my arm in his elbow and together we made our way to the far eastern corner of the room, where tables of food were laid out for us to eat. We were parted more than once—the ballroom was long and vast, and Idris was popular. I should not have been surprised when Furat made an appearance before me.

She sank prettily to her knees, and then rose just as gracefully. She was wearing a gown in the old Zidane style, in shades of gold that came close to red and brown, with wide sleeves and a beautiful waist piece. Her hands were dark with henna, a tradition Maram had never indulged in. She resembled Idris more than Maram with her high forehead and olive skin. Where Maram's hair—my hair—curled uncontrollably, hers fell in waves around her face, thick and brown with a red sheen in the sun. She had the roundness in face common to the Kushaila, and a hint of rounded cheeks. Her daan must have been striking when she had them, dark black against her skin, impossible to ignore.

I eyed her warily, trying to make sense of what I knew. If she had given up her daan, why choose to dress so? Why not blend in?

I could see, suddenly, why Maram disliked her so. She was effortlessly poised, fearless, despite all she'd lost and all she still had to lose. Maram clung to her Vathek gloss like a shield. Furat, on the other hand, was fully Andalaan despite being stripped of her daan. And she managed to produce the same hard shine as any Vathek courtier.

Maram, I imagined, would hate her twice over—first for effortlessly embodying our dying traditions, despite Vathek mandate, and second for her calm.

Me, I envied her. She was everything I wanted to be—free, despite being completely under someone else's control.

"Cousin," she said when she was standing again.

"I didn't think you would come," I said. "You seem to enjoy your provincial traditions far more."

"I was invited," she said. "And I thought I should see such a celebration at least once. You cannot judge what you do not know."

I hummed, thoughtful, then moved around her.

"We should learn to be around each other," she said as I passed by.

"I don't see that we should," I replied, voice flat, and tried to continue on.

Instead, I ran headlong into a servant.

"Are you alright?" I asked without thinking, then realized my mistake. Her head jerked up, eyes wide and face white.

Maram would never ask such a thing.

"Maram?" Idris said from behind me. He did not spare the

serving girl a look, and instead held out an arm to me. I held my breath, but he said nothing.

Idris and I were led to a table on a dais, raised up over everyone else. There was a single large plate between us, along with a tea set, the glasses etched with feathers in silver. The food itself was from various regions, all of it finger food. Small Vathek biscuits, Kushaila briouat stuffed with lamb, Norgak vilgotzi. Ringing the edge of the plate Kushaila chebakiyya, a favorite of Maram's. To our right and left were other tables, a little below us, but the seating arrangement had effectively closed us off into our own little bubble.

He bent his head toward me when he wanted to speak, mouth close to my ear, as I'd seen him do with Maram. I stiffened, unsure what he would say, but he merely wanted to gossip. He pointed out dignitaries and their children, telling me the latest news from far-off places.

"The king has confiscated all of House Dion's holdings," he said to me, and set a piece of honey-drenched chebakiyya on my plate. "They're not penniless, but none of them want to go back to Luna-Vaxor."

I resisted the urge to pick up the chebakiyya, lest the honey drip onto my dress. "Why not? It's home to them."

"Oh, my dear," he said, and I fought the instinct to raise my eyebrows. "They wouldn't be half as wealthy on their moon mining excelsior as they would be here inheriting lands that were liberated in the occupation."

His voice dripped with sarcasm. Did he really speak to Maram in such a way? I struggled for a moment, casting him a sidelong glance. Was it his security as a lord at Maram's side that allowed him to speak so, or was he taking a risk?

I'd never considered what it might be like, to be a makhzen

and hostage of the Vath at the same time. I wanted to know where his loyalties lay. Did he want to be a king among the Vath? Or did his status as hostage necessitate play-acting as mine did?

I was unsure how Maram would respond to such a statement and settled on saying nothing at all. I looked out over the ballroom and the mix of people—Vathek and Taifa and Norgak and every tribe and culture across all of Andala and its moons were gathered here tonight.

He was still smiling, but there was a sharpness to it now, as if my cold reaction had put him on the defensive. We fell into an uneasy silence until he lay a hand on my shoulder.

"Another dance?" It felt like both a challenge and a peace offering. Did he placate Maram like that? Did she enjoy dancing so much? I let him lead me onto the dance floor as the music started up again.

"Would you like to hear a story? It's a Kushaila one. An old one."

I couldn't stop my head from jerking up at that. He was playing with me, I was sure—though whether it was because the statement would annoy Maram, or because he had a notion something was off about me, I couldn't tell. He smiled just a little, with an edge of triumph. My fingers tightened painfully on his shoulder without thinking.

"Now you're interested," he said.

I held my tongue, though he deserved a tongue lashing. I was angry—at myself for being so easily baited with the mention of home, and at him for gaining this small victory.

"It's about Massinia," he continued. "And her marriage."

I restrained myself from closing my eyes. I knew the story—most people knew the story. But I had memorized the poetic forms it had taken, the formalized prose by Ibn Saj', the varying anecdotes in biographies. I didn't want to hear the story. Not to-night. But if I stopped him, he'd grow suspicious.

He lowered his head to mine while we danced, his voice even and melodic.

"Massinia was of the Tazalghit, horse masters of the desert," he began. "They were tribal, and all their tribes were ruled over by women."

His voice was strong and even, though hearing the story in Vathekaar was not ideal. Kushaila had a rhythm to it, and the sto-ries were told in verse, so by the end you felt you were hearing a song you'd heard all your life. Idris's telling of the story brought me no comfort. Instead, nostalgia for home rose up in me, bitter and hard. I didn't want to hear the story in this cold, alien tongue. I wanted Ibn Saj's prose or the poetry I'd kept back in the Ziyaana.

"She fell in love with a shepherd," he continued. "And for a time she was happy."

"But?" I prompted.

His hand tightened on my waist. "But Massinia's heart did not belong to her," he said. "It belonged to her tribe and her family. And their discovery might spark a war."

"Did it?" I asked. I knew the answer, but Maram likely didn't.

"Her sisters discovered her and killed him," he answered. "And a war with his family followed."

I shut my eyes and allowed Idris to guide me through the last steps of the dance. Likely I would never find a love like Massinia's. When I was younger I'd dreamed of such a thing—quiet moments that built on each other into something lasting. But I lived in the Ziyaana now. Though my heart belonged to me, my body no lon-ger did. Finding such love would be impossible.

"What a sad story you've told me," I said at last, looking up at him.

He grinned. "She gets a happy ending."

"Oh?"

"Do you know what happened to her? At the end of her life?" he asked.

I did know, but by all accounts Maram was not religious, so I waited for him to continue.

"She disappeared," he said.

I was hard put to not snort. She hadn't disappeared, at least not in the way historians meant. The tesleet who'd first saved her, Azoul, returned to her—after the wars of unification, after the transcription of Dihya's Book, after her love died—and offered her a feathered cloak.

Return, oh mourner, he said to her. *Set your feet in our Citadel.*

And she'd donned the cloak and slipped out of the hands of everyone who'd ever wanted to make use of her and her legacy.

I was pulled out of my reverie by Idris's voice. "The Steward-ess is here to escort you away."

Idris and I finished our dance with one last twirl. Then with-out another word he escorted me across the floor to Nadine, who stood in her customary black, her ever-present droid at her side.

"The king requests an audience," she said when I reached her.

I forced myself to stand tall and not waver. If I couldn't pass muster with His Grace, then all was lost. I heard Maram's voice again, her comment to me during our very first meeting: *your very life depends on it.* Yet she needn't have said the words aloud for me to understand what was at stake. I knew how the Vath worked; we all did. Failure was not an option.

Idris brushed a kiss over my cheek, then let me go.

My heart beat erratically as I let her lead me away, toward the throne at the far end of the chamber—it had long been unoccu-pied as the night wore on, but now I saw that the king was indeed in his place. King Mathis, Maram's father. King Mathis, Conqueror of the Stars.

I hated him more than I had ever hated anyone.

"You are in fine form tonight," she said as we walked through the crowds, which parted as they saw us approach. "I hope you are enjoying the ball."

"Thank you, my lady, I am."

I had managed an entire room full of courtiers, I thought to myself. Even Idris, who seemed to know Maram best of all, didn't appear to suspect I was a stand-in. Surely I could brave one more trial.

My breath did not come any easier, but I stiffened my spine despite that. I could go without breath if it meant I would live to see the next morning.

A man in a high-backed chair spoke urgently to the advisor next to him. At our approach, he turned and waved the advisor away.

Mathis, son of Hergof, High King of the Vath, Emperor of the Outer Ouamalich System, Protector and Inheritor of the Stars of the Inner Reach, sat before me.

I had seen his face before, of course. It was impossible to escape our king. His profile graced our new currency and most administrative buildings. He was taller than I expected, his chest and shoulders broad, hard beneath the black of his military jacket. His silver hair gleamed in the torchlight, cropped short and close to his skull. His eyes, blue, seemed to glow, and every story about the Vathek alienness rushed to the forefront of my mind.

I sank to my knees slowly, as I had done before Nadine not so long ago, and cast my gaze to the floor. I could feel his eyes on me.

"Your Eminence," I breathed.

Silence.

I forced my hands to relax in my lap, though I heard the sound of the king turning back around to his advisor, whispering something. My life depended on the outcome of this meeting. My world had narrowed to this moment and all the steps leading up to it.

"Nadine," he said after a moment. "Notify my servants. I go to Rif tomorrow, once this festival has ended."

"Yes, Your Eminence."

"And Maram?"

My head jerked up and I met his eyes. I felt nearly blasphemous looking at him. My face, I hoped, was blank. I willed my heart and my thoughts to calm. His eyes seemed to knife through all my pretending to see inside me. For a moment my mind was blank with fear that he'd seen through me.

I wrestled myself into calm, and forced myself to continue.

"Yes, Your Eminence?"

He held out a gloved hand. For a moment, I stared at it, uncomprehending. Nadine said nothing, but I could feel her behind me, berating me for my slowness and stupidity. I slid my hand into his and let him help me gracefully to my feet.

"What do you intend to do about securing your confirmation?" he asked me.

"Your Eminence?" I felt like a glitching holoreel.

He frowned, a fearsome, angry expression. He was so unlike my own father, who even in his angriest moments never frightened me.

"Last we spoke," he said, "you agreed to produce a plan to handle the senate and confirm your status as heir. I ask so little of you already—"

Nadine, at last, coughed softly. "Your Eminence, we discussed the small matter of . . ." She never finished her sentence, and I was not foolish enough to turn my back on the king, but his expression smoothed as he understood. He turned a new gaze on me, critical and sharp, as if he meant to peel away all the layers of my self.

"Come here," he said, his voice soft.

I stepped forward.

His gloves were soft against my chin. I did not know if it was the Vathek way to touch those below you, turning them this way and that to see if they met the measure they'd set. I felt like a bauble, constantly held up to the light to determine clarity. At last, he leaned back and rested his hands on the armrests of his chair. I hadn't lowered my gaze and watched him almost as closely as he watched me.

"We are curious to see if you will survive the Ziyaana," he said, whisper-soft. Then he raised a hand and waved me away.

I sank to my knees gracefully, my mind still, rose to my feet again, and walked away. But I could not resist a glance over my shoulder—he had turned his chair so that he was facing the wide picture window. The last I saw of him was his back and too-broad shoulders, outlined by the moonlight.

Nadine delivered me back to my table, whispering a few words of approval. Nerves still singing, I sat and watched the dancing couples as they stepped and spun. The night had taken on an otherworldly feel, and the lights seemed to reflect off the ice sculptures and windows in strange ways, making shapes on the floor out of shadow and iced flame.

I had succeeded in the impossible. Pride swelled inside me. I'd succeeded where everyone had expected failure. And my success meant that I would live. Long enough, I hoped, to escape. Long enough to find a way out of the Ziyaana, and to another life.

Return, oh mourner, return.

the ziyaana,
andala

12

Maram was waiting for me in my chambers as soon as we returned to the Ziyaana. She stood in front of a window, haloed by the bright orb light.

The door creaked open and then shut before she turned around to look at me. It was still disorienting to see myself in another person. I had become so much like her, had learned to carry her expressions over mine like a second skin, that sometimes I forgot there was an original.

She sighed and sat on the pillowed bench behind her.

"Well," she said. "You seem to have had a good time."

"I danced," I replied, voice flat. "It was enjoyable."

She lifted an eyebrow. "So. Tell me how it went."

I didn't know what to tell her. No one, not even her father or fiancé, had been able to divine the difference between the two of us. Her father had been warned, and still failed to notice a double in his daughter's place. Her peers had given me a wide berth, had spoken to Idris first before looking at me.

I wondered, for a moment, how such a life might feel. Isolated from everyone except the person you were meant to marry, and he a prisoner of the state in every way but name. Feared by your peers. Ignored by your father. Orphaned by your mother.

For a brief moment, I felt something like pity.

It died quickly.

"It was as you said," I spoke finally. "Dazzling. Far more fun than I thought it would be."

"Different from your small country parties, I gather?" she said, leaning back.

"We don't dance with one another on Cadiz," I said. "At least not in such close quarters."

The dances on Cadiz had none of the manufactured polish of the waltz I'd shared with Idris. They weren't about closeness or about looking close—they were about joy. They were about experiencing joy with your family and community. The waltz felt as if it were about secrets—Idris's voice in my ear, his breath on my neck, his hair brushing my cheek.

A manufactured closeness, but an effective one.

"How . . . quaint."

The gown she wore made it seem as though she poured herself onto the divan, as if she were a flood, when she sat down.

"The king?"

"Could not tell the difference," I said quickly. "It was a complete success."

I hated that she flinched. "Come here," she said, and patted a spot on the divan.

I watched her as I would watch a viper, but did as I was commanded. In the moonlight she looked soft and young and vulnerable. She was young, I remembered. Seventeen, nearly the same age as me. I wondered how often Idris saw her like this. Did this make it easier to be kind to her? Was this the girl he remembered when he told her stories?

"You do look very much like me," she said, and tilted her head. "One could almost forget you were a farmer's daughter."

"Am I meant to be flattered?" I asked.

She laughed, loud and bright. "You're developing a sharp tongue," she said. "Tell me, at least. Did he speak to you?"

For a moment, I blinked, confused. "Ah—His Eminence. No, not more than a few words. He asked about your plan for your inheritance, but—he seemed quite busy."

"Yes," she said, her smile slipping. "Though not too busy to remind me I still haven't secured my own inheritance from my half sister."

My eyes widened. "You have a half sister?"

Maram nodded, her gaze far-off. "Galene, from my father's first marriage. His only Vathek marriage, as everyone is kind enough to point out whenever given half a chance. We were brought to Andala at the same time, though she's been relegated to its northern climes. Technically she doesn't qualify for the line of inheritance—a stipulation of the peace treaty is that only my mother's children can. But it doesn't keep her from trying to supplant me."

"But—" I started.

"But Mathis, Conqueror of Stars, has never been held back by the laws of others." She waved her hand dismissively. "Do you know the story of how my father came to power?"

I shook my head; I'd never heard it before.

"He was a second son," she began. "His father expected him to be a second general as befitting his order of birth. My father refused—he killed his father and took control of both the planet and its military. Mathis stops at nothing to secure his power and rule. He will disinherit me if he believes it suits his aims better."

I stared at her, unable to comprehend such ruthlessness.

"I imagine a farmer is not so merciless or single-minded, hm?" Maram asked, apparently done with her story.

"My father . . ." I'd seen my father often, but that happened when you lived in a small house and worked a small farm in a small village. Still, I knew what Maram meant. Some fathers, like Mathis, did not have time for their children. Baba had always been present, had encouraged the dreamer in me despite my mother's insistence that he not. I never doubted that he loved me, and I never felt as though I'd disappointed him.

"He loved poetry," I said without meaning to and turned to look out the window. "He wrote poetry for my mother before they were married. It was a necessary skill in courting—and he taught me." I smiled.

My parents were not a showy couple. Some of my friends' parents brought one another flowers or re-declared their love every festival. My parents on the outside were very close friends, though the heat and passion that characterized most love poetry was absent. When I was young, I'd wondered sometimes if theirs had been a marriage of convenience or of love. But then when I was eleven or twelve I'd returned from the orchards earlier than either of my parents expected me. I'd found them sitting quietly in the living room, my father's head in my mother's lap as he slept. When he opened his eyes to look up at her he smiled and she'd leaned down and pressed a gentle kiss to his forehead. My father was gentle by nature—my mother was not. But in that moment I'd seen what she might have been like when she was young, and what she was like when she was with my father.

Maram raised an eyebrow. "What need does a farmer have for poetry?"

"Every Kushaila is a poet," I said. "Poetry is our way. It's how we court, how we tease, how we—"

She raised a hand. "Enough," she said, voice threaded with laughter. "Don't break into vapors. My, my—you look pleased at such a heritage."

"Aren't you pleased with yours?"

I'd said the wrong thing. Her smile turned hard and brittle, and her warmth evaporated. She stood up as if to remind me that I was the lesser of the two of us.

"Well," she said, and her smile made me shrink back. "Congratulations on your success. You needn't look so suspicious."

She made her way to the door. For a moment she stood in the entryway, framed by the faint light coming from the courtyard. What a lonely figure she struck, I thought. Without family or friends.

And then she lifted the hood of her cloak over her head and was gone.

13

A few weeks after my return from Atalasia, I watched Tala's fingers in my hair as she wove in semiprecious stones polished down into beads. The first time she'd shown me what she meant to put into my hair, I'd gaped in astonishment. But time had done its work and now the fineries afforded to a body double no longer shocked me.

"Tala," I said softly.

She looked up from my hair and caught my eye in the mirror with a smile. "Hm?"

"I never thanked you."

"For what?"

"For . . . saving my majority night dress," I said. I couldn't thank her for the poetry. That seemed a dangerous thing to speak out loud, and I knew in all likeliness she wouldn't acknowledge it. But it had carried me through all my weeks here ever since I'd found it. And I wanted her to know how grateful I was to have it. "I know you didn't have to."

She looked back down at my braids, the smile gone. "Say nothing of it," she said at last.

I watched her for a moment, then nodded. "Of course."

We sat in companionable silence for a few minutes. I imagined this was the way Tala preferred it. She had shown kindness to me, to be sure, but she had never tried to be my friend. I imagined she knew firsthand the costs of friendship in the Ziyaana.

"I meant to ask," she started. "How was the ball? How was the amir?"

I raised my eyebrows in surprise. She'd never asked me about how I spent my days, and I wasn't sure whether this was meant to be an opening.

"Oh, come now," she said with a sweet smile. "Maram is the envy of every Andalaan girl in the world. Idris ibn Salih is handsome and tragic. How did he seem to you?"

To my horror, I flushed. Handsome had seemed an understatement to me. But he was too charming by half, with his elegant dancing and his light touches and his quick rejoinders, and I knew he had to be clever to have survived in Maram's presence for so long. Still, even knowing that, I'd been hard pressed to resist his charm.

I smiled without meaning to. "He was a prince," I said at last. "What else is there to say?"

She made a soft chiding sound. "How vague." And then, "Oh," she said, as a droid arrived, summoning me away.

I'd never visited Maram's royal apartments. In truth, I'd rarely left the deserted east wing. It seemed dangerous to venture out, but the droid had offered a veil before we left, and I wore it now, terrified it would slip.

Maram's apartments were, I suspected, unchanged from their Kushaila stylings since before the occupation. The walls were layered in red and orange and green tiles, the ceilings and moldings along the wall were carved with geometric shapes in the zelij style and the old Kushaila script. There were no carpets, just cool stone floors beneath my feet, and dark wood furniture, upholstered in rich fabrics, stuffed full with feathers. Everything was situated low, in the Kushaila style, and there was a tea table to my left with floor cushions, and a Kushaila tea set.

I had imagined that she, with all her hate for her own blood, would have stripped the room of any Kushaila design. The script, at least, which I knew had to be from the Book, I thought she would have sanded down. And yet . . .

Maram herself was sprawled out on a divan, and facing the open balcony doors. I could see the wooden trellis, and hear birdsong and a babbling fountain, the rustle of leaves as a false wind passed through the courtyard below. It carried with it the smell of fruit—fig, I thought, and oranges. It smelled like home.

"It's so beautiful here," I said without thinking, forgetting for a moment that this was not a casual interaction between friends. But Maram seemed pleased.

"I've always wanted to hold our sessions here, but Nadine refused," she said, more to herself than to me.

I slid the cloak from my shoulders, and the veil I wore with it, and hung it over the back of a chair, before sitting next to her.

"Aren't you the princess?" I said without thinking. "Why don't you decide?"

Her mouth quirked briefly into a smile. "If—when—I am queen, I will do as I please," she said with a shrug. "Nadine is

Father's steward." Her mouth twisted at the word. "She can do as she likes whenever she likes."

Again, I could not control my mouth. "That seems—"

"She is High Vathek. Pure," she interrupted, staring into the distance. "My father . . . he values that. They all do."

There was nothing I could say to that. We sat in awkward silence as she seemed to mull over what she'd said, and I was uncomfortably reminded why we looked like one another. Maram was not only Vathek. I could imagine, suddenly, the neglect she'd suffered at the hands of her father, and how it might have been a result of the circumstances of her birth. Few of those outside the Ziyaana believed the old queen had married Mathis willingly. It had been a necessary thing; the only way to stave off the bloodshed, to save the last families remaining, to ensure peace.

Peace among the makhzen, at least.

A bird cried out from the courtyard, and Maram startled, coming out of her reverie.

"That isn't why I called you here," she said, standing.

I straightened.

"We have an assignment for you."

"Some plan to send me to my death, then?" I asked, before I could think better of it.

The words hung between us, said in her voice, in her dry humor, perfectly sharp and royal. If only they hadn't come out of my mouth.

She laughed, a burst of crystalline sound. I eyed her uneasily, but her shoulders relaxed and she dropped back into the seat beside me.

"I like you better when your tongue is sharp, village girl," she said, a smile still tugging at the corners of her mouth.

I had the sense to not say "*today*," and kept my eyes on her hands, instead of meeting her gaze.

"The assignment, Your Highness?" I said.

Her laughter had not transformed the tension in the room, at least not for me. I knew by now how mercurial her moods were, how quickly a smile or the appearance of friendship could turn. She would remember something, or I would move in a particular way, or she would simply change her mind about the way she wanted to be.

So I waited, and I watched.

"Oh, yes," she said, and pulled her braid over her shoulder. "My grandmother, the Dowager Sultana—in exchange for remaining off-world, I must visit her. It's meant to demonstrate"—she waved her hand dismissively—"something. Continued good will between savages and conquerors. You are being sent in my place this year."

There was no way to hide my confusion. I was meant to be a stand-in when there was trouble. What harm could there possibly be in going to her grandmother's estate? Too late, I noticed the clench in her jaw. For once it was not me she was looking at, but a tapestry hung on the far wall in the room. I watched her, hands clenched in my lap, as she made her way around the divan and onto the balcony.

She didn't brace her hands on the railing as I would have. Instead, again, she stood perfectly still, one hand twisted easily in the folds of her gown, the other idle. She looked picturesque—a vision of Andalaan royalty, burning in red.

"There are rebels on the moon where she resides," she said at last, her voice dangerously flat. "Some suspect they have flourished because of her idleness."

I didn't know how to respond. Maram was universally reviled

by Andalaans—there was no way around that. But her grandmother, no matter how much a patriot, could not condone a rebel
plot to assassinate her only grandchild.

Maram flicked her gaze to me, and then back to the garden
below, uncaring. "You needn't look so shocked. It's your way, isn't
it—tribal infighting?" she sighed. "Go. I tire of you. Nadine will
tell you the rest."

I forced myself to speak as I stood, the words tight with fury.
"It's in our blood, I suppose," I said, and left.

14

The day of my departure dawned early. I sat at the vanity while Tala moved between the wardrobe to the many open chests spread around the room.

"What are the Gates?" Tala said. She was quizzing me as she worked.

"The Gates of Ouzdad are the unassailable walls of the Dowager's estate, brought from an ancient temple on Andala to the moon Gibra at the time of its terraformation. It predates the space age."

"Name the Dowager's living relatives," Tala said, with a brisk nod.

"She had two younger sisters and a younger brother before the invasion," I said. "The brother rebelled in the twelfth year of her reign, sparking the civil war. He was banished to Cadiz and was among the dead in the first wave."

"And her sisters?"

"Died in the third wave of the invasion," I said.

"The populations on Gibra," she prompted.

"Largely Kushaila," I replied. "Though a coterie of the Tazalghit settled there some two hundred years ago."

Tala made a soft noise of approval, her quizzing over.

I stared at myself, hair twisted like Maram's, a circlet wrapped around my forehead, the dark green of the qaftan gleaming in the soft light of a lantern.

I set the stick of kohl down and stood, finished with my preparations. Small earrings, two rings, instead of Maram's customary four or five, and a single bracelet. I'd forgone even a necklace in light of the Dowager Sultana's tastes.

A droid waited for me in the courtyard, one of Maram's cloaks draped over an arm. It was not alone.

Maram stood beside the droid, uncharacteristically quiet and patient. She was dressed as I normally dressed—an austere dark blue qaftan, with little embroidery, no jewelry, and a cloak with its hood raised over her hair. A veil hung limp from one of her hands, waiting to go back over her face.

She cracked a smile when she saw me. "Oh, don't look so stoic," she said, coming forward. She reached over and pulled the loose braid from over my left shoulder to my right. "You'll have a great deal of fun on Gibra and then you'll come back, and that'll be that."

She seemed in a great mood, her smile wide enough that her left cheek dimpled. There was no edge to her today, no anger or sarcasm in reserve. I didn't trust it for a second.

"Where will you go?" I said, rather than poke at her mood.

She beamed at me. "Somewhere far. I don't mean to be a caged bird while you go traipsing through my grandmother's catacombs."

"Oh," I said. I hadn't thought about that, really. I was certainly caged in when she was cavorting through the Ziyaana or traveling the system. Still, I was not a princess. There was no reason allowances should have been made for me.

"Somewhere cooler, then?" I asked.

She hummed, lifting a shoulder, and plucked at my gown. "Perhaps. It's not for you to know."

The droid beside her lifted my cloak, a signal to prepare to leave. I draped it over my shoulders, slid my arms through the small openings in its fabric, and raised the hood.

"Village girl," she said, as I turned away.

I paused, the hairs on the back of my neck raised in warning.

"Take care of Idris," Maram said, and came around to face me.

My eyes widened. I hadn't realized he was coming. I'd barely managed when we'd only spent a few hours together. Now I would have to manage him—fooling him—for weeks. "He . . . Gibra is often difficult for him."

I frowned. "Difficult?"

For a moment, she stared at me, as if trying to discern a hidden truth. Then she shook her head. "He is—we are friends," she said, as if it pained her to admit it. "But he gets bored easily and there's nothing but sand and rocks on Gibra."

My eyes widened further and I considered pushing. Idris seemed to have little difficulty, no matter what it was. I could not imagine that being on Gibra, free of the machinations of the Ziyaana, would prove difficult for him.

"Village girl," she said, and gripped my arm. "Do you understand?"

I nodded, the warning in the back of my mind rising. "Yes, Your Highness."

She nodded back. "Good."

We were not departing from the main concourse, as we had when leaving for Atalasia. Our group was much smaller this time around; all of Maram's ladies in waiting were staying behind, so that it was myself, Idris, Tala, and a handful of handmaidens. This landing zone looked more like a garden than a place to leave the planet. There were trees everywhere, heavy with out-of-season fruit. The cruiser we were taking off-world was smaller than the luxury liner we'd boarded only a month ago. Shaped like an ocean floor-dwelling creature with wide, curved wings, and a bulbous center, it was only two levels high, long enough that the serving girls and boys would remain separate from the handmaidens, and they separate from Idris and I.

Idris, for his part, stood on the other side of the concourse flanked by two droids. He'd not bothered to tie his hair back this morning, and there was something missing—as though he had not put on all his armor as he usually did. He looked tired, I realized. There were no bags under his eyes, and he stood up straight, as though there were a rod of steel in his spine, but he lacked his usual gloss.

I was used to quiet, so I thought little of Idris's silence when he offered me a hand as we boarded. We were led to a sitting room, lushly carpeted, with a wide window at the far end. There was a low table in the Kushaila style, and several cushions for sitting. Idris and I settled ourselves into our seat, and waited while a droid put down a tea set and poured.

We were very quickly clearing the cloud cover on the surface of Andala. The only time I'd been so high up was my journey to the planet's surface, and I remembered that only in bits and pieces. The sun was only just rising, and the air above the clouds was velvet blue and pink and violet. I could see Cadiz, pale green, threaded with gold lights of the dozen cities on its surface.

A soft pang twisted itself in my chest. I'd had few opportunities to look up at the sky in the last months and had not seen my home since leaving. Now I looked for it hungrily. I missed the image of the mountains painted against a sunrise, missed the sounds of my village, and the smell of snow just a few days away. I was determined to get back to it somehow, Dihya willing.

Of the two moons, Gibra was the larger, a round rusted red giant. Botanists had settled Cadiz, and I didn't know who terraformed Gibra, but none of the verdant and lush life clear on Cadiz from millions of miles away showed on Gibra's surface. There was no evidence of water, though I'd heard a large portion of it existed underground. The lights that twined around Cadiz were largely absent on its sister moon. Fewer cities, fewer citizens, and populated by an altogether harsher people.

I could not imagine what sort of life the Dowager Sultana lived on its surface. I knew that her continued survival depended on her removal from Andalaan politics, both physically and in spirit. But to go from queen of the free people, to their freedom fighter, to a prisoner on a faraway moon—it would have been a difficult, bitter pill to swallow. In her long life she'd battled would-be usurpers, civil war, traitorous family, and our Vathek conquerers. To be exiled after all that . . .

No one ever saw her in the public eye. The few times I'd glimpsed her face were in old holos from before the occupation. She lived a quiet life, away from her past, away from the present.

A prickling on my scalp prompted me to pull my gaze from

the window. Idris was watching me. He was leaning away from the table just a little, one hand resting idle, the other playing with his signet ring. When my eyes landed on it he stopped and folded his fingers over it. I raised my eyes back to his face and found him just as focused as he'd been moments ago.

"Do you know why I told you the story of Massinia?" he said at last. "I wanted to see how much you would remember."

"Remember?" If he'd been telling the stories to Maram, she'd failed to mention it to me. I was in dangerous territory here.

"From your childhood," he said.

I raised my eyebrows. "You were testing me?"

He smiled. "Yes."

"Did I pass?" I forced myself to say.

"You didn't contribute," he said.

"It is my understanding that it is rude to interrupt a story-teller," I said. "No matter how poor the telling."

His smile deepened. I'd amused him. Lovely.

"Did I not measure up?"

I looked away. I wouldn't take the bait. I'd amused myself in the quiet hours by cataloguing his mistakes, both in the story and in its telling. Poor diction, no sentence variance, no interest—Idris didn't care about the story of Massinia. Why should any-one care about her when her story was a series of dates and historical moments, devoid of passion or care?

"Silence is the most damning criticism," he said with a laugh.

We were approaching the moon now, and I watched its rusty red resolve into something more complex. The surface was a shift-ing tapestry of orange, yellows, and reds, pushed this way and that by the currents of the wind. Sand everywhere, with few breaks in its surface for anything else.

A strange place, but home for the next three weeks.

the ouzdad estate

GIBRA,

A MOON OF ANDALA

15

It wasn't long before we made the descent to Gibra's surface. The blurry tapestry of sand didn't resolve itself into anything as we approached our landing port. There were a few buildings, some lampposts, and the tarmac.

The cruiser hissed and bumped as it touched ground. For miles outside our window all I could see was desert, sand dunes, and an impossibly pale blue sky, unbroken by clouds.

There was a greeting party on the tarmac. I held back, still close to the ramp, as Maram would have, and watched as Idris grinned, and grabbed the leader of our greeting party in a hug.

"What's happened to your face?" the man said, clapping Idris on the shoulder. It took me a moment to recognize him from the holoreader—Nabil, a lesser illegitimate son. Maram hated him, as she did Furat. Despite the status of their birth, they were favored by the Dowager and allowed to live with her.

"It's what always happens," Idris said, grinning. "I shaved."

Nabil snorted in disbelief and shook his head. "One day, we're going to get you to keep the beard, friend."

For a moment I felt as if I were back on Cadiz listening to my brothers. Husnain had only just been able to grow a beard in recent months, and to call it that was to be generous. Aziz had teased him mercilessly over it. I'd not expected to find the same sort of ribbing here, and had to fight down a smile. Maram seldom found Nabil amusing on these visits.

His eyes drifted over Idris's shoulder and settled on me. The smile broadened, though I had the sense he'd reminded himself where he was and what he was meant to do.

"Your Highness," he said, polite and easy. "As always, we are delighted to welcome you back to Gibra."

I said nothing, but held my hand out for Idris.

There was a slender transport, similar to the street carriages I'd seen on Andala, with an open hood. The rest of the party was seated on horses instead of the desert bikes I would have expected.

For a long while there were only the sounds of the carriage cutting through the sand, and the soft thud of hooves cantering along beside us. The landscape was unchanging, and it was a wonder to me that our drivers knew where they were going. They seemed determined, even without landmarks or compasses.

And then the ground changed. The carriage jolted, and the soft thuds turned to clops. The land dipped smooth and easy, and led us down, away from the sand and its moveable mountains. Rock walls rose up on either side of us, impossibly high, peach colored and shadowed. From the entrance to the canyon, it looked as if some great hand had shoved itself into the ground and split the earth in two.

We rolled over the smooth path quickly, and it seemed that after no time at all, the scenery—and the air—changed yet again. I could feel water in the air, cool, thin, but there. It carried with it the smell of lemons and oranges, and the sound of a hundred trees, waving gently in the wind.

I did not gasp, because Maram had seen this before, but my body stiffened in wonder and awe all the same.

The Gates of Ouzdad were the stuff of legend. As high as the canyon walls were tall, made of bricks as tall and wide as men, its doors studded with gleaming silver pikes, they had withstood a hundred thousand assaults. No one had ever been able to tear them away from the canyon walls, nor breach the doors. Like the spikes on the door, the tiles overlaying the walls gleamed—orange, green, blue, and white, they were arranged to look like flowers with sharp petals. The Dowager Sultana's flag flew from the top, merry in the weak breeze, and her soldiers marched along the walkway, keeping watch over those inside and out.

I followed its edge along the canyon wall, seamless, all the way to the top. It stopped several dozen meters shy of the ledge, but my eyes continued to climb. There was nothing like this in Walili, the capital city where the Ziyaana sat, or on Cadiz.

A dozen mounted horsewomen lined the left edge, robed in black. They were stark figures in a barren landscape, outlined against the blue of the sky. Several of the horses shook their heads, and the light bent off the silver on their bridles. The Tazalghit. The tribes of the Tazalghit were Massinia's people, united under her mother, and powerful horsewomen who'd ruled the desert before the rise of the Ziyadis.

They looked as fierce and fearless as the stories made them

sound. I knew it was still the custom of villages and cities alike in their lands to pay tithe to them. I tried not to stare too much— they couldn't see me, but our escort could, and Maram had made clear nearly everything on Gibra bored her.

We pulled to a stop several meters shy of the gate, and waited as Nabil flashed identification and for the doors to groan open. A flash of birds burst into the air on the other side of the gate, shrieking angrily, their cries pierced every now and then by the sound of happy children.

I had not thought of the Ziyaana as a Vathek-washed version of the traditional Kushaila styles, but entering the Ouzdad estate made it strikingly clear. The sun shined down on a wide, two-story structure built against the left side of the canyon. A single tower rose on the far end, capped in gold, its walls inlaid with shining green stone. It was obvious the white walls were regularly cleaned—they had none of the Ziyaana's rusted pallor and gleamed almost as brightly as the tiles weaving their way through them. The gates to the town were impressive, but Ouzdad itself, its many windows and turrets, its single, high gold doorway, was beautiful. Treetops peeked over the edges of terraces, birds roosted where they could, and the doors were ajar, letting in a steady flow of people.

The town itself spilled from the palace, instead of from the gates, a well-organized cluster of buildings, none more than two stories, all clean and well kept. The avenues were wide, the roads smooth and lined with lanterns. Beyond the town itself were yet more orchards, and beyond that another tower, which I knew was attached to the Dihyan temple at the outskirts.

The inside of the palace was equally beautiful. Gleaming white walkways, high carved arches, ornate pillars—everything the Ziyaana had but brighter, more real, as though the Ziyaana were attempting an imitation of something else. I'd found something real here.

There were orange trees, heavy with their fruit, inside the palace as well, fig trees waiting to bloom, thin, skeletal olive trees, their bright and glossy leaves waving slowly as we made our way further into the palace. Maram's quarters—my quarters—shared a courtyard with Idris's, a round, paved space, with a fountain babbling happily in the center. The fountain tile was inlaid at the bottom with orange and blue tiles, arranged to look like flowers sprouting from the ground. The entrances to our rooms were framed by pillars made from orange canyon stone, carved with the old Kushaila script.

I remained standing by the courtyard as Tala directed serving girls to unload our things. The collection of chambers was built like a small kasbah—all of the living spaces oriented around the courtyard, including an upper floor with a portico, its engraved shutters wide open to let in the breeze. I could see the sky from here, a novelty I didn't know I'd been missing until I looked up.

For a moment I worried. I hadn't thought they would put Idris and I so close together, though why they should house us apart I had no idea. He was engaged to Maram, and it made sense to be so close—to dine and break fast together, to be able to wander easily into each other's spaces. But . . .

He'd retired almost immediately, claiming a headache. Perhaps we'd be able to go our separate ways, and I would not have to worry about keeping up pretenses with a prince.

This place felt loved, airy—the opposite of everything my quarters in the Ziyaana were. In the very back of the quarters was a small door, unobtrusive, made of dark wood. A lit lantern hung beside it, which I took, and after a glance around I pulled the door open. A breeze puffed out, and when I shone my lantern in I saw a series of stone steps leading down.

I knew they had to lead down to the catacombs. Ouzdad was famous for them, miles of passageways linking different wells beneath the surface, that led out of the palace. Hundreds of stories about royals in peril ended with them escaping into the catacombs, and coming out far away in the desert. For the first time in months I would be alone for a few hours, with no demands on my time. I could explore. I could wander the catacombs, masterless for the first time in ages.

I heard water before I reached the bottom. I'd expected an enormous cavern, wide open space with stalagmites jutting up from the ground. Instead the stairway led down to a passage lit with flickering sconces. On one side lay a waterway, waves sloshing up against the sides of pillars, and on the other side a mural of Massinia that seemed to roll forward, endlessly, into the gloom.

From the staircase I'd descended and onward the mural depicted Massinia throughout her life. Her childhood in the desert, her kidnapping and escape, her encounter with the tesleet, her adolescence, and on and on. I was transfixed by the image of her on a horse, her black robes whipping in an unseen wind. It was her face, dark and austere, her eyes furious and piercing, that held me. I didn't know how to describe Massinia—she was beautiful, as if a piece of night sky had come down to us. Her skin was dark, her forehead high, and her cheeks looked as if they'd been chiseled from stone. Always, her wiry hair was bound into a single braid from the crown of her head, threaded with silver pieces.

Her horse reared back and yet she kept her seat, unafraid of falling. Etched in gold across her forehead was the crown of

Dihya. Instead of the desert sky, the tesleet was spread behind her, its wings outstretched, its head held high.

At every turn in her life, Massinia took control of the narrative. She escaped her slavers, she found her love even if she couldn't save him, she united the tribes. And at the end of her life, when she'd had enough, she'd simply stepped out of the story and up into the sky.

My life had been a series of events happening to me, and I wanted so desperately to be able to exert the control Massinia managed on my own life. To see my family, to see Husnain, again. To have her power, her determination, her faith.

"There you are," Idris said from behind me, and I spun around, startled.

"What are you doing here?" My heart was racing and my voice trembled. The question came out as a demand, and an angry one at that.

He raised an eyebrow and took the lantern from me. "Your maidservant said you were down here. You've never liked the catacombs before, so I wanted to see what you found so fascinating," he replied. His gaze narrowed at me. "I did not peg you for a Massinite, cousin."

I frowned. "A what?" Maram wouldn't know that word, even if I did.

He gestured to the mural. "An acolyte of Massinia."

I shook my head and turned back to the wall. "I don't pray to her, if that's what you mean. She's dead—she can't hear me."

"Then why do you look as if you love her?"

Even my mother had commented that how I felt about Massinia was stronger than what most of the faithful felt, and I chided myself for showing it.

"I'm not," I said at last, and picked up my lantern.

As far as I could gather, Maram had no faith. Her mother died before she could teach her, and her Vathek family had not bothered.

He caught my wrist, and raised an eyebrow at me. "We've never kept secrets."

I hardened myself against his smile and shook my head.

"I'm not keeping a secret," I said. "The murals are beautiful and I came down to look."

He wandered a little way down the mural and traced a finger over the lines of Kushaila. It depicted her first revelation—hidden away in a cave with a blank book open in her lap, and the first lines of our Book swirling around her.

Hear and recite, the words read, *for We know things you do not.*

"*One day you shall return to the stronghold.* That's how her poem ends," Idris said.

I paused, confused, then realized what he was referring to—the poem we'd talked about during the ball. Massinia's flight.

"That is a horrible translation," I said flatly.

He turned to look at me a second before I realized my mistake.

Maram didn't speak Kushaila—and even if she did, she would not have known the poem he'd tried—and failed—to translate.

"You are almost as easy to bait as Maram," he said at last. He wasn't smiling.

I felt the blood drain from my face.

Maram. The name hung in the air.

I'd been caught.

16

I stood in the gloom of the catacombs, head spinning.

"When—?"

"When did I know?" he asked. "I suspected at the ball, when you asked that servant if she was all right. Maram doesn't see servants, as a rule. But a million little things have told me since. Your face is far too open—Maram is never so unguarded. You look at people when you talk to them, instead of through them, as is her practice. You listen—everything I said elicited a reaction from you, no matter how small or benign. You seemed awed when we landed in Gibra, though Maram has never spared it a glance. Perhaps most telling of all is you listened and catalogued my mistakes during my . . . uninspired . . . telling of Massinia's stories. I could see it in your face, even if you had the grace not to share your true feelings with me."

Horror crept up my spine. Had I been so transparent? Were my mistakes so easily pinpointed and catalogued? A small part of me was impressed—I knew Idris had to be clever to have survived in the Ziyaana all these years, but this . . . How closely did he watch everyone around him to spot a difference even Maram's father had missed?

"If you were so sure," I said angrily, "why bait me at all?"

"Because you never would have admitted to being other than Maram if I'd asked nicely." He huffed a humorless laugh. "So, then. Who are you? And why are you here instead of Maram?"

I clenched my jaw. All my work, all I'd suffered, had come to nothing in a single moment. And Idris hadn't proven himself trustworthy, only clever. "And if I refuse to tell you?"

For the first time he looked surprised, and took a step forward. I quickly stepped back.

"You're frightened," he said, eyes widening.

"Of course I'm frightened," I said, my voice breaking. "You live in the Ziyaana! You know the cost—"

"Of failure," he finished. "I didn't think—"

"Of course you didn't. This was just a game to you. A puzzle to decipher." I drew in a trembling breath. "This is no game to me. My life depends on my success."

He nodded, eyes searching me, missing nothing. "I understand. But I can't help you unless—"

I scoffed before I could think better of it. "Help? You can't help. My old life is over. There is no escape, no respite from that truth. This is my life now. If this is a life at all."

He stared and I raised my chin, daring him to disagree with me.

"You speak like one of us," he said instead.

My jaw clenched harder in anger. "Thank you, sayidi," I said, the highborn Kushaila title a pointed reminder that I was *not* one of them. "A high compliment."

"That isn't—"

I held up a hand. I was so angry—at myself for being caught in this trap, at him for not understanding what it meant to be caught, at fate for landing me in the Ziyaana all those months ago.

The fountain further into the gloom turned on and the sudden flow of water disturbed a small bird, no larger than the palm of my hand. She chirped, offended, then winged her way past us and up the stairs toward the sun. The light flashed off her jewel-toned wings and then she was gone. I sympathized with her, disturbed after finally finding a place to rest. And I envied her for her quick and easy escape.

"You look so much like her," he said. "Did you always?"

I fixed my eyes on a flower just over his left shoulder.

"I had daan," I replied. Had I ever spoken—thought—about them in the past tense? "They were taken from me."

He had nothing to say to that.

In the quiet I felt my anger rise up again, resisted the urge to touch my cheeks and my forehead. There was no phantom pain where the ink once was, no lingering feeling. They had simply been a part of me, and now they weren't. I had reconciled myself to that.

His voice was softer when he spoke. He understood, then, the high price I'd paid. "How did you end up here?"

"How does anyone end up in the Ziyaana?" I asked, folding my arms over my stomach.

"You were kidnapped," he said. I remained silent. "We will be here, together, for some time. It may be to your benefit to trust me, sayidati."

The Kushaila word wasn't nearly as clumsy in his mouth as I'd expected.

I shook my head. "You should know better than me how difficult trust is in the Ziyaana."

He approached me as if I were a frightened animal. "You can trust me—it is not to my benefit to reveal your secret."

I forced myself to look at him.

"If I meant to use my knowledge against you," he said quietly, "I would have done so already."

I paused, considering. He was right. If he'd known the night of the ball, or on the flight from Andala to Gibra—he'd had opportunities to turn me in, to make use of the knowledge. To ruin me. He had not. That, at least, counted for something.

"They stole me on my majority night," I whispered, looking sightlessly into the dark water. "While my friends and family watched. While my brother watched. I didn't know why they wanted me until I saw her."

"Maram," he said.

I nodded. "My life has been defined by her since I've come to the Ziyaana." Once the words were out of my mouth it seemed they couldn't stop. They poured out of me—coming to the Ziyaana, being sealed away as if I were a girl in a tomb. Part of me felt like a girl detached describing everything I'd experienced— the isolation, the loss of my daan, living under Maram's and Nadine's eyes. But the girl who'd wept on her first night alone still lived in me, and I felt my voice waver and break.

Idris leaned against the wall beside me, quiet and observing, and let me talk, prompting me with questions, or giving me space to pause when I felt overcome. A strange lightness filled me as I spoke, as if I'd been waiting to unburden myself. I hadn't spoken about what happened to me to anyone. Who was there to listen? Tala, who had shown me small kindnesses, but feared getting too close to me. The droids, who could show neither sympathy nor understanding.

"How long have you been a prisoner?" he asked as I finished.

I let out a broken laugh. "I don't know. Weeks? Months? The ball was the first time I was allowed outside of the Ziyaana."

"These weeks might be a respite for us both," he said thoughtfully. "Without the Ziyaana to watch our every move."

I didn't smile, but the idea of it took hold of me. Time as myself, without a mask; without the threat of Nadine or Maram to darken my days.

"Yes," I said softly. "It could be."

The silence filled the space, more comfortable now, tempting me to accept his offer—of respite, of trust.

"What shall I call you?" he asked at last.

I raised my chin, making a decision. "You may call me by my name. Amani."

17

I woke to the sound of a loutar. The strings hummed slowly, leisurely, as though whoever were playing had all the time in the
world. No one sang, and there was no accompanying thump of a
bendir. I lay in bed for long moments with my eyes closed, luxu-
riating in it, hearing old tunes give rise to newer innovations.
There had been one loutar player in my entire village, an older
grandfather who'd passed away two years before my majority
night.

My room was full of shadows, the curtains drawn tightly shut.
Two lanterns flickered weakly, and their lights cast strange starry
shapes against the floor and walls. It was early yet in the morning.
The night's desert chill still lingered, and the birds were quiet. But
I could hear serving girls moving quietly outside my room, their

soft whispers, the sweep of a broom over the floor. Tala would not come to wake me while I was at Ouzdad; the royals could sleep as long as they liked.

The music faded and my mind turned to the night before, and my confession to Idris.

A small part of me whispered not to trust him. There was no trust in the Ziyaana—its inhabitants couldn't afford it. But we weren't in the Ziyaana. The proof of his trust was in my continued safety. For now, at least, my secret was safe, and so was I.

For a moment I worried what would happen if my trust were misplaced. Could I take such a risk? But it didn't matter, I reminded myself—I didn't have a choice.

I rose from bed and found a mantle to wrap myself in against the morning chill. The serving girls paused and lowered their heads as I passed through the main rooms and out of the garden. My feet carried me out of the garden suite and down halls painted in cheery colors, with high ceilings hung with lanterns.

Maram and Idris's suites were closer to the center of the palace, but it was an airy place filled with open courtyards and walkways everywhere. I plucked one of the many books off a shelf in my room and ventured outside. After some direction from a serving girl, I made my way to one of the few swimming areas in Ouzdad. The catacombs didn't always empty out into hidden rooms and temples. This passage opened up into a grotto carved out from the canyon wall. The walls had been smoothed, and the bottom of the pool was paved with bright orange and green stones. Someone had pruned the ground around it, clearing paths and setting up pavilions. I could see Idris's shape on the far end of the pool, near its entrance, twisting lazily beneath the water.

Neither I nor Maram could swim, so I settled into the cushioned seat and stretched along its length, the book in my lap. I'd pulled it off the shelf without looking at it, but now I realized it was a child's book, written completely in Kushaila. It was a collection of folk and fairy tales, the pages' edges gilt, with a hundred fanciful illustrations of mythological creatures.

I lost myself in the stories. I'd not read Kushaila script since my arrival in the Ziyaana, and like so much else at Ouzdad the experience was part grief, part elation. Part of me felt transported back to the marketplace in Cadiz. Old khaltous had sat in its center, telling old tales, harmless as far as the Vath were concerned. Khadija and I snuck away from our chores regularly to sit at the feet of one storyteller or another and listen to stories about tesleet and 'afareet come to our world to carry one person or another away. Khadija always liked the most romantic tales; her favorite was the story of Badr, who found his way to the gate-city of the tesleet and married one of its princesses.

The sound of water sloshing over the edges of the pool and a grunt broke my reverie. Idris had pulled himself out of the water, and now stood at the edge of the pool facing me, combing his dark hair out of his face. I was used to the broad-shouldered build of farmers in my village. My friends and I had spied on them, harvesting in the fields, reclining shirtless in the sun, beautiful and brown and perhaps one day husbands. Khadija had flirted with propriety the closer our majority night came. First bringing them food or water, and then later bringing nothing but herself. She'd been braver than me and more willing to grab what—and who— she wanted without ever looking back.

I'd never been such a girl—the arguments with my brothers had always loomed large in my mind. And besides, I'd never wanted any of them. Not truly. I'd flirted, to be sure, but fled anything serious. I was content with my parents' farm and my poetry.

But today my cheeks warmed and I could not pull my eyes away from the spread of Idris's back as he turned away from me, or the water trailing from his hair and over his shoulders. I'd never realized how long it was, it curled so at his ears and chin, but wet it clung to the back of his neck, and nearly reached past his shoulders. Idris's skin was a warm, dark gold, but already the few hours on Gibra had warmed it closer to bronze. Drenched in water and struck by sunlight, he seemed to glow as if he'd emerged out of another realm entirely. The spirits—'afareet—that stole spouses into their realm were normally women, but today I could believe it of Idris, come to Ouzdad to find a bride.

He turned to pick up a towel, still unaware that I sat on the pavilion behind him. There was a black circle about the size of the palm of my hand inked on his upper arm. I frowned, trying to make sense of it. I couldn't keep the noise of surprise inside when I realized what it was.

Idris jerked up in shock, and his eyes locked with mine. I felt like a child with her hand caught in the pantry. The heat in my cheeks spread, and no matter how much I willed myself to I couldn't break the stare. For his part, he seemed to fare just as poorly. His eyes were wide, his mouth slack with surprise. A bird cried out overhead, and just like that we both jerked our eyes away from the other. I pulled my knees up, as though they might shield me from him, and turned my eyes to my book, hoping that he would return to the water or to the palace.

The sound of bare feet slapping against stone moved away from me and toward the palace, and after a moment I breathed a sigh of relief and tried to return to my book. No matter how hard I tried, I couldn't follow the words on the page.

I knew that I had to have imagined the mark on his arm, or at the very least misunderstood what it was. It looked like a khitaam, a royal seal. Before the occupation, the members of the royal families bore them just below the neck. They were normally twice the size of the mark on Idris's arm, and like the daan they denoted family, faith, and ancestry. But the khitaam were more than that. When a member of a royal family came of age their family inked their hopes for them into their skin. May you be just, may you be kind, may you be strong, and on and on. When Mathis outlawed the daan among the nobility, he outlawed khitaams right along with them. The old families would not be recognized except through him, ancestral ties would not be recognized except through him.

The appearance of Idris's khitaam distracted me enough that I did not realize he'd returned until his shadow fell across my lap. He'd changed from his swimming shorts to a pair of trousers, and a white shirt that still stuck to his skin. His hair was bound away from his face, still wet, the shorter strands clinging and curling against his cheeks. There was a wooden board under his arm, and a velvet bag in his hand.

"Do you mean to take the whole couch?" he asked, staring pointedly at my outstretched feet.

And just like that, the nervous flutter in my chest disappeared. I resisted the urge to sigh, and pulled my feet underneath me, rearranging myself so that there was room for him.

"Thank you," he said. All traces of his earlier shock were gone, though when my gaze darted to where the shirt stuck to his chest he caught my eye and then looked away. He took the seat beside me, and without saying anything unfolded the board and set it on the table in front of us. From the bag, he pulled what looked like more than two dozen pieces split evenly between red and green.

"Have you played before?" he asked. I flushed again, caught staring a second time.

The board was set, but in mid-play. "Shatranj? Yes. It's popular with children."

He raised an eyebrow again. "The elder among us enjoy the game too."

I picked up one of the red pieces, shaped like an old chariot. The piece was well worn, though I could still see gold flakes in the grooves. "Not," I said, setting it down, "if they do not want to be accused of treason and sedition."

Idris snorted, a half smile lifting the corner of his mouth.

"What do farmers need to understand strategy for, if not to revolt?" I leaned away from the board.

He pursed his mouth, as if resisting the urge to bite on his bottom lip. My skin prickled just looking at his mouth when it had no business doing so.

"Well," he said, interrupting my thoughts, "a princess needs to know strategy, and you more than most. When did you play last?"

I lifted a shoulder.

"Then it will be easy to beat you?" I didn't rise to the bait. He sighed. "I really am trying to help you. You give away too much with your face, and so far you haven't been faced with Maram's peers alone. You will need to think strategically to survive."

"Alright," I said after a moment. I set my book aside and put my feet on the ground. "You will have to set the board from the beginning."

He shook his head. "It's a mansuba," he explained. "A problem board. Your pieces are trapped like so. How do you get them out?"

I could not have been more than nine or ten the last time I played shatranj, but the rules and strategies I'd learned came back easily. Idris was an engaging player. I was not surprised to learn that he was just as good as masking his emotions while we played as he was everywhere else. He was clever and distracting, and more than once I lost track of the board laughing.

"You are not thinking more than two moves ahead," he said when I reached for an elephant piece. "You need to be anticipating the end—you won't solve the problem any other way."

"I would have to know the other player extraordinarily well," I pointed out, picking up the piece.

He grinned when I moved. "You could if you weren't distracted. Like this." It was a single move, but it landed him on my side of the board. I could see, clearly, how he would win in four or five more turns. And there was no move I could make to stop him.

"You cheated." Even I could hear the undercurrent of whining in my voice.

"I used the skills available to me," he said, and plucked one of my viziers from the board. "It isn't my fault you enjoy laughing. Shall we try another?"

I nodded. The book of fairy tales lay on the table beside me, so I opened it while he cleared the board and rearranged the pieces into another mansuba.

"You can read?"

I stilled, and waited for him to repeat the question. When he didn't, I lifted my eyes from the page, still silent. He frowned, obviously confused, and then at last his eyes widened.

"No—I didn't mean at all," he said.

"What did you mean?" I said, and let some of Maram's frostiness seep into my voice.

His eyes fell to the book. "Kushaila. You can read Kushaila?"

"My mother taught me," I said and closed the book.

I didn't ask if he could read Kushaila. It was becoming abundantly clear that while the lower classes had suffered beneath the occupation, the royal families had suffered a different kind of cruelty. He might have learned when he was young and then been made to forget. I watched him reset the pieces and tried to think of what to say. I knew what I would want. A piece of myself, of my family, back. A taste, no matter how bitter, was better than knowing that a piece of you was missing and having no way to fill it.

He gave me another half smile. "You're staring."

Idris had offered me respite. Telling him my name, speaking of my life in Cadiz—in some small measure, he'd helped me find a way back to myself. Didn't I owe him the same?

"I could read it," I said.

It was his turn to go still, a hand poised on a red horse piece. He knew I meant the ink on his arm. "It's in the formal script," he said eventually.

"What do you think the Book is written in?"

I thought he would reject the offer, he was quiet for so long. His nod was sharp and fast, as though he were afraid that he would change his mind before the movement was complete. He didn't look at me when he gripped the bottom of his shirt and pulled it up over his head. Idris wouldn't meet my eyes, and his jaw was tight almost as if he were bracing himself against a blow.

I'd guessed right; it was a khitaam. I brushed my fingers over his arm, and he flinched, then stiffened.

"I don't even know what it is," he said. His voice was hoarse, and his right hand was clenched tightly in his lap. I was seeing him without a mask, without his usual polish and distance. I wanted to avert my eyes, as if I'd caught him in a worse state of undress than when he'd emerged from the water.

I took his arm instead and redirected my gaze to the tattoo.

It was beautiful and elaborate, clear despite the abundance of lettering crammed into such a small space.

"It's a khitaam," I said. "A royal seal."

He sucked in a sharp breath. "Those are usually on your back."

"They are," I said. "This was done just after the surrender, wasn't it?"

He was quiet, staring at the chess board.

"Idris?"

"Yes," he said. "Just after."

"They probably put it on your arm to hide it from the Vath. They would be looking for daan and khitaams on your back. But barbaric writing on your arm would go unremarked on."

"That's ridiculous," he said.

"You still have it," I pointed out. "And you're engaged to the Imperial Heir."

He had no reply to that.

The seal was split into three parts—the top half was broken in two while the bottom remained whole. I traced the left corner.

"This is ancestry. Descent from an ancient house, always royal." I smiled. "Half the families claim to be direct descendants of Kansa el Uwla."

"Mine as well?" he asked.

"Yes," I said, and pressed a finger to the narrow point of that section. "This is her name, here. All the writing flows from her."

He nodded, as if it made sense.

"Here," I said, touching the right section, "is your immediate descent. Mother, father, grandmother."

"Their names? They're there?"

"Yes," I said again. His eyes closed. "This bottom half—your name is in the center, here. There's a Dihyan blessing. These are the hopes of your family—kindness and justice. I think this is for health."

"Enough," he said, and tugged his arm out of my grasp. He wasn't rough or abrupt, though I would not have blamed him. The color had drained from his face, and the tendons in his throat stood out from the tension in his jaw. He scrubbed his hands over his face and raked them through his hair.

"Idris," I said, and hated that my voice came out so soft. He was not a wild animal I could spook.

He looked so tired with his elbows balanced on his knees, slouched forward as if suddenly bowed beneath the weight of what he'd learned. I shouldn't have offered, I thought.

"You should know," I said. "Whoever inked that khitaam for you loves you beyond imagining."

"I don't understand."

"It's a crime to ink daan or khitaam on royal skin. Someone risked their life so you would always know where you came from."

I reached for him without thinking, placing my hand over his and leaning in close. He let out a slow breath. For a moment, I was transfixed by the image of our hands, mine covered in henna over his larger one. I'd indulged, despite Maram disdaining the practice. When I looked up he was watching me, his face close to mine, openly curious. I had the feeling he was seeing me as I'd seen him—as me, not the person I had to be as Maram, not the girl in between. His hand turned beneath mine, and our fingers intertwined.

The winged pulse at the bottom of my throat beat its wings faster, hard enough that I could feel it echoing through the rest of me.

"You have given me a gift," he said when I lifted my eyes to look at him. "I didn't know I carried them with me. A hazard of having forgotten your mother tongue."

Don't stare, I thought. He hadn't shaved, and he looked more Kushaila for it. Like a boy I could see walking down a road in my village.

He brushed a touch over my cheek and trailed his thumb down to the corner of my mouth. It felt as if he had as little control over his hands as I did.

His hand settled on my neck, and his thumb grazed just over the pulse in my throat. It beat faster, fast and hard enough, I knew, for him to feel it.

"I . . ." he started.

"Cousin?"

It wasn't a spell broken, but I saw him remember just as I did where we were. Who we were. We pulled apart easily, without comment or fluster, though I could feel the flutter of my pulse at the base of my throat, like a bird trying to escape.

Furat stood on the steps to the pavilion, smiling as though she'd discovered a secret. When our eyes met, her smile widened.

"Are you teaching her to play shatranj?"

"Teaching her to get better," he said, and managed a half-hearted smile.

"Were you betting clothes?" she asked, raising an eyebrow.

The heat of embarrassment returned twice as strong.

"Yes," Idris said, managing a real grin, and leaned back on his hands. "I lost the first round."

"I think," I said, rising to my feet, pulling Maram's brusque manner over me like a second skin, "that is all I care to play today."

Idris didn't look at me, though his lashes trembled just a moment when I gathered up my book. I—we—were playing a dangerous game. Idris was as Tala had said: beautiful and tragic. But he wasn't mine, and there was no world or reality where he ever could be.

I saw logic, and yet I could not shake the feeling that he was as aware of me as I was of him as I walked all the way out of the grotto and back into the open air.

18

I slept and I dreamed.

My majority night wound down to a close. Touched with the ether of dreams, the festivities went on uninterrupted. The trees were strung with small orbs of light, and the trill of a loutar filled the air, punctuated by the sound of someone beating a bendir. The loud rush of wings against air came and went, though no birds appeared. From my shoulders fell a cloak, black embroidered with feathers in gold thread. Like Massinia's cloak, my mother's voice said. I laughed, though at what I had no idea. In the center of the courtyard, my friends danced, beckoning me to join them.

"Look," Husnain whispered, sitting beside me. "To your right."

Idris.

He stood beside my eldest brother, dressed like one of us,

smiling easily. Aziz was taller than him, I knew this for a fact, but they seemed of a height with one another tonight. My eldest brother clapped a hand on his shoulder, then pointed at me.

Idris's smile changed when our eyes met. Sweeter, bolder, touched with a different kind of happiness.

And then the dream faded away. I was coaxed into wakefulness by the soft notes of another loutar. The sound that played in my dream had not stopped. I rose from bed as though there were a string tied to my breastbone that drew me gently closer and closer to the sound.

In the back corner of the courtyard was a short wooden gate that led to a small garden. There I found Idris, seated at a table, on a collection of cushions. The garden was less than half the size of our courtyard, and boxed in by wooden trellises on all sides. A tree grew just beside him, and he cradled his loutar in its shade.

He lay his hands over its strings, quieting them, when the wooden gate shut behind me. "Did I wake you?"

I shook my head. He looked so much like the version I'd dreamed. His hair fell down just below his chin, and the bristle of his beard had grown just a little more. He wore a djellaba, though the sleeves had been shortened and there was no hood.

"I . . . I'll let you play," I said at last, and turned to leave.

"You're welcome to stay," he said.

I paused. *I should leave*, I thought. The longer I spent with Idris, the easier it was to forget who we were. He a prince and I a slave in all but name. There was no happy ending to this story, no way for the two of us to make one.

And yet . . .

"Have you eaten?" I asked, instead.

I brought back a tray with tea and bread, and a spread of butter. He fiddled with the strings on his loutar as I poured tea and set a glass close to his elbow. He'd arranged a cushion against the tree, and gestured that I could take my seat there. Comfortably seated, with a glass of tea warming my hands, I closed my eyes and listened as he began to play again.

It was easy to welcome the answering shivers in my heart as the music built and changed, rising and falling softly. I wondered who had taught him to play. He couldn't speak or read Kushaila, so who would have taken the time to teach him how to play a Kushaila instrument so well? Procuring it would not have been difficult for a prince, but learning it was another matter. The Vath had not outlawed all our cultural and religious practices, but their stance on it was clear. And among the makhzen, especially, such a hobby would have been quickly snuffed out.

The tune changed again and I opened my eyes. "I know this song," I said, smiling.

He smiled back. "Will you sing it?"

I laughed. "I have a villager's voice."

"Beautiful, then, I'm sure."

I resisted the urge to call him a flatterer, though his eyes told me he noticed the wry twisting of my mouth, and began to sing. It was an old song that had come to the Kushaila by way of the south. A girl wandered a garden and found a man swaying and singing, and though she asked for mercy, nothing could free her from love, nor was she sure she wanted to be free. The sound of the loutar faded away before the song was done, and I let the sentence hang, unfinished.

"You—" he began, then stopped.

"I?"

It unsettled me when he looked at me as he was doing now. Not critical, but sharp. He missed nothing when he looked at me like that, and he always came away having learned something I had not offered. I thought of how he'd guessed who I was, how he'd seen through weeks of hard-earned training. Could another have done the same? I'd been angry with myself for my failure, but the truth was he hadn't only seen that I wasn't Maram—he'd picked up on the clues of who I was.

We sat close enough that he could reach over and sweep my hair over my shoulder and pull at the chain hanging around my neck. I caught his wrist to stop him, but he'd already found the pendant hanging on the end. The pendant was half the length of my thumb, and just a little wider. On one side it was etched to look like an ornate hand, and on the other someone had carved a verse from the Book.

Believe, for We know things you do not. And We see what you do not.

Maram would never have worn such a thing.

"Something from your old life?" he murmured.

The sharpness softened when I met his gaze. "I have nothing from my old life."

I'd found it two nights ago, stashed among Maram's jewelry. Likely it had been a gift from the Dowager that she'd never worn, or a piece of jewelry commissioned before her mother's death. Such charms were common among Dihyaans, and the Kushaila in particular. They were worn to ward off evil and invite good, to turn away envious gazes, to safeguard the fortunes in your life.

He lowered his gaze to examine the charm again.

"Do you dislike it?" I asked.

"I don't trust in such things to protect me."

"Then in what?"

"Myself," he said, letting it slip from his fingers.

"None of us can survive alone, Idris," I said.

He watched me for a moment. "You were alone."

"Not entirely." My fingers wrapped around the charm. "I had hope."

"Amani," he started. I went still. It still felt novel to hear him—anyone—say my name. "I have a request."

"Yes?"

"I want you to reveal yourself to the Dowager when you meet her today," he said. "And to Furat. I'll keep your secret. We all will. But they deserve to know. This is their home."

I'd already risked my life trusting him with who I was. To tell others was— It didn't bear thinking on. "You know you ask too much—so why ask at all?"

"The Dowager is as a grandmother to me," he said. "I love her very much. And she's suffered a great deal. She is Kushaila, but none of her descendants speak her mother tongue. None of them know the old songs or stories. It's too dangerous. She has given up her home and her throne to aliens."

We'd all given our homes over to aliens. That was the state of the world. But most of us had family to comfort us in difficult times, grandparents or grandchildren, friends who'd suffered through the war. We had our language to give us respite and our stories to keep us warm.

The Dowager had none of that. And she hadn't been queen on a small farm—she'd ruled the world and was now trapped on this moon. I felt my heart soften—a dangerous thing.

"And Furat?"

"Surely you know how Maram feels about her," he said. "When Maram visits Ouzdad . . . She hates being here, and she takes it out on Furat. My cousin feels like every moment is a landmine waiting to go off. I want to give her respite from all that."

He laid his hand over mine and lowered his eyes just a little.

"Don't do that," I said with a laugh. "We aren't in the Ziyaana."

He grinned and squeezed my hand. "Is that a yes?"

"Has that ever worked with anyone?"

"Amani."

I resisted the urge to bite my lower lip.

"It's such a risk," I said softly.

"I'll make sure nothing happens to you."

"How gallant," I said dryly, and his grin widened.

"Is that a yes?" he said again.

"Yes," I said at last. "I'll do it."

"Thank you. You have no idea how much this means to me," he said, his grin near blinding in its brilliance, and kissed my cheek.

I froze, my hand still in his, and stared at him for a moment, uncomprehending. It took him a moment to realize what he'd done. He raised a hand to my cheek, his thumb brushing over the spot he'd kissed.

I didn't move, nor could I tear my gaze away from his. We seemed balanced on a knife's edge, in territory I'd warned myself away from. He watched me as closely as I'd watched him, his hand still on my cheek, his eyes locked with mine.

"There you are," Tala said, out of breath. "I have been looking for you everywhere! You're expected at the Dowager's for lunch. Dihya, you're not even dressed."

Idris helped me to my feet as Tala waited, but didn't release my hand when I made to walk away. He looked at me as he had yesterday, as if he meant to find answers in my silence. His fingers were feather light on my cheeks as they drifted down and over my throat. There was a hot, tight feeling in my belly, my fingers itched, and I couldn't look away from him. The sharpness had gone completely from his gaze, but I liked what had replaced it even less. It was the look of someone gone too far.

It called to its sibling in me, waiting for it to reply.

"Your Highness," Tala snapped. Even that couldn't shock us apart.

"You will tell the Dowager today?" he asked, voice low enough that Tala couldn't hear.

I nodded, still unable to speak. I took a step back but he held fast to my hand.

Idris smiled, and gestured to Tala. "She is becoming impatient."

I did not look back as I walked away.

Tala oiled and combed my hair. I saw her glance at me in concern more than once, but said nothing.

"Shall I braid it in the Gibrani style?" she asked me, setting the comb down.

"What does that mean?"

"Smaller braids, wound with fabric," she explained.

I nodded.

For a long time the rooms were quiet except for the sound of the comb going through my hair and faint music, strings and drums wafting through the air from a distant corridor. I felt a knot in my chest ease as the moments ticked by. In the Ziyaana it felt as though I spent half my time splitting the world between Maram's and mine. The lines were never clear, or at least never seemed so to me. I knew part of this was because I could not remove myself from the part I played. Every time I emerged from my room as Maram, I felt more pieces of myself woven into the fabric of Her Highness. But this moment felt as if it belonged to me. Idris knew me now, by name, and soon, the Dowager and Furat would too. The request frightened me; it was a risk, no matter how much I trusted Idris. But a part of me was excited, too, at the thought that more people would know who I really was; that I could be Amani again, that this seed of relief and contentment that Idris had planted could flourish.

There was a bower of incense on a table, newly lit, and its smoke rose into the air, curling lazily, its path lit by late-morning sunlight.

"Tala?"

She hummed.

"What happened to Idris's parents?"

She paused in her braiding, and met my eyes in the mirror again. "You don't know?" Her fingers began to move again.

"A farmer's daughter from a backwater moon, remember?"

Her smile faded quickly. "You remember the second siege of Walili?" I nodded. "The Salihis—Idris's family—led it. There were others, of course, but before the occupation they were the great military strength of the world. When they took a stand, it meant something."

"They died during the siege?"

Tala shook her head. "They surrendered after Queen Najat died, to honor her last wishes. But we all knew that Mathis wouldn't pardon them. He'd never exercised mercy, and it was early yet in the regime. It couldn't stand."

I nodded again, understanding, as dread welled up inside me. Whoever survived the siege would have inked the khitaam into Idris's skin, knowing that a worse storm was on the horizon. That the Imperial Garda might come, that another war could break out, that Mathis would enact an irreversible cruelty.

"There was no trial. No warning. A year passed. And then one night Vathek forces stormed the strongholds of all the dissident families, pulled them from their beds, and shot them."

My heart gave a single, painful thud. The Purge.

"Idris survived?"

"Idris was allowed to live," Tala corrected. "Anyone who survived the Purge did so to serve as a reminder to everyone else."

"He couldn't have been more than—"

"He was ten," Tala interrupted, tying a bright red ribbon at the end of a braid. Old enough to remember. Not the haze of knowing you've experienced something, but memory, bright and sharp in his mind. And in my ignorance I'd stirred up those memories. I'd given him a bittersweet taste of what he'd lost. His heritage, yes, but his heritage bound up in blood and misery.

It felt as though I'd discovered a bruise over my own ribs, new and tender, soft and waiting for blood to break through.

"Amani?"

I blinked, and focused, looking at Tala in the mirror. My bottom lip was caught between my teeth, red from worrying. She watched me with concern and a measure of her usual censure. The final braid was tied off, and she twisted the collection together into a bun low at the back of my head. Red ribbons fluttered and wove through it, and over it she draped a silver net hung with small coins. She rose from behind me and came to sit beside me.

"You cannot fix this," she said, taking hold of my chin. "Do you understand? He is not yours to help—he belongs to another."

"I know," I said, rising from the vanity. How much was writ on my face for her to see? I supposed it was not a difficult guess to make.

Tala was silent as I dressed. It was only when I stood in front of the mirror and caught my expression that I understood her concern. I looked dazed, my kohl-lined eyes wide, my bottom lip red from worrying. I didn't recognize the girl, as near to love struck as I'd ever been, staring back at me. When I looked at Tala she shook her head.

"Amani," Tala called as I began to make my way down to the Dowager's. She looked truly worried. "Stop. While you can."

I thought of Idris's hand over mine and felt something tighten painfully in my chest. Even if I could, I wasn't sure that I wanted to.

Tala's gaze didn't leave my face, so at last I nodded and continued on.

❧ 19 ❧

I paced in front of the entrance to the Dowager's wing of the palace. The Dowager's quarters were in the far end of Ouzdad, their back walls flush against the canyon wall. To enter them, a person had to pass through an enormous pair of doors that sealed the entire wing off from the rest of the palace. Like much of the palace, they were beautiful, but they stood out for the paintings framing the doors. A pair of tesleet, each with a single wing extended, stood guard. The feathers in their wings glimmered, shining in jeweled tones: green, red, blue, purple, and their heads were crowned with white feathers.

Idris appeared behind me, silent as a shadow, and caught my wrist. I'd twisted my fingers into the chain of my necklace without realizing it, but even that couldn't distract me. We were both quiet as he untangled the chain from around my fingers.

His voice was low as he said, "Thank you for doing this. I know you're risking a lot. But I wouldn't ask if it wasn't important."

I nodded without looking up. "I know. It's not any less—I still worry."

The Dowager didn't rise when we entered, but Furat did. I eased myself onto a floor cushion, and a moment later Idris and Furat followed suit. The Dowager didn't shift her gaze from the open window or greet either of us.

Itou bint Ziyad's resemblance to her granddaughter, to me, had shocked me into silence. The angular sweep of her chin, the wide mouth, the eyes framed by wrinkles. She could have been my grandmother, we resembled one another so.

I was still staring at her when she looked up and caught my eye. It was difficult not to flinch away from the look on her face—age and grief weighed heavily on her and I couldn't tell if she always looked this way, or if she only ever seemed so when Maram was around. I couldn't imagine what it must be like for either Maram or the Dowager. One to be confronted with proof of her failure to defend her people, and the other with how much her grandmother must see her as a representation of that failure.

"Ya'bnati," she said in Kushaila. Child.

I wasn't sure what inspired me to say the words in Kushaila, but I did. "Dowager Sultana," I said. "I'm not Maram."

Furat jerked back as though she'd been struck. I imagined she'd never heard Maram speak in Kushaila. The Dowager for her part leaned back, her face calm and grave, the grief and fatigue wiped away.

I imagined that after the war very little could shock her, or move her to reveal her shock.

"Then who," she replied in Kushaila, "are you?"

"I am your granddaughter's body double."

Her eyes remained on my face. She looked at me contempla-
tively, as if appraising every one of my features.

"Name?"

"Amani, sayidati."

"Qadissiya?" she asked at last. Cadissian?

I nodded hesitantly.

Her mouth quirked in a smile. "My brother was fostered on
Cadiz," she said, still speaking in Kushaila. "They drop letters in
their Kushaila frequently; it took him years to lose the habit. Aji."

Come here.

She waved me over. After darting a glance at Idris, who smiled
at me encouragingly, I rose to my feet and came to sit beside her.
Her hands were dry on my face, and the rings she wore were cool
against my skin.

"How strange," she said when she let go. "How did you come
to be in my granddaughter's place?"

Furat watched the two of us curiously. She couldn't understand
what we were saying, I realized, and I switched to Vathekaar.

"Imperial droids stormed my majority night," I started. The
words came easier now that I'd said them before. "My face was
scanned and I was kidnapped and taken to the Ziyaana. I—I was
trained to be Maram so that I could take her place."

The Dowager raised her eyebrows. "Her place?"

I cast my eyes down. I didn't want to offend the Dowager,
though she likely knew the violent responses Maram elicited in
the general public. "It's not safe for her to go outside," I said.

"The people hate her," the Dowager said wearily. "Since she
has done little to earn their love."

"Yes, sayidati."

"The Vath are not good at inspiring love," she said. "Or receiving it, I gather."

"Sayidati?"

"Coyness is not our way," she said and I heard a little of Maram's brusqueness in her tone. "My granddaughter and I are estranged. Which I imagine is why she sent you in her place—it is difficult for us both. That and the rebels."

"Sayidati?" I prompted again.

"The rebels her father believes I have something to do with." The weariness had crept back into her voice. I could hear what she didn't say. *The rebels I don't consort with.* She'd fought her own brother in a civil war, but looking at her now, I didn't think she had the stomach to hunt down all that was left of her family.

I bowed my head. What could I say? There were no reassurances I could offer. Maram had demonstrated all the things the Dowager knew to me repeatedly.

"Well," she said. "Tell me about yourself. Your family?"

"Still in Cadiz," I said. She tilted her head, waiting for me to continue. "My mother and father run a farm there, with my brothers."

"More than one?"

My burgeoning smile wavered. "Two," I continued, more somber. I missed them every moment of every day—how could I not? I prayed for the millionth time that Husnain was unharmed from the night in the kasbah. That they all were. "I am the youngest."

"Ah," she said. "The apple of your father's eye, then?"

For the first time in a long time, I grinned. "Maybe," I said. "He favored me. We had much in common."

"Oh?"

"He was a botanist before the occupation—he was teaching me before— Well, before." Idris squeezed my hand under the table and I found myself smiling a little. "He liked poetry as much as I did and taught me that, too, when my mother wasn't looking."

Furat made a small noise under her breath, but shook her head when I looked at her.

"I was the same," the Dowager told me. "My brother took after my mother, and I after my father. We hunted together often."

My cheeks ached from smiling so. "We don't have that sort of thing on Cadiz. At least not now."

"No. I suppose not. We used to be able to hunt here, but my comings and goings are restricted now. I'm—the Vath refuse me the right to journey to my old estates in the south." She closed her eyes for a moment. "There was a time when I wouldn't have accepted anyone's refusal. When I would have gone anywhere in the stars that I wished."

"I'm sorry, sayidati."

She smiled. "Save your pity for the young and the dead, girl," she said. "It won't help me."

The minutes ticked by as we spoke. I thought I'd said all I had to say to Idris, but the more questions the Dowager asked of my life and my family, the more I had to say. In kind, I learned about her childhood and upbringing. I could see it pained her, to speak of her life before the Vath, a bittersweet joy to remember the good times knowing they would never come again.

It felt—I couldn't express how it felt to sit with her and speak in Kushaila. Like slipping back into my old skin. I knew this girl who smiled and talked of her family without bitterness. Who canted her head when the music started in the courtyard and recognized the tune. Who laughed when a boy made a joke for her benefit.

Idris was more relaxed than I'd ever seen him. His shoulders were loose and he kept smiling at the Dowager, refilling her tea glass without being asked. Had he been denied this during his visits with Maram?

"I haven't seen you smile so in a long time, cousin," Furat said.

He made a dismissive sound in the back of his throat. "Don't be ridiculous," he said. "I smile all the time."

"There is smiling," the Dowager said, lifting her tea glass. "And then there is smiling."

He lifted a shoulder but ducked his head.

"You are called Amani, yes?" Furat said. I nodded. "Was it you or my cousin I met at the Terminus ball?"

"Me."

She leaned back, her eyes a little wide. "Consider me suitably impressed," she said with a laugh. "You were every inch Her Royal Highness."

I grinned. "Your cousin disagrees."

She waved a hand. "We are not all looking for the next trap in a waltz."

"We do not all have reason to be," Idris chimed in. "But you were very good, Amani. I almost didn't believe it until your incisive critique of my storytelling abilities."

"Don't be so excruciatingly boring, then," I said, trying not to laugh.

If Husnain were with me he would be having a good time, I thought—he loved laughter and loved it more over tea and good food. He and Idris would get along. At the very least Husnain would enjoy making fun of him for his talentless translations and storytelling.

The Dowager watched us, at last relaxed into her seat, a soft smile on her face.

"You must miss your old life very much," Furat said carefully. "Your old . . . self."

"It has been difficult. More difficult than anything I thought to endure in my life," I told her honestly. I had not been so relaxed, I realized, since my majority night. "Ouzdad has been a reprieve."

"A deserved one," Furat said. "We are happy to have you with us."

The Dowager rose to her feet with a creak of old bones. Idris rose with her and reached for her cane. She waved him off.

"No," she said. "The girl. Amani. It's been some time since I've walked the garden."

He held the cane out to me with a smile. I felt the corners of my mouth rising without my say-so in response. When I rose to my feet and took the cane, he squeezed my arm.

"Thank you," he murmured.

"No gratitude is required for what is freely given," I said.

"It wasn't free. I know that."

For a moment we stared at each other, and I felt warmth flow through me, new and strong.

"Go," he said at last. "The Dowager is waiting."

❧ 20 ❧

I slept soundly that night. I could hear the whistle of wind through the canyon, and the babbling of our courtyard fountain, and a hundred other sounds of a large estate settling into sleep. Sounds largely absent from my wing of the Ziyaana. I woke refreshed before the sun had risen and the palace woke. I didn't bother waking Tala, and dressed on my own. She would likely have a fit when she realized I'd gone out of my quarters in the simple steel-gray qaftan, with little jewelry, and my hair twisted into a simple braid.

I donned a cloak and made my way through the palace and toward the temple.

The Dihyaan temple was austere when compared to the rest of Ouzdad. Its entrance was an archway carved with script from the Book, borne up by two simple white pillars. The courtyard was laid with simple gray and green marble tiles, with a single stone fountain at its center, and ringed with benches and reed mats. It was lined on three sides by corridors, whose white columns were capped with dark wood. The roof tiles were a bright, cheery green and stood out even in the murky dawn light. It was a legendary structure. Half its walls had been hauled from the wreck of an ancient civil war and to the moon's surface.

There were no icons here, no murals depicting our leaders or followers. The walls and pillars were carved with old script, verses from our Book, reminders of Dihya and peace and faith. I heard the patter of bare feet against stone, the whisper of robes, the rising murmur of people in prayer. On the other end of the courtyard stood a pair of dark wooden doors, carved with fruit bearing trees: the doors to the zaouia. On the other side of those doors anyone who needed shelter would find it, anyone who needed a place to rest or alms or help would be welcome.

I smelled incense, freshly burned, and the clear sharp scent of the temple itself that emerged from stone and people and worship. I couldn't make myself enter the temple proper, so I took a seat in the courtyard beneath the awning, and breathed.

For the first time in months I felt something like peace settle over me. The tightness in my chest, in my muscles, unwound. When I exhaled it felt as though a hundred small pebbles fell away. For a sliver of a moment I wasn't Maram or Amani. I was a girl in a temple, filled with nothing but want and expectation. The sun was rising, and the light carved its way across the courtyard, splitting it between light and shadow. A bird perched on the curved edge of the fountain, warbling at the water as though it might warble back.

A ringed hand landed on my shoulder. I jerked to a stand in surprise and spun around to find Furat on the other side of the bench. Her hair curled loose over her shoulders, as plain as mine, and in the same simple cut of qaftan that I'd donned. I was not the only one who'd dodged her handmaiden this morning.

She smiled. "I didn't mean to startle you, Amani," she said. She was calm and collected, deeply at ease in this temple. There was a serenity to her, a deep composure that I knew I would never be able to unseat. I doubted very many people could.

We both took a seat on the bench, quiet as the morning light slowly brightened the courtyard.

"This is my favorite place in the whole world," she said. "There is no other place that fills me with such stillness."

"You seem to be at home here," I noted. "I mean, in Ouzdad."

"The truth is I never wanted to leave Ouzdad," she said without looking at me. "I cried when my grandmother suggested it. My whole life I'd avoided the Vath and my cousin—they have no power here. And then all of a sudden . . ."

"Then why leave?" I couldn't understand it. If given the chance I would remain at Ouzdad forever. It wasn't perfect, but it was a haven away from Vathek politics and machinations.

Furat paused, considering me. I realized with a jolt that she was someone who wouldn't be forced into doing anything—not unless it served her own ends.

"Duty. I have a duty to my family, to my grandmother, to Andala. I hate what our planet has become, and I can't stay here and complain. I should have gone sooner, but . . ."

"Can I ask . . . why does Maram dislike you?"

Furat scoffed. "Your time in the Ziyaana is turning you into a diplomat," she said. "Maram hates me. I'm fairly certain if she could she would have me executed."

"Why?"

"Before Najat died—Idris's and my—our mothers led the

loyalists in a coup hoping to depose Mathis and put my brother on the throne."

The beginning of the Purge, I thought.

"It failed," I said, as though it needed clarification.

"It failed," she repeated. "The entire Wattasi branch was snuffed out. Except for me, to remind everyone else what was at stake when you lost against the Vath."

"That doesn't explain why Maram hates you," I said, frowning. "Or why Idris is engaged to her and you were exiled."

"Maram—she is incapable of viewing this half of her family rationally. Her father sent her to Luna-Vaxor after the coup, and I think it only made her more paranoid. The Vath have no love for her, you know. She is a half-breed, so far as they are concerned, and those who do not outright hate her for her heritage resent her for being the presumed heir to the imperial throne. But they bred a deep mistrust of us in her—she believes if I am allowed freedom I will take up arms against her."

"Idris won't?"

"We are two sides of the same coin," she said softly. "Mercy and ruthlessness. We have been raised to pray for Vathek mercy and to do anything to keep it."

I couldn't imagine what it must have been like for Maram to grow up in such a way, reviled for the circumstances of her birth, hunted by one half of her family, targeted by her blood. What kind of person emerged from such a childhood? What sort of woman would that create? Constantly afraid and hateful and cruel, all in the name of self-preservation.

Nor could I imagine growing up as Idris and Furat had, terrified that whatever stability they'd managed would be snatched away from them in an instant. Their poise despite that astonished me.

"Is she wrong?" I asked her carefully. "About you?"

She took her time answering. "If I believed I could—that any-one could—turn her against the Vath, I would not be so afraid of her coming reign. I would try to befriend her, to help. I would even swear fealty to her. But she's turned the whole planet against herself. Hope that patience will win us the day has waned."

I turned my gaze to the sky. We were coming dangerously close to treason. There would be no new regime, King Mathis made sure of that every day. And Furat's peers among the makhzen would not support her, no matter the state of the world.

She rested a hand on my arm. "Do you know what my grand-mother said to me before I went to the Ziyaana?"

I shook my head.

"She told me, everyone in the Ziyaana will tell you to resign yourself to being crushed," she said. "Do not. Even your happi-ness is rebellion."

I couldn't stop myself from speaking. "Happiness may be re-bellion, but it won't win the war."

Furat eyed me, still considering. "No, it won't," she said at last. The wind blew through the courtyard.

"But there is another way." Furat squeezed my arm. The bells heralding the opening of the outer gates rang, followed by the sound of hooves beating against the ground. "Come. There is someone I'd like you to meet."

21

Riding through the gates were three Tazalghit women, robed and veiled, dressed in dark blue. Two rode on black horses, but the rider in the front, the one climbing off her horse, rode a white stallion. She tugged the veil from her face and pulled the turban from her head as she walked toward us. She made no sound, and unlike the two women who remained astride their horses, bore no sword at her waist, nor any charms.

I struggled to control my expression when I saw her face.

This young woman looked exactly like Massinia.

She couldn't have been much older than me, though she was significantly taller. Sunlight reflected off her dark skin, and caught on the silver coins hanging from her ears. Her mass of tightly curled hair was tied down to a single braid that ran from the crown of her forehead and in a thick rope down her back. She bore two black daan, one on each cheek, though her forehead was clear of the crown of Dihya. There was a scar that ran from the corner of her ear and disappeared beneath her jaw.

I could not dismiss her resemblance to Massinia any more than I could dismiss my own resemblance to Maram. She was younger than most depictions of her, but the fierceness of her features, the hard line of her mouth, her face—the resemblance was not uncanny, it was exact.

Furat lowered her mouth to my ear. "They are not here to hurt you," she murmured, then walked away.

Gooseflesh pimpled up and down my arms as a revelation shot through me. The whispers about the rebels on Cadiz came hurtling back to me in flashes: Massinia reborn, and rallying the rebels. It couldn't be true—could it? And yet . . . I was looking at living proof of it. Here she was, the rebel leader. *The blood never dies* wasn't a figure of speech. It was the reality.

I almost spun around as a second wave of shock hit me. Furat. Her determination to return to the Ziyaana was suddenly made clear. Duty, she'd said. A different sort of duty than I'd imagined. She was spying. She was spying for Massinia. My head spun thinking about it.

But why had she brought me here?

The girl made a sharp movement with her hand and her party turned their horses, including the white stallion, and rode away. A smile spread across her face, as though she found something in my appearance amusing.

"Join me," she said in Kushaila. It was clear she was used to being obeyed.

There was a table further in the garden bearing a metal chest and two small goblets. She took a seat on one side, folding her legs beneath her, and I took the other. The chest held shaved ice; she filled the goblets and set them between us so the ice could melt, then set her hands flat on the table deliberately, as if to do otherwise would invite the loss of control.

"Were you born with your face?" she asked. Her Kushaila sounded different from mine, sharper, slicker.

"Yes." My voice was thick with shock.

Like everything about her, the gaze she directed at me was sharp and critical. Perhaps it was her way, the Tazalghit way, to search out weaknesses in everyone she met. Or perhaps, like me, she could not believe I was a double.

She huffed a laugh when I lifted my chin. "You must feel quite lucky, then, to have been raised out of poverty."

I could not contain my derision. "Only a fool would hope to be raised to the Ziyaana. A cage is a cage even if gilded. Even if it softens my hands."

She smiled and her face transformed—younger, more radiant, the daan in her left cheek creased inside a dimple. "You are not stupid, then," she said, and pulled one of the goblets to herself. "How old are you?"

"Eighteen."

"And your given name?"

I was wary of her. "Amani."

"Pretty," she replied. "My mother named me Arinaas, though few people use that name anymore. I was nine when my mother realized the rebels were tracking our camp through the plains. You can guess what they wanted."

"Massinia reborn."

She lifted the goblet in confirmation. "They'd seen the mark on my shoulder, and took it as a sign from Dihya."

My eyes widened. Surely she didn't mean—? "The mark?"

She set the goblet down and pulled at the collar of her robe until she'd revealed most of her collarbone and shoulder. Warmth drained out of my face. The scar started just below her throat, a starburst of white, and stretched out across her shoulder in a dozen thin lines. It looked as if a company of flares had erupted from the scar, searing her flesh. And woven through all of it was gold. Not paler flesh or inked lines, but gold, shining and glittering in her skin.

"And did the rebels get what they wanted?"

She lifted an eyebrow, her mouth curling in amusement. "My mother was not a fool. She knew what would happen—I would survive perhaps a year as they paraded me around. Then the Vath would find me and execute me."

"But now—"

"She told them if she found them following our camp again, she would kill them. And then she went to Andala just after the Purge to see what had driven desperate men to this moon looking for a savior."

It was not hard to imagine what she found. Even if I did not remember the Purge, I remembered that year. It felt as if the mothers in our village would never stop crying. As if the Garda would never leave. As if there was never enough food or water or money. My mother's last living brother and his family disappeared that year.

"What happened when she came back?"

"She called the other queens of the Tazalghit," Arinaas said, meeting my eyes. "And they planned. The rest of my life, the future of our world, the destiny of billions."

The newly emerged softness on her face turned hard. Her anger was likely a constant thing, always banked just below the surface, fighting for air against all the demands her body represented.

I knew, Dihya I knew, what that felt like. Neither of us asked for such faces, for marks, for fate, and they'd been thrust on us anyway.

"Tell me," she began. "Do you believe in Dihya?"

"I do," I responded.

"I wasn't so sure I believed in Dihya when I was your age," she said. "I couldn't understand why I'd been given Massinia's face and her mark and nothing else. I don't wake up from dreams of a past life. I have none of her patience, nor her sight. The Book doesn't reveal hidden meanings. I have only her face, and most days it felt as if I were being punished. People came to my mother's camp once word spread, looking for faith or relief or reassurance, and I had none of that." She was staring into her cup, gaze unfocused, as though she could see the girl she'd been, young and bitter and alone. "Do you know what I realized?"

I shook my head.

"It doesn't matter if I'm really Massinia, any more than it matters if you are the Imperial Princess."

"I don't understand."

"A princess and a prophetess can do incredible things. We can bring justice to millions. We can do what ordinary people cannot."

And what was it that ordinary people couldn't do? My heart pounded out a fast rhythm as my mind raced, trying to pin down all of the things she thought we—I—could do.

"What is it you want of me?"

"We need a spy in the Ziyaana."

"You have Furat," I said suspiciously.

"Furat is a lesser cousin in disgrace," Arinaas said. "You are a body double. You have access to places and information she does not."

I said nothing. There was no need for me to speak—she knew

the risk she was asking me to take. She set a small black box on the table between us.

"Inside the box is a communicator—undetectable by the Ziyaana's security system. All we want now is information. Watch, listen, report anything of interest."

"All you want now," I repeated, staring at the box. The idea thrilled and frightened me at the same time. Spying was not a game—I knew what would happen if I were discovered. I couldn't be rash or foolish and throw myself into something without considering the consequences.

"We may call on you," she replied. "It is the nature of our work."

"Rebellion," I clarified.

"Freedom," she countered.

"So." She gazed at me. "Will you do it?"

As childish as it might have been, I wished for my mother. I wanted her advice, but more than that I wanted her shoulder to lay my head against. I could almost see her, smell the rose water she put in her hair some days, see the firm line of her mouth. I wanted her hand on my shoulder as it had been countless times, wanted the squeeze of reassurance.

Arinaas's face looked as though it was carved from stone. She wouldn't have room for softness—not if she had stayed alive for as long as she had. Not if she had spent her life evading the whispers and rumors that led the Vath to her. She had a fire in her, an unquenchable flame that would devour all that stood in her path. This, I thought, had to be what kept people at her side. Once they found out she had none of Massinia's memories and only her appearance, it would have inspired those around her. This was what made me lean forward, as if I were helpless to resist the flame of hope that burned in her.

Whatever people might have expected her to be, Arinaas had forged herself out of that fire. She'd become someone worth rallying around.

Hope. Hard won, soaked in blood, a hope that burned as much as it lit her way. The opposite of what I'd nurtured while still on Cadiz. That had been a bright, gleaming thing, reflective like a moon in the sky. Harmless, but without its own warmth. Could I live my life knowing I'd never stepped close to such a flame? Could I exist in the Ziyaana knowing I had chosen my shadowed half life, had accepted a horrible changing in my soul, instead of reaching out with both hands with something that might remake me? Arinaas's flame might char my skin and break my bones, but in the end I would emerge remade, newer and stronger and a version of myself no one could snuff out.

I'd prayed for a sign, for hope, for a purpose in being sent to the Ziyaana. I'd been answered with something I hadn't even imagined.

"I will do as you ask."

"Good," she said, as if she'd expected it. She held out a hand, palm turned upward, and after a moment I realized what she wanted. I'd only ever seen soldiers greet or depart in this way. I reached across the space between us, laid my arm over hers and grasped her elbow, and she did the same to mine.

❧ 22 ❧

Dawn hadn't yet broken, but I stood staring into the fountain in our courtyard. My presence had triggered the water so that it flowed, lapping gently. I thought of Furat's words to me from yesterday, *Happiness is rebellion.* Since arriving at Ouzdad I'd found both—happiness and an ease with Idris I hadn't felt since the days before my majority night, and rebellion—the rebellion I'd heard about since I was small, but hadn't believed in. I knew the possible cost. If I were caught I would find no mercy in the Ziyaana. But I also thought of the night I had been taken from my family; of the look on Husnain's face as he cried out that the Vath could not have me.

If he could see me now, I thought, he would be proud.

In the lantern light my reflection peered back up at me, broken up by waves and ripples. I recognized this girl, with her round cheeks and round chin, her wide eyes, always lined with kohl now. She was not a farmer's daughter, not with the gold chain hanging from her neck and bejeweled earrings. And she wasn't Maram, either; she would never look so vulnerable as I did now.

I realized, with surprise, that she was me.

"Your Highness."

I was too tired to be shocked or frightened, though Idris's feet had made no sound on the stone floor. He stood in the entry to the bower dressed as simply as I was, in a dark green jacket edged with white thread, and loose matching trousers. His hair was loose as it always seemed to be here, and his face was still shadowed with beginnings of a beard. One of my—Maram's, I reminded myself—mantles hung over his arm.

"Why are you awake?"

He raised an eyebrow. "Why are you?"

When I said nothing he came forward and settled the mantle over my shoulders. It wasn't particularly heavy, but it would keep the dissipating morning chill at bay. I clutched it around my shoulders and tried not to stare at him. I'd thought of him too often since the morning I'd sung for him. And as the realization that I could choose who I was grew in my mind, so had my feelings for him.

He pulled my braid from under the mantle and settled it over my shoulder.

"Idris—"

"I want to show you something," he said at last. "Will you come with me?"

He took me down into the catacombs. His hand, dry and cool, wrapped around mine and pulled me gently through the half dark. There were no lanterns, but when I looked up, there were small light orbs hovering close to the cavern ceiling. They hushed and whispered at us in rhythm, as if keeping time. The walkway extended well beyond the Massinite murals. He led me down a path that forked to the left, and then another. At last there was a doorway of light at the end of the tunnel.

We emerged into an impossibly large cavern whose ceiling had caved in years ago. Just below the opening was a lake, its water dark and still. The air was heady, filled with the scent of flowers and greenery. Everywhere I looked, plants and trees grew, twining themselves around stalagmites, crawling up the walls.

"What is this place?" I breathed.

"The oasis Janat," Idris said. "Furat and I discovered it when we were young. The moon is filled with such underground oases. It's how the settlers terraformed it."

"Are—are we safe here? Alone?"

He nodded and tugged on my hand. "The Tazalghit control nearly all the oases, but this one they ceded to the Ziyadis as a gift centuries ago. The Dowager's men guard it well. We'll be safe."

We followed a path that led us up a ledge and onto a cliff overlooking the entire cavern. For a while we stood there, watching sunlight fill the cavern, quiet as the sound of birdsong rose. When I wandered off, Idris let me be. I appreciated this—bringing me here, not asking questions—more than he would ever know. In the Ziyaana, no one wanted or tried to put me at ease. Even here at Ouzdad, the Dowager liked me because I spoke Kushaila, while Furat watched me because of how I could serve the rebellion, and Tala despaired constantly of my inability to follow rules.

This was the first time anyone had offered me respite without asking for anything in return.

Eventually I found a small pool, flush against the cavern wall. I slid off my slippers and with a grateful sigh, hung my feet over the edge of the rock and into the water. It was cold, but the air was heating quickly and it didn't take long for me to shrug off the mantle I'd clung to earlier. Janat was hushed, as if waiting for something holy. There was birdsong and the sound of flowing water and the rushing of leaves, but there were no people here, or so it seemed. It was like being in a temple, waiting for the call to prayer, for the sun to rise, for the sound of worship. I closed my eyes, breathed, and felt the weight of the last week slip from my heart.

Idris found me like that, leaning back on my hands, my face upturned to the cavern's ceiling. He said nothing, but pulled his shoes off as I had, and took up a spot on the rock beside me. Our silences too often felt weighted, as if we were both replaying the afternoon in the grotto or the morning in the courtyard. I shouldn't have touched him, shouldn't have let him touch me. I should have kept my distance. And because I hadn't, I was now faced with a choice.

When I looked over at him, he was watching me.

"What?"

He smiled. "I could teach you to swim."

I snorted and his smile widened. "Her Highness doesn't swim," I reminded him. "And I will only ever go where she needs to be. Besides, it's a terrible idea."

"You've never lived by the water?"

I shook my head and turned away. "It was a valley," I said after a moment. "The Vath dammed up the river twenty years ago. There's no place to swim."

"Ah," was all he said.

I hadn't thought of the valley that had been my home in so

long. Always my thoughts were with Husnain or with Aziz and my parents. I'd never thought to miss it, and yet here I was, my chest squeezing tight as I thought of its mountains and smoky skies.

"I have been wondering," Idris started again, and I tried not to sigh.

"Yes, sayidi?"

"The song you sang that morning. What did it mean?"

I felt the flush working its way up my throat before I even looked at him. He truly didn't know, that much I could tell from his expression. But what a fool I'd been, singing an old love song. He knew what it was, even if he didn't know what the words meant. He'd been lulled into it as much as I had, had stared at me as though I were the only person in the garden, even as Tala berated us for being alone.

Don't let your thoughts stray so, I told myself. There was no future for us together. Any and every end I imagined for the two of us was one mired in tragedy. No matter how beautiful or kind Idris was, he was not mine. And yet the happiness that had taken root in my heart refused to listen. I watched him as he watched me, caught and unable to look away.

I turned around just as he lost his balance on the ledge. I watched it as if in slow motion: his realization, his hand reaching out, his fingers grabbing the mantle. I hadn't counted on his weight or his strength, so when he pulled me along with him, I screamed.

I fell into the pool with a splash. Somehow, it seemed, the water had gotten colder since I'd pulled my feet out. It was only knee deep, and after flailing and struggling against Idris I managed to right myself onto my feet. Idris followed suit a few seconds later. We stared at one another in shock, bedraggled and soaked to the bone. His clothes stuck to him now like a second skin, and when I looked down at myself—

I groaned. Tala would be so angry when she saw me. Simple as the blue qaftan was, it was ruined. When I looked up at Idris again he was grinning.

"What?" I snapped. I was wet and uncomfortable and his delight did nothing to help.

"Nothing, you just—" He laughed. "You look very angry. Come on, there's a spot we can dry off."

He led me away from the cliff ledge and down to the beach itself. It was warmer on the beach, below the open cavern ceiling, and the sun had fully risen, turning the lake a brilliant turquoise. The water rushed and pulled away from the shore with the soft shushing noise the orbs had made on our way here. There was a flat, wide rock a few feet away and that was where Idris led me. I stretched out the mantle against it, hoping it would dry quickly, and sighed.

A moment later there was a wet plop and when I looked up Idris had removed his shirt. In the morning light, his wet hair and skin seemed to glimmer. The khitaam on his arm looked bolder and darker than it had the last time I'd seen it. He looked at it as if remembering and then looked at me. His eyes widened a little and he froze, as if he hadn't expected to catch me staring.

I should have looked away. But I was tied to where I stood, as I always seemed to be when Idris was around. His skin was warm beneath my palm, and I imagined for a moment that I could feel his heart beating beneath it. When his forehead touched mine I closed my eyes and breathed out a sigh.

All our time at Ouzdad we'd been inching our way toward one another, fingers brushing, tucking back strands of hair, stealing glances at one another. I knew what I wanted. My own happiness, not tied to his, but alongside it. I could see what I could have, secret, furtive, but real. He'd shown me a little of who he was and now—

His hands tangled in the wet mass of my hair. I could feel the whole world between us waiting for us to choose. For me to choose. His smile wasn't so wide as his grin, but it was slower, sweeter, and pulled an answering one from me. I tucked a stray lock of hair behind his ear and let my thumb brush over his cheek.

I felt as though my whole body were waiting for his kiss. My fingers tightened in his and I rose up on my toes to meet him. His hand cradled the back of my head just as his mouth brushed over mine once, then again. It felt like an entire conversation unto itself—questions I had but couldn't articulate, answers I wanted to give but didn't know how. He drew me closer until the lines of our bodies were pressed against one another, until I had to put my arms around him to keep my balance.

I had kissed other people before and the things I remembered were strange—the taste of a mouth, the bee humming around our heads, the sun beating down on us.

I thought of none of those things with Idris. The sharp heat I'd felt every time we were together, the tightness in my breath, the pinprick of need over and over—they roared to life, pushing me closer to him, opening my mouth beneath his. They told me to answer his questions, tell him what I wanted, how I felt, give him the respite he sought and I would have mine, too. The world disappeared even when we parted. All I heard, all I felt, was the two of us and the little space in between.

For the second time that day, Furat's words came back to me. Happiness is rebellion, I thought.

23

The morning of our departure came before I was ready. A strong wind blew through the canyon, howling angrily, warning everyone of the sandstorms to come. Ouzdad itself was hushed, shadowed by the clouds in the sky. I stood in front of a mirror in the early morning as Tala dressed me in a gift from the Dowager. The serving girl who delivered the qaftan stood aside, eyes critical as Tala's hands moved here and there, adjusting the belt and the cape.

It was a beautiful dove gray qaftan with elbow-length sleeves cuffed with dark crystals and dark purple embroidery. A sleeveless, floor-length jacket of the same purple sat over it, with a stream of layered gray silk chiffon falling back from my shoulders to pool on the floor behind me. Tala had stripped the henna from my hands the night before, and they looked naked in the mirror, even though they were laden with rings.

"There," Tala said, coming around to look at me. "Beautiful."

"The Dowager has requested her presence before she leaves," the serving girl said in Kushaila.

Tala translated before I could respond, and after a moment I nodded.

I made my way to the Dowager's quarters, and paused at the entrance. It would be a long while before I saw the image of the tesleet bird again, and I wanted to commit the way they framed her doors to memory. Massinia had carried such a bird for most of her long life, its crown of feathers a shocking, brilliant emerald green. Some thought the bird Azoul, the tesleet she'd encountered in the desert, and that the mark she bore was its gift to her, tying them together. I didn't know if I believed that, but the bird had always heralded change and power. And now it was gone from the world.

"My lady?" the serving girl said in accented Vathekaar.

I nodded and the doors groaned open.

The Dowager Sultana sat in her customary throne-like seat, her face turned to an open window.

"I will be sorry to see you go, girl," she said in Kushaila. "I should have liked to walk the garden paths a little longer with you. The few afternoon walks weren't enough."

I made myself smile and leaned over to kiss both her cheeks and the backs of her hands.

"If I am still living," I said in Kushaila, "you will likely see me again next year."

She grunted and waved her hand. "A year is too long for an old woman like me."

Furat swept in, still in her sleeping robes, her hair flowing behind her. "I thought I'd missed your departure."

I barely had time to stand before she pulled me toward her for a hug. Gratitude flowed through me as I hugged her back. We'd not spent much time together, but what I'd learned about her comforted me. She was a good ally to have, here and in the Ziyaana. And now I felt we were sisters-in-arms, too. She would watch my back as I watched hers.

I wished, briefly, for a true sister—one who watched my back for no other reason than she wanted to. But I didn't live that life, and the wish came and went, flashing and dying as quickly as lightning.

"When we return to the Ziyaana we will be enemies," she said, pulling away.

"But we will know the truth," I replied, squeezing her hand. The next time we saw each other, I would be spying on the Vath. The notion sparked both fear and excitement in me, but the idea that I would have an ally—that mattered to me more than anything else.

We set off soon after the same way we'd come, with Nabil and his guards leading us out of the canyon and through the desert. I felt a pang in my chest and forced myself not to look back. I'd spent three weeks in the shadow of those canyon walls, happy, and safe. I was used to feeling that way now, and the prospect of returning to the Ziyaana, a place wreathed in suffering, frightened me.

Far in the distance I saw the shape of half a dozen Tazalghit women astride their horses. One of the horses reared up on its hind legs, whinnying angrily. I didn't know if it was Arinaas, if she'd even sent those women to watch as we departed the palace. But the sight of them heartened me nonetheless.

I knew I wasn't alone.

I retired to my chamber once our cruiser took to the air. I had no desire to spend the next few hours constantly aware of Idris, to wonder when I might see him next.

I dozed on and off until Tala woke me and helped me to freshen up.

"Alright?" she asked.

I nodded and settled the light cloak over my shoulders. "I don't think I'm ready to go back."

Tala smiled. "I would find it strange if you were."

The cruiser had begun its descent to Walili and the Ziyaana landing by the time I emerged from the chamber to the receiving room. Idris was already there, standing at the large window, framed by a stream of clouds and the planet's afternoon light. His hair was held back as it always was in the Ziyaana, and his navy blue jacket was buttoned up to his throat. He struck a severe figure with his clean-shaven face, wiped of expression. The sarcastic rise of his eyebrows and small creases at the corners of his eyes were absent.

When he turned away from the window and saw me, something in his expression eased. I found myself smiling, just a little, in response. And when he held out a hand to me I took it without hesitation.

His hands were dry and warm, the hands of a makhzen with few scars and no callouses. Idris had likely never plowed a field or hauled wheat into a warehouse. His struggles were altogether different.

I stilled when his hand brushed against my cheek. His fingers slid over the hairline behind my ear and into my hair. "The next time we see each other," he began, "we won't be ourselves."

I wound my fingers around his. I'd known from the beginning our moments would be stolen and few. Hoarded and measured out between engagements, while all the world watched me thinking I was Maram. I knew it wouldn't be enough, but right now it was something, and that was more than I'd had before I'd gone to Ouzdad.

"We all have parts we must play," I told him. "It doesn't change—"

"Anything," he interrupted and smiled. "The ties they forged have broken and Fate has led our feet to freedom."

I couldn't keep my grin off my face. "That was a very good translation. And from a lesser-known poem, no less."

"The Dowager helped." My laugh was stopped by a wave of emotion. By his own admission he couldn't read Kushaila very well, but he'd struggled through it to find something to bring to me. It was a gift more precious than he knew.

My hand tightened around his. I didn't know when we'd see each other again, how many weeks or months we'd have to wait before we were brought together next.

"We will see each other again?" I said softly, leaning my forehead against his.

"Yes," he replied, his words a promise. "Yes."

the ziyaana,
andala

❖ 24 ❖

"Will you swoon like Bayad?" Tala muttered to me one afternoon, startling a laugh out of me. I blinked at her, clearing the daydream from my mind.

"That ends happily, doesn't it?" I asked.

Bayad and Riyad's story was one of a love that had managed to transcend and conquer class and difference. Bayad, a merchant's son, fell in love with Riyad, a girl serving in a vizier's court. It was not a favorite of mine—Bayad swooned more than I liked—but it was beautiful nonetheless.

She snorted. "The question still stands."

The Ziyaana had felt quiet since I'd returned from Ouzdad three days ago. Maram, surprisingly, had left me alone, nor had I seen Nadine. I wasn't lovesick, or so I told myself, but I spent an inordinate amount of time daydreaming and missing Idris. The longer I was away from Ouzdad, the more my time there seemed like a beautiful dream.

The only proof I had that it wasn't was the communicator Arinaas gave me. I tested it my first night in the Ziyaana, as she had instructed me, to make sure the signal worked. I'd hidden it against the lettering on the back of the charm, so that the quote from the book seemed to be alive with nano-circuitry.

Believe, for We know things you do not. And We see what you do not.

It was a strange thing to carry around my neck, its tiny gel-like surface pressed to my skin. But it felt safer to keep it there than to risk Tala or a droid noticing it.

The reading of fairy tales I'd started at Ouzdad continued in the Ziyaana and branched out to include whatever poetry I could get my hands on. I had more time than I knew what to do with— there were no goats I needed to attend to, no orchards to pick, no food to be made in the village oven. My success, first at the ball, and now at Ouzdad, meant that Nadine and Maram largely left me to my own devices. I spent as much of my time as possible avoiding thoughts of the next engagement. Thus far, they'd been uneventful—but I knew that the rebels and the world hated her. I knew I'd been brought to die in her place. My mind sobered and my thoughts grew grim whenever I remembered.

I kept Husnain's gift close to me as often as I could, and ofttimes I thought of what he'd said to me the last time I'd seen him. Part of me wanted to try my hand at writing my own poetry— in the old days there would have been salons full of Kushaila competing to produce the best verse for rewards from the town magistrates. But here, there was only myself, and no one to hear. Still—I tried.

Destiny shadows her footsteps . . .

"I won't swoon," I assured Tala now, and patted her hand. And then, "Are you the go-between for divided lovers, then?"

She shuddered, but was smiling. "Dihya forbid you should ever truly be divided lovers, and that I should be your go-between, Amani."

I was still grinning when the droid appeared to summon me to Maram.

The light in my heart dimmed just a little as I drew the cloak over my shoulders and took the veil from Tala's proffered hand. I knew I wouldn't receive a lesson; Maram and Nadine believed I'd performed admirably at Ouzdad, and they had no way of knowing what had transpired between Furat and I, or the Dowager and Idris.

Still, if my mind's distance was so easily discernible to Tala, what would Maram glean from looking at me?

All the while we walked toward her quarters I tried to ready myself for another assignment. It would likely be in Greater Walili; I could not imagine that she would need to journey somewhere as far as Gibra a second time. There were enough scorpions hiding in the desert around Walili. The droid led me past her door, and down a set of steps. We emerged into the courtyard I'd glimpsed when I visited her last.

We continued toward a secluded bower surrounded by trees, and filled with floating orbs of light. Maram was seated on a cushion on the grass, a low table set with a shatranj game spread out before her. She was clearly lost in thought, but as soon as the droid stepped into view her gaze cleared and she lifted her eyes to me.

"You may go," she said to the droid.

After a moment she gestured to my veil and waited for me to pull it off.

"Well," she said, raising her eyebrows. "Shall you sit or must I command you?"

My mind swung back and forth between fear and suspicion. But as I settled down onto the cushion and shrugged the cloak from my shoulders, I had the impression she was bored. The board was set in the middle of one of the problem puzzles Idris had shown me while at Ouzdad, only half solved.

"You and his lordship enjoy this game, then?" I asked.

"You played at Ouzdad?" Maram's bright smile didn't set me at ease.

"It served as a distraction," I said. Not a total lie. It had certainly produced a distraction for us both.

She hummed her ascent. "So—how did you like him?"

I raised my eyebrows in surprise. "Like him?"

She balanced her chin on her fist. "I've heard my fiancé is quite the Kushaila catch," she said. "Do you disagree?"

Like so much with Maram, this felt like a trap. I turned my words over carefully before I spoke. "His lordship was kind and gracious. Very easygoing."

"Diplomatically stated," she said dryly. "And not a word to his handsomeness."

"Does his lordship need reassurance?" I asked in the same tone.

She laughed. "I could stand to be warmer, or so I've been told."

"Why?" I said, surprised. "It's a matter of state. Not love."

"You surprise me, village girl. I would have thought a provincial sort would have been all for love."

I shook my head. "My parents were a love match," I said. I had countless memories stored away of the small things they did for one another that spoke more loudly than the declarations many spouses made during our festivals. His hand on the small of her back, the soft look in her eyes sometimes as she watched him move around the house. I'd always felt lucky to grow up in a house with such love, even knowing that it was likely not in my future. "But I knew I wouldn't have that luxury. That I'd likely have to pick someone who wouldn't impoverish me further over someone who loved me."

"That's quite mercenary," she said. She sounded delighted.

I shrugged. "An empty belly makes one mercenary, I suppose."

The board went ignored between us while she stared at me as though I were an interesting puzzle. "We are not in love," she said at last, matter-of-factly. "The marriage is a stipulation in the peace treaty that granted my father stewardship of this planet." A pause. "What a strange puzzle you are," she said and returned to the board.

I laughed. "Are your companions so uninteresting, Your Highness?"

She grimaced and leaned away from the table. "You have no idea." I must have looked skeptical, because she continued. "All they can talk about is my upcoming eighteenth birthday."

"I imagine they are excited," I said and watched her reset the board. "Certainly such chatter is more interesting than me."

A corner of her mouth lifted, an echo of Idris's own self-satisfied smile. "It would be if they didn't spend half their time giving me sideways glances they thought were discreet."

"Oh?"

She finished setting the board, and tilted her head at me. "Stupidity is a poor look on you—or me, I suppose. On us. My inheritance of this planet and its ancillaries has not been confirmed. It needs to be by the time I turn eighteen or it will pass to my elder half sister, Galene."

"Oh." I tried to wrap my mind around what she'd told me. That she might not actually inherit Andala. That someone worse could rule over us. I wanted to ask why she would be passed over, but held my tongue. My curiosity would be a strange thing to her, and I didn't need her prying into the new secrets I had to keep.

Maram's shatranj set was done up in sapphire blue and white. She set the blue pieces on my half of the board, and the white on hers. Where Idris's set had elephants, hers had birds. I lifted one into my hand to examine it more closely.

"Why birds?"

She shrugged. "The set came with the apartments," she said. "Whoever lived here before must have liked birds."

I rubbed a thumb over the beak, and then the crown and froze. There was a spring of feathers swooping back over its head, smoothed out and nearly disappeared with time.

"What?" she said, then plucked the piece from my fingers. She frowned again. "What is this?"

"I think it was a tesleet bird," I said, then drew a finger up over the center of my forehead. "It's nearly gone, but . . ."

"Why should that matter?"

"It doesn't, I suppose."

It was the royal bird—or had been before the Vath. How strange that Maram had kept these pieces—kept all the old trappings of the Ziyadi order.

Maram set the piece back on the board. "White always has first move."

We were quiet after. It seemed she truly had been bored, and didn't want to play against an AI or a courtier that would have to let her win. We were evenly matched, which was to say neither of us was particularly good. Like me, Maram never thought

more than a few moves ahead and eventually we found ourselves
locked into an unsolvable board.

She huffed a laugh. "Reset?"

I shrugged.

"How was Ouzdad?" she asked. "How was my grandmother?"

I should have been prepared for such a question, but I wasn't.
I'd assumed she wanted to avoid all mention of it, of ever having
to go. Another lesson, then. Always be prepared to report to
Maram.

"Old," I managed, tamping down the image of Idris, just before our first game.

She hummed. "Yes, well."

Her hum turned to a noise of surprise when I captured one
of her birds.

"And Furat? She returned there just before you set out."

I remembered the last time Maram and I discussed Furat.
"Briefly," was all I said.

"And?" Maram asked, impatient.

I pulled away from the board. "Perhaps if you were more specific with your questions, Your Highness."

She looked away from me, and for a moment I had an image
of her as a small child, short arms folded across her chest. I
imagined she had been used to getting anything she wanted. At
least for a short time. Had Najat doted on Maram, despite who
her father was? Would she have been able to resist a child made
in her image, unaware of all the horrors that surrounded her con-
ception?

Perhaps not. Perhaps Najat had been a woman who could forgive her daughter the sins of her father.

"How did Furat seem?" Maram asked finally.

I thought of my walk with Furat, and our shared conspiracy.

We were allies now, tied in our rebellion against the crown. Against Maram. "She wanted to play shatranj with me. With you. I declined. I imagine you would have done the same."

She nodded after a moment and returned her eyes to the board between us. I couldn't resist watching her, though I should have been watching her advance across the shatranj board. In this moment she seemed normal, though that felt like a weak word. She was only my age and worried about how her cousin and grandmother had received her, resentful of those her grandmother favored.

No one had given her a chance to be raised among them, and by the time she'd returned from the Vathek homeworld her mind had been poisoned against that part of her family. And I imagined that her cousins had not reached out to her when she returned. They all viewed her with fear and suspicion now, but her complete hatred might not have stood against kindness.

Or perhaps I was a fool who expected too much.

Maram caught me staring and narrowed her eyes. "What?"

I knew better, and yet . . . "I don't think your grandmother is . . . is seeding a rebellion."

"I told you stupidity was a bad look," she said. "What would a village girl know about what the Dowager planned?"

"I speak Kushaila, remember? You do not. They didn't say much around me." I shrugged. "Her head of security is too cautious for that. But it did sound like they were trying to protect you."

It wasn't a complete lie. The Dowager missed her granddaughter; she missed what they could have been. She grieved their relationship. She would not have turned on her, not in such a violent way. And the longer I'd been there, the more I'd served as a holdover, a way to assuage all her grief at losing her only grandchild.

Maram balanced a chariot piece in one hand, weighing it. "You're sure."

"As sure as I can be."

She smiled suddenly and set the piece back on the board.

I didn't want to plumb Maram's hidden depths. There was nothing that could change what she'd done to me when I first arrived, or the way she treated those around her. Despite that, I couldn't forget how the Vath had shaped her. How early she'd lost her mother. How terrible such an upbringing would be. They'd shaped her into the cruel, hateful creature she was now. I imagined she didn't believe she had a choice in how she behaved. Survival among the Vath would have ensured that.

She made a sound of triumph and my gaze returned to the board.

She'd won.

"I never beat Idris," she said, grinning. "We will have to play again."

I thought to bite my smile back too late. Our eyes met and I watched as she tried to remember herself, remember who we were. Not friends, not twins. Master and servant.

"A droid will escort you back," she said, gesturing to the walkway from which I'd come.

I rose to my feet, bowed, and collected my cloak. I knew she would not invite me back. I'd seen her come back to herself, the strange flicker of anger in her eyes. But I couldn't help wondering what life in the Ziyaana might have been like if she were always like this; what the future might be like if she softened just a little.

25

I sat on the cushion Maram offered me, hands folded in my lap, my eyes fixed on the ground.

It had been a week since Maram and I played shatranj. Maram and Nadine had not been in the same room with me for a long while, and I could not work the itch from my back. Whenever they'd been together, I'd paid for an offhand comment or a tantrum Nadine could not or would not control.

So I waited, hoping they'd forgotten Maram had invited me to her apartments. Praying that neither thought I had any opinion on their argument.

"She is not a doll," Nadine said. "You may not dress her up and send her where you please. She is a shield."

"Galene's parties are dangerously dull, then," Maram said.

I'd been summoned earlier without warning to prepare to take Maram's place at her half sister's ball. She'd tossed a holopad in my lap and commanded me to learn the names and faces of those who would be present, then settled herself on her divan.

Even Nadine's arrival had not stirred her from it. How odd that she and I sat close, though I was at her feet, while Nadine stood. It did not escape my notice that Maram had not offered her a seat. In fact, any place where she might sit was conspicuously absent.

"And what will you do if the fool girl exposes herself?"

"She fooled my grandmother, Nadine," Maram said. I didn't have to raise my head to know the look she gave Nadine implied a measure of stupidity. "She is clearly quite adept at her job."

"Your Highness—"

"Are you forbidding me?"

"Have a care, Your Highness. It would be to your detriment to lose her."

I held my breath as Nadine spun away, the silver lining of her skirt flashing in the afternoon sunlight. Only when the door clicked shut did I release it and the tension in my shoulders.

"Now," Maram said, swinging her feet to the floor. I looked up; she was smiling. "Shall we?"

Maram had a closet large enough to be its own room. Aside from the clothes hanging along the walls, there was a sitting area, a vanity, and a small alcove with a stand and a mirror. I hovered in the doorway while she dived in, flipping through qaftans and gowns.

"So," I started. "A party?"

She sighed and rolled her eyes, as if the very mention of it pained her. "Galene is throwing a party to celebrate her profitable year in the north. It's a desperate, last-minute bid to be considered for inheritor of the realm. Vathek visitors only, barring spouses and fiancés."

"You dislike her so much?"

"Do you like all of your siblings?" she asked archly.

I managed to stifle the desire to laugh. "Yes."

A strange look came over her face, as if she were reliving a memory. "Galene was—is—the height of imperial breeding. Everything in her life was assured until I was born, and she's never forgiven me for that, nor for being a half-breed. She turned the Vathek court on Luna-Vaxor against me before I ever set foot there."

"Blood is so important to the Vath?"

She cut me a withering look. "You say that as if blood is unimportant to Kushaila. But to Galene, yes. She hates foreigners, and my mother's people most of all." There was still a shadow in her gaze, as if the things Galene had done were worse than what Maram wanted to say.

Her own sister, I thought, and fought the creep of pity. It was no wonder she trusted no one. I kept my thoughts to myself— Maram would never condescend to accept my sympathy.

Instead I said, "And you can't decline?"

"To decline would be to appear weak."

I frowned. "Weak?"

"Is the word beyond your comprehension?"

I struggled not to scoff. "It is not. But if you don't want to go to the party, then don't go."

"Galene would have been a natural contender if the galactic treaty hadn't locked my father into having to declare me as heir," Maram said.

"Alright," I said, skeptical.

"You don't know anything about the history of your own world, do you?"

I said nothing, lest I snap.

"When my father conquered Andala, he violated galactic law. The only way to keep the planet—the whole system—was to legitimize his rule. Marry the queen or one of her children, and ensure that her line inherited the planet." She waved a hand. "At any rate, Galene is still convinced that she has a chance to inherit the protectorate of Andala over me."

I took a seat beside her. "But—"

"But it's my inheritance?" She looked away. "It is not the Vathek way to let those conquered rule themselves, and with my Andalaan fiancé—people say . . . things. They say my father will have to sign over the center of Vathek rule to someone else."

"Ah," I said, ignoring the uneasy turn in my stomach. This was how Vathek rule worked—we, the conquered, were prizes in a game to be won or lost among people who didn't care about us. "This is a bid to unseat you."

"Yes," she said. "And I cannot avoid her. If I don't go, my father will know I didn't have the stomach for it, and it will prove them all right—that I'm unfit to be the heir."

I was too much a fool not to laugh. It seemed in keeping with the absurdities of my life that it now included a rivalry between sisters played out on a cosmic scale.

"What?" she asked, furious.

"I just," I said, coughing. "I didn't expect such a problem from you."

"Such a problem?" she said coolly.

"You're rivals," I said. " It happens."

"You've had this problem?"

"No. But I never had anything anyone coveted."

She sniffed and leaned back. "Then how do you know? That this is such a normal problem?"

I shrugged. "I had friends, hard as it may be for you to believe. And in a village as small as ours, rivalries happen." Khadija had often found herself the target of one girl or another's ire. She was beautiful and loved to smile—heads turned for her, sometimes when they should have been looking at someone else.

"So what would you do?"

"Really?"

"I'm asking, aren't I? Don't make me repeat myself."

I hesitated, searching her face to see if she would take it back.

I worried at my bottom lip, searching the room. "The best way to unsettle her is to behave as though you've already won. You're the one living in the Ziyaana. You're the one born here and meant to inherit. She is the foreigner. Do you have jewelry that would remind her of the Andalaan royal seal?"

"Like a crown?"

It was difficult to restrain my skepticism. "Something more subtle."

"The royal tesleet is not very subtle, village girl."

"Birds have feathers," I reminded her. "And you had a necklace—a talon gripping a jewel."

"And she'll associate those things with the inheritance?"

"She wants to inherit the whole planet," I said. "She's spent her life resenting your birth. She's likely spent hours imagining her wardrobe and the seal and all the things related to the office in the event of her success."

"Hm," was all Maram said, but she rose from her seat. "You are not as stupid as you seem, village girl."

I tamped down a smile, and returned my eyes to the holopad still clutched in one hand. The list of guests was quite long, but I recognized them all. All Vathek, all silver-haired and pale. Maram would stand out in such a crowd.

I frowned. "His lordship isn't on the guest list."

She made an unprincess-like sound. "He is skulking and so was removed," she said without turning around.

"What?"

"We had an argument. So he refused to accompany me."

My eyes widened just a little. I hadn't imagined that the two of them ever argued. Fighting with Maram seemed to me a dangerous thing, and my curiosity was close to getting the best of me and asking what they could have argued about.

There was a sharp twist of disappointment in me too. I hadn't seen Idris since our return from Ouzdad, and I'd hoped— But then, things rarely went so easily in the Ziyaana. "Is that why you planned to send me in your place?"

"Are you asking me if I was avoiding my fiancé?" she said, and stilled in her rummaging.

I lowered my eyes. "No, Your Highness."

"Good," she said, then tossed a gown toward me. "Try this on."

galene's estate,
andala

26

Galene's estate was far to the north, across the sea. Farther north than Atalasia. It was situated against a mountain range and made of white stone that shined even against the snow. High turrets and coned roofs marked it apart from the architecture many of the visitors would have been used to from the south. Even on board the ship I could hear the mountain wind screaming as it bore ice and snow down the mountainside.

I was placed in tower apartments on the north side facing the steep slope leading away from the castle. A fire roared in the bedroom, already stoked by a northern serving girl. For a moment I wondered who had lived here before the property had been confiscated and given to Galene. I didn't even know the name of the people that lived so far north. Who had the will to build such a castle in such a place? Who had the will to stay?

A knock on the door roused me from my seat. It opened before I reached the door, revealing my visitor.

"Idris!" I couldn't stop myself from smiling.

He frowned and looked over his shoulder as though he'd knocked on the wrong door. I closed the door behind him and touched his arm. A moment later he broke out into a wide grin as he realized it wasn't Maram who greeted him, but me. A wave of happiness washed over me. Being recognized—and being recognized by Idris—would never lose its wonder.

"I didn't think . . ." he started once he was inside.

"I thought I was coming alone," I said.

He was still frowning. "I've just arrived. Maram and I had an argument and I wasn't going to come."

"You've come to apologize," I said, amused.

"Something like that. What are you doing here? There's no danger here."

"My half sister's bid for the crown poses a danger to my sanity," I said. "Or something to that effect."

"You are cheerier than I've seen you in some time."

He was right. Twice now Maram and I had sat together and talked and I'd come away from it unharmed. A low bar for friendship, to be sure. But she seemed more real to me now, and I imagined—or hoped—that I seemed more real to her. We would never be friends, but—

But what? I didn't know.

A serving girl knocked on the door and poked her head through.

"We've unpacked your gown, Your Highness," she said. "Shall we bring it in?"

"Yes," I said, and flashed Idris a look.

His face cleared immediately. He bowed a moment later. "I will see you when you're ready."

The gown Maram had settled on was more Vathek than Ku-shaila; it was a black gown with an oval neckline and black lace sleeves. The skirt clung to my hips and then widened just slightly at the knees, spilling into a pool of fabric at my ankles. There were silver epaulets at the shoulders and a thin silver belt of interlock-ing wings no wider than my smallest finger. She'd managed to find the necklace I'd mentioned—a dark silver talon clutching an emerald, and it swung from my neck, bumping against my ribs every now and then. The earrings were the same dark metal shaped and etched to look like feathers, and smelted so that when they moved, they glimmered with a rainbow of color.

All in all, I thought as I examined myself in the mirror, the effect was striking. The serving girl pulled my hair away from my face so that the earrings would not be hidden, but it hung low on my back, curling freely.

Idris's eyes widened when he saw me. "You're—" he began.

"Thank you," I said, grinning. "Shall we?"

Galene held the party in the central courtyard, a place that was part garden and part ballroom, with a high glass ceiling to trap the heat. The walls were covered in ornate mirrors, and hovering high above were several chandeliers rising and falling, as though a wind flowed beneath them. White flowers hung from every-thing, twining over bannisters and around sconces.

I managed to keep my expression serene and apathetic as we made our way through the crowd. Most faces I recognized, and when there was one I didn't, I squeezed Idris's arm. It seemed Galene had invited not only the Vathek courtiers who resided on Andala, but some Vath from other places in the system. I couldn't understand why they would make such a journey, but then I imagined a noble with no occupation had the time.

"Maram!"

Theo. And his Moranite wife. The two of them peeled away from their circle; Theo kissed me as he had in Atalasia, and his wife remained at his side, silent.

"You look a vision," he said. "Idris."

"Theo," he replied. "You're looking well. Marriage agrees with you."

Theo grinned. "It agrees with us. Doesn't it, my dear?"

The girl seemed to have eyes only for her new husband, and beamed up at him. Still, she'd not spoken a single word.

I smiled at her. "Does she speak Vathekaar?" I asked.

Theo didn't look offended. "She's only shy. She still hasn't got used to the Vathek way of doing things."

"A Moranite hardly has reason to fear us." I looked at her critically. The planet Moran had been conquered not so much earlier than Andala, but they'd fallen quicker, surrendered faster. "Is Moran so different from Andala?"

I thought she wouldn't respond. But she shook her head, her eyes still focused on her feet. "No, Your Highness." And then, "You look well, Your Highness, you and his lordship."

I raised my eyebrows in bewilderment and looked to Idris, who smiled faintly.

"She only means you look happy," Theo cut in. "You do, cousin—lighter."

I forced myself to smile despite the alarm ringing in my head. "Thank you," I managed.

I should have released Idris's arm, but I worried it would bring more attention to it. Did we look closer than Maram and Idris normally did? Had I done such a poor job of hiding how I felt?

"Don't look now," Idris said into my ear. "But here comes Galene."

"Well," I said, making sure not to look around. "Here goes nothing."

Advising Maram had been one thing. But faced with the prospect of holding my own against Galene, my advice seemed flimsy and ill thought. I knew little of royals, and less about envious half sisters.

Your life depends on this, I reminded myself.

I had perfected passing as Maram. But if she found that I'd failed to hold my ground against Galene, I'd pay for it. Friendly overtures or not.

Before Galene reached us a hand touched my elbow.

"My dear," a voice said as I turned around.

Ofal vak Miranous was a favorite cousin of Maram's. I recognized her from the holopad, wide-set eyes and unusual dark hair, a spread of freckles over her nose and cheeks so thick it seemed sometimes to be a mask. She was older than Maram and Idris, and had snuck Maram treats when they were small, and later taught her to train her hunting roc.

She smiled at me, warm and lovely, and I could not control the answering smile back. Maram warned me that Ofal had that effect on people.

"Ofal," I greeted her and let her kiss my cheek.

"I don't think I've yet seen you in something so sleek," she said, holding me at arm's length. "It suits you. Makes you all the more striking."

My grin widened, and I pulled my arm out of Idris's grip and linked it with hers.

"How are your hounds?" I asked her as we walked away.

She laughed. "Oh, come now, that's not the question you want to ask."

"Fine," I conceded. "How does she look?"

"Furious. You know she doesn't like to give chase."

"More's the pity," I said. "She might have had more than her inheritance if she'd learned."

Ofal grinned down at me. "I can't tell if your tongue's gotten sharper or you're just always nice to me."

I had no response to that. Maram's tongue always seemed razor sharp to me, honed so fine it was as likely to break as it was to cut someone.

"Perhaps my half sister just brings out the worst in me."

She looked at me sidelong, smirking, and shook her head. For a split second I felt as though the world tilted. I was not Maram, I knew that. There was no way to forget. But I didn't know when I'd gotten so good at being her, at being her around other people. I hadn't committed a great wrong against Galene, but I was enjoying the careless baiting. Perhaps more than I should have.

"Let's find a seat," I said to Ofal. "You know she'll hate to greet me so."

I'd lost track of Idris, but by the time Ofal and I settled on a bench wreathed in white flowers, he'd returned. He handed each of us small goblets filled with steaming hot chocolate, and kissed my cheek.

"Careful," he murmured.

I considered saying nothing. "You," I said. "Should sit."

Ofal snorted into her cup. "She'll hate that whenever she arrives."

A small measure of satisfaction rose up in me. "Good."

Idris did not resist or argue, but there was a pause while he met my eyes. He sat, leaned back on his hands, nonchalant as ever.

I could imagine the picture the three of us made. Regal, laughing. Idris severe in his distance, as if he were looking out for danger. When I was younger I'd imagined such parties and such laughter, beyond carefree. Maram and Ofal were without the troubles of a village girl. They had never gone hungry or developed calluses on their hands from picking fruit. Neither of them had ever cowered in fear of outsiders.

When Galene arrived, she paused at the edge of our circle, waiting. I imagine she waited for Idris to stand, but I set a hand on his thigh to keep him in place. I turned to acknowledge her at last and saw the moment she understood. Saw her weigh the cost of walking away against the cost to her dignity.

In the end, protocol won, and she came forward and sank gracefully to her knees.

"Maram," she murmured. "You honor me with your presence."

Her hair was near silver in the High Vathek way, her gown done in the style of antiquity, a long flowing gown, gathered at one shoulder. A large pendant swung from her neck bearing the crest of the Vath. She looked every inch a conqueror.

I drew on all my rage since coming to the Ziyaana, all the rage of being taken on my majority night—at losing my own inheritance—to harden my voice.

"Galene," I replied coolly. "You remember the Lady Ofal and my fiancé, the Lord Idris."

I had not given her leave to rise.

"Of course," she said.

She raised her head and I let her stare, waiting for her eyes to drift down to my necklace. She was far more practiced in keeping her emotions in check. Her jaw tightened when she saw it, but nothing else.

"Thank you for your invitation," I said, and at last gave her leave to rise. When she stood, I held out the near empty goblet, waiting for her to take it. "The food is delightful."

And then I turned back to Ofal, dismissing Galene. Ofal for her part could hardly contain her laughter. Her lower lip trembled until she bit it.

I heard no footsteps marking Galene's departure so I turned back and tilted my head.

"Had you need of something?"

Her grip turned white knuckled around the goblet.

"No, Your Highness," she said through clenched teeth. "Enjoy the festivities."

I spent the rest of the night giddy on my success, giggling with Ofal and a few other friends. It was easy to forget I wasn't Maram, these weren't my friends, this wasn't my life. Easy to enjoy it all, especially when Idris took me out onto the dance floor. By the time we retired for the evening I was dizzy with success.

"You've had too much sugar," Idris said as he led us upstairs.

"I have not," I replied. "It's only that tonight feels like a triumph."

He sighed but said nothing.

I bathed, in the hopes that the warm water would pull me closer to sleep, but it did nothing. When I emerged robed, with my hair down, I could not force myself into bed.

I'd discovered that the living room attached to my apartment linked my rooms to Idris's. He was standing over the table, his hair wet, arranging a shatranj board.

"I thought we might play," he said. "If you're not too exhausted."

"Do we have to play at the table?" I asked. I hated the tall table and the equally tall chairs the Vath preferred. He was quiet as he moved the board to the floor and retrieved a pair of cushions.

"You look tired," I said.

He settled on the floor and gave me a faint smile. "These engagements exhaust me," he said. "I'm not as tired as I could be, though."

"Oh?"

"I've never been able to look across the room and know I have an ally," he said without looking at me. "It was . . . novel."

"Really?" I said.

"Did you know none of my peers are friends?" he said with a sad smile, his eyes distant for a moment. "We tried at first. We thought—we thought that we were all hostages. But if we stuck together, eventually we would grow old enough to resist the Vath. We would take back our strongholds, avenge our families. The Vath had only won because we didn't work together. Or so we reasoned."

I reached out for his hand. His gaze grew more distant, but his hand gripped mine as if it were an anchor.

"It took three months for us to realize that fear was stronger than loyalty. A boy would disappear or a minor house would be raided, and we'd know the Vath had gotten to someone. Had pressed fear into them and turned them against the rest of us. By the end of our first year none of us trusted each other."

I couldn't keep the horror from my face. Imagining such a world seemed impossible, even though I lived in it now. I had never second-guessed any of my friends, never wondered if one would sell me to the Vath in exchange for safety or mercy. I knew in the early days of the occupation such a thing had been common, but by now—

"I'm sorry," I finally said. It was all I could think of to say.

He shook his head and looked down at the board.

"And Maram . . . she isn't an ally?"

At that he looked up as if to say, *really?*

"She . . . she isn't reliable. Most days we're friends. Or as close to friends as we can be. But she values the respect of her Vathek peers far more than mine. It puts me in difficult positions regularly."

"More or less difficult than when you argue with her?" I asked, my curiosity getting the better of me.

He grinned. "I wondered when you were going to ask."

I couldn't help smiling back and brushed a curl behind his ear. "Well? I didn't think she was the type one argued with."

"Normally she isn't," he said with a sigh. "I don't know what got into me. She made a comment about Furat and I snapped."

"You snapped?" I gasped.

"Furat's and my circumstances are much the same," he said. "You know that. I asked her if she felt the same about me and she became angry."

I leaned back in surprise. "I'm surprised she didn't claw your eyes out. Or that you risked her clawing your eyes out at all."

"It felt worth it," he said, looking at me. "As if now . . . I have more at stake. More reason to . . . care, I suppose. It's easy to do or say nothing," he continued quietly. "I don't want to take the easy path anymore."

I felt a flush work its way up my throat and looked away. We were both silent and the room quiet, but for the crackle of the fire. He broke the silence first.

"You want first move?" he asked.

We didn't speak for a while after that. My skill had not progressed as much as I would have liked, and more than once I leaned forward, trying to plan an escape. Idris was methodical, working his way slowly over the board and into my territory. If he was ever given command of real armies, I imagined he could do a great deal of damage. His patience astonished me.

"You're cheating," he chided.

"I'm not!"

"Your hair is obscuring the board," he said, and flicked a finger at a lock.

For a moment I had no idea what he meant. And then I laughed and leaned back.

"Sorry," I said, and began to gather the hair spilling over my shoulders and down my back into one hand. He watched, eyes sharp, as though he expected to find a shatranj piece hidden in my curls. "It's never been so long before. I forget."

His mouth curled with skepticism.

"Frown all you like," I said. "Farmer's daughters do not have the time that noble women do to tend to an excess of hair. My mother cut it in the winter. Why are you staring?"

The braid was only half finished but I knew the sudden tremor in my fingers would keep me from completing it. He watched me as if all his patience had been honed and transformed into a gaze that could cut through metal. It was the same look he'd given me at Ouzdad. We had not seen each other since that afternoon, and a part of me thrilled to think what might happen. The rest of me, however—

"I don't understand how anyone can mistake you for her," he said at last.

My eyes widened. "Is this about Galene? Did I not do well?"

He breathed out a half laugh. "No, in that you were Maram to perfection."

"Then what do you mean?"

He rested his chin on a fist. The firelight cast his face in shadow so that I could see the ghost of his lashes against his cheeks, but not his eyes. He mesmerized me as no one ever had. It wasn't only that I wanted to look, I wanted to touch.

My fingers itched with the desire to reach forward and comb through his hair.

He shook his head as if coming out of a dream. "My apologies," he said. "I'm being—I'm more tired than I thought."

I could breathe again, though I watched him still. He did look suddenly tired, his shoulders slumped, a hand shielding his eyes.

"We can pick up the game next time we see one another if you like."

"We don't know when the next time will be," he replied.

I laid my forehead against his and linked our hands firmly together. The only sound in the room was the crackle of the fire. Its flame cast him in sharp relief—the flecks of dark brown in his eyes, a thin faded scar on his chin, the black-red in his hair.

"I never—I used to not think about having to marry Maram," he said. "It always seemed so far away."

"How far?" I asked, though I didn't want the answer.

"After she turned eighteen and her inheritance was confirmed," he said. "I always—" His grip tightened around my hands.

"What?"

"My marriage felt necessary." His voice had dropped to a near whisper as if he were struggling to admit something to himself. "For Andala. For its future. But now . . ."

I raised my hands to his face. "Now?" I wasn't sure I wanted the answer to that, either.

He didn't complete his sentence. Instead, he leaned forward and kissed me. It felt like relief and desire. I—we—had avoided thinking about our future, about what it meant that I was a stand-in for his fiancée. I'd avoided examining my feelings too closely. But I wanted him for myself, for all time. I could admit that much at least.

I poured all that feeling into this, my fingers tight in the folds of his robe as his hands found the tangle of my braid and undid it, as if he'd been planning to since I'd put it up.

When at last we parted, I struggled to breathe and laid my head on his shoulder.

"Every time I see you, Amani, feels like a gift and a reprieve," he said, threading a hand through my hair. "But every moment together means that her confirmation, and our marriage, draws closer."

The thought gave me pause, and I felt my earlier excitement drain away. Did we have a choice, I wondered. We lived in the world of the Vath, and their chains had tied him to Maram. He was welded to her and to the throne in the same way I was welded to her shadow.

"We have this," I said, and laid a hand on his heart. "But the world will decide what becomes of us."

He pressed a kiss to my forehead. "I am tired of being at the mercy of the world."

the ziyaana,
andala

27

"What is the matter with you?" Maram snapped, pulling back enough to get a full look at me. "Are you even listening?"

"What?" I was too distracted. As in most things, Tala was right; I could not allow Maram's basic kindness to lull me into a false sense of security. I could not afford to not pay attention while in her presence. "I'm sorry."

"What in the worlds could possibly be distracting you?"

"The dress?" I volunteered weakly, trying to marshal my thoughts. It wouldn't do to be caught thinking of Idris, or what he'd revealed to me. That the more I helped Maram, the more successful we were, the sooner I would lose him.

She snorted.

For the second time in a row I would be required to dress in the Vathek style. This costume was not as stark as the last gown, but it had no sleeves, and a heavy cape that descended from the front of my shoulders instead of from the back. I felt exposed and uncomfortable, but I was expected at a Vathek council meeting. Maram could show up in Kushaila dress, but it made a stronger statement if she didn't.

"Perhaps if you cut your hair?" she suggested, tugging on the cape.

"Then you would have to cut your hair as well," I pointed out.

"Hm. No, this is fine. You pass muster." She threw herself back into a seat beside the mirror. "Remember, *you* are not to speak. Listen, and nothing more. I can't afford you saying something foolish and risking my position."

"And if you were there?"

"I would have notes and be prepared to participate," she drawled. "I will be queen—I need to know how to rule my planet."

"Why is this meeting such a security risk for you?"

"Trade delegations are coming from outside the system," she explained. "Everyone is screened, but Nadine deemed it an unnecessary risk."

"Then why go at all?"

"It's a test from my father . . . He wants to know I have the stomach for this kind of thing. If I'm to inherit, it will be one of my responsibilities."

I nodded. Though Galene's party had been a success, Maram's father had said nothing about the state of her inheritance. Every day until her birthday was an opportunity to prove herself to Mathis and the rest of the High Vath.

"Besides," she continued. "If I'm not present, it makes us look weak. If the Vath do not have enough security to protect the Imperial Heir, why trade with them exclusively, and on and on." She waved a hand lazily.

"Exclusively? I don't understand. Who else could they trade with?"

"The rebels," she drawled. "If they gathered the funds, they could build an arsenal. Everyone must be dissuaded from doing business with them."

I fought down a smile. I hadn't realized others in the galaxy needed to be dissuaded from allying with the rebels—it always seemed like a fight we'd soldiered through on our own. That people needed to be dissuaded from helping us pleased me more than I could say, though I kept my gaze fixed on the floor.

The council chamber had been gutted and completely refurnished by the Vath. Gone were the red and orange pillars and the old script craved along the halfway point of the walls. The walls were white, carved with opulent gilt floral designs in the corners. There were mirrors all along the walls, and upholstered seats around an oval table. It was missing its center, and hovering over that opening was a holograph of the Ouamalich System.

The members of the council and their visitors milled around the opening, waiting for someone to call them to order. Several of Maram's distant relatives were present, and greeted me with a small smile or a touch to the elbow. Galene, I noted, was also present, though seated at the far end of the table. She nodded when she saw me, once, a cool tilt of the head.

It was easy to pay attention and affect Maram's usual sharp demeanor. The discussion crawled as the trade delegates argued and negotiated taxes, what they were legally allowed to import into the system, and what would be in direct competition with Vathek production. More than once I had to consciously keep my face impassive—there was no way to become used to the casual ease with which the Vath discussed our lives and our planet. We were numbers in a profit gained and lost column, nothing more.

It seemed to adjourn as slowly as it had started, but I didn't rise from my seat. Some of the Vathek councilors left, while others procured drink. But all too soon the military commander, a man named Isidor, reconvened the meeting, this time with only the Vath in attendance. He was now flanked by several other lower directors, each wearing the midnight black jacket of the Vathek military, their collars pinned with the silver lightning bolt denoting their rank.

There was no more talk of trade. Instead, the image of the world hovering above us expanded until it focused on the eastern end of the main continent of Andala. The sharp Vathek letters spelled out the name of the largest city on the coast: Ghazlan. Before the occupation it had been a profitable city and a center for the arts, renowned for its beauty. It had been under the aegis of the Salihi clan, but without a central stronghold, and had been saved from the Purge. Under the Salihis it had been a cultural jewel and reminder of what we'd been. I kept myself still as those on either side of me leaned forward and began to murmur.

"Where shall we start?" Isidor said, his voice gruff.

"Ghazlan is our immediate problem. Though the whole of the Eastern Reach is brewing with dissent." The woman who spoke was called Kora. Maram didn't know her well; she was normally stationed at another planetary outpost.

Isidor gestured for her to continue. Kora's hands moved quickly over her workstation and the image of the Eastern Reach faded and was replaced with a holoreel. Ghazlan's stone towers were stark against the ocean just behind them. Smoke plumed up into the air, curling its way around the pale blue of the Vathek flags flying from the towers. I held my breath as a small figure climbed quickly up the side of the tower, an assault rifle strapped across his back. There was no sound but I could imagine the screaming—raucous and loud—in the streets below him as he tore the Vathek flag down. The old Andalaan flag, before the occupation, had been white, with a green crescent moon pointing up, and a spray of stars rising up like a fountain from between its two points. White for prosperity and longevity. Green for rebirth and growth. This was not the flag the rebel hoisted onto the tower.

Since the occupation, the flag had been replaced by the Vathek one, and the rebellion had refashioned themselves a new flag. A green full moon with the silhouette of a bird streaking halfway across its surface against a red field.

Green for rebirth and growth. Red for blood. Our blood.

No one had flown the rebel flag since the Purge, almost a decade ago. The bloodshed that followed their surrender was catastrophic, and most of us believed that it was over. There was no resistance to be had against our new masters. Cruel as they were, as hard as life was, they'd won. Gooseflesh rose on my arms as the image of the flag became clearer, as Kushaila letters formed just below it.

The ocean wind picked it up, straightening the fabric so that everyone below could see it. Beneath the full moon in green was Kushaila script.

The blood never dies.

The blood never forgets.

The same part of me that froze when long misshapen shadows appeared in the fields, when I heard the whiz of Vathek fighters in the air, screamed at me now. I had agreed to spy for the rebellion, but while they celebrated their first victory, the Vath were here, plotting their undoing.

How could they—how could *we*—survive such a thing?

"So far they've managed to take Ghazlan and Sidi Walid, a city on a major trade route, and a collection of estates with acres of verdant farmland." The hair on the back of my neck stood up. Sidi Walid was a holy city. The first Dihyan temple was built there and it was the last place Massinia was seen.

"They're peasants," Galene spoke for the first time, her voice dripping with disdain. "How is this possible?"

"They're clever," Kora sighed. "They never hit a place with a large Vathek presence. And it's two cities, hardly the rebellion we're worried about."

"If we don't crush it . . ." Isidor started.

"Yes," Kora agreed. "For now it's contained to this region. But if they get hold of the entire region? It will become a bigger problem."

"Why was it not crushed from the start?" Galene insisted once more.

I still hadn't moved. In fact, I feared to breathe lest I give myself away. They were right; it was only three cities. But no one had succeeded in taking anything back from the Vath in more than twenty years. What they took, they kept.

"We are stretched thin," Isidor said. "Andala requires a heavier military presence than we anticipated. Between that and the losses we suffered during the second siege . . ."

"The siege is eight years past now," the minister of finance said, frowning. "It's high time we repair the holes in our military."

"With what? We have neglected the infrastructure of this planet in favor of quashing dissent. And Luna-Vaxor does not have the resources to build us back up. Not in the numbers we need."

Isidor raised a hand, forestalling the minister. "How long would it take to get the resources we need in place?"

"With droids, and assuming no sabotage? The mines would

take six months, the factories three or four. To replace what we lost in the war, a year perhaps. But that doesn't account for the bodies we will need to man our ships."

A chill spread through me as they spoke. Was this how our fates were decided? By cold High Vathek directors who were not interested in the planet itself but the resources we might yield? They had said nothing of this world, or Gibra, or even the whispers of Massinia's rebirth. The rebels would become more than a problem for the Vath, that much was clear. And yet they skirted the issue, as if to speak of it would give it power.

The ministers continued to quibble among one another, citing cost and loss of Vathek life for and against campaigns in reclaiming the Eastern Reach.

"Bomb the coastal cities," a voice said. It cut through the rising tide of argument as clean as a sharp knife, and as one our heads swung toward the source.

Mathis, king of all, sat at the far end of the table, his broad form leaning back as languid as a lion. None of us had seen or heard him walk into the meeting room, so absorbed had we been in the arguments. Not for the first time, I thought of the story Maram had told me. Mathis had committed patricide to secure his throne; he'd done worse to secure this system.

I was not a child, I knew that the very beautiful could hide evil. But Mathis's strength, his menace, seemed to radiate from him. He cast a long shadow, frigid and dark; it seemed as though I could feel the chill of it all the way down the table. Even Galene seemed to pale just a little in her father's presence.

"Your Grace?" Kora said.

"Was I unclear in my meaning?" he asked. "We can no longer afford such bald dissent. Not if we mean to continue to control this and all the other planets within our empire. We began the

226 * somaiya daud

Andalaan conquest for profit and resettlement, and we've lost more money than is acceptable."

His voice was even tempered, his face impassive. Despite that, I felt fear rope its way around my neck, as if at any moment he might explode into violence.

"Leave Ghazlan," he said. "We cannot afford to rebuild its infrastructure. But we can afford to lose Tairout and Sidi Walid."

I forced myself to think even as I felt grief twist in my chest. This was why I was one of Arinaas's spies, so that I could pass information on to her. And it was all here, sitting in a data packet plugged into my workstation. Galene smiled at me from down the table, cool and mocking, as if she could sense my weakness.

I knew what I had to do, though I was terrified to do it. My hands worked, fiddling with the console, as I kept my eyes on the king.

"Sidi Walid is home to one of the oldest zaouias on the planet," I said. My voice came out clear and as even as the king's. Galene looked at me in surprise, as if shocked that Maram might speak at all, much less with authority. "It will be a moral blow to the dissidents."

I felt ill suggesting the destruction of the zaouia. Even after the occupation, most of them had fulfilled their duties— giving shelter to the poor and needy, offering a place for respite and prayer. But Maram had to seem hard, and I needed people to focus on my words, not what I was still doing with my hands.

Mathis stared at me, and smiled. "An excellent point, Maram." He turned back to the council. "Deploy the fleet."

I returned to my apartments in a fugue. Tala offered me food and tea, but I shook my head and returned to my room. Somehow I got out of the Vathek gown and Maram's circlet and jewelry and into my own clothes. The chill had not gone, and I found I had to wrap myself in a heavier robe to stave it off.

"Amani?" I jumped when Tala laid a hand on my shoulder. "What's wrong?"

I stared up at her, wide eyed. What could I tell her? Only, I imagined, what she already knew. That the Vath did not see us as people. That any method to keep us down and obedient was and would always be used. That the conquered people were not the priority, only the resources we sat on.

Bile burned in my throat. I'd helped them—given them advice on how to conduct a campaign that would kill yet more of us. They would target the zaouias, I thought. Because I had pointed them there. The places were ancient, and still home to the poor and needy. I'd done that.

I'd done that. Oh, Dihya.

I drew in a deep breath. "Nothing," I said at last. "The Vath are . . . overwhelming. The council meeting was . . . I was not prepared."

It was necessary, I reminded myself. I'd needed the information. The *rebels* needed the information.

She smiled in sympathy. "Shall I bring you in some tea?"

I shook my head. "I just need to rest, is all. I may stay in my room the rest of the day."

"Alright," she replied. "You know where to find me if you need me."

I waited until her footsteps faded away before I rose from my seat and locked the door behind her. My hands reached for the charm I'd worn at Ouzdad, peeling back the thin, gel-like tab attached to the back. It emitted a brief, blue light when I pulled it off, then stuck it beneath my ear. It did not take long for a voice to speak.

"Yes?"

Something like a smile pulled at the corners of my mouth. "Have you given me your direct line?"

Arinaas laughed. "I can reroute the call to someone else if you like."

I leaned back into my cushioned seat, and allowed myself a true smile. "No, thank you."

"Ah," she said, an echo of laughter still in her voice.

I liked Arinaas, I realized. She seemed straightforward and had a dry sense of humor I enjoyed. I never questioned where I stood with her and she never rode circles around what she wanted out of me. I had so few of those relationships now.

"What news?"

I sobered. "The Vath are going to bomb the coastal cities in the Eastern Reach."

She muttered something under her breath that sounded like a swear. "Mouha!" A name. "Get me Sa'ad. Quickly."

A low murmur.

"Drag him across the desert if you have to."

"Arinaas?"

"Amani." Her voice had gentled.

"It's as bad as I imagined?"

"No," she said. "Not yet. There is still time to weaken their assault. You have proven very useful, my friend."

"I have a data packet with troop numbers and weapon depots, but I need someone to collect the information from me."

"Well done, Amani," she said warmly, despite the news I'd given her. "We'll find a way to get it from you. I'll be in touch."

"'There's something else," I said. "They're . . . they'll be target-ing the zaouias in Sidi Walid."

Arinaas swore. "We'll take care of it. Contact me if you learn more."

"I will," I promised.

The line went dead without a goodbye.

☙ 28 ❧

It felt as if the data packet were burning a hole in my pocket and in my mind. Nothing could keep me still, and my mind went round in circles, cataloguing what I knew—the bombing campaign, the cost in life—against my helplessness as I waited for Arinaas to arrange a handoff. I needed something to distract me, to occupy my time.

I thought I might have forgotten how to cook, especially in a strange kitchen. But the moves and measurements came to me easily. My family always ended the summer with a sweeter tajine— instead of olives, my mother added figs or apricots, whichever was more handy that year. I wondered if she would do so this year. If Aziz would hover as he did every year, trying to sneak a taste. Or if it would be harder for them to acquire the fruits with all the setbacks the village had suffered this year.

I'd set the tajine to simmer and was kneading dough, lost in thought, when a droid's whistle echoed in the kitchen.

Maram stood in the center of the courtyard, her cloak pooled on the ground around her feet and her veil thrown over her shoulder. She examined the open space with a distant curiosity. The sparsely planted courtyard paled in comparison to her lush garden. But she didn't sneer, which I found a small victory.

"Your Highness?" I called, announcing myself. "What are you—what can I do for you?"

She looked a little longer before settling her gaze on me. "No," she replied. "Nothing you can do for me. I realized I'd not been to this part of the palace in a long while and wanted to look."

"Oh."

Her eyes narrowed. "Why are you covered in flour?"

"It happens, Your Highness, when one is cooking bread."

At that she seemed delighted. "I thought I smelled food," she said and wandered past me. "You cook. How provincial."

"Your Highness," I called, trying to stop her; the data packet was hidden in my chamber, but her proximity to it raised a hundred alarm bells. Instead she made her way past my chambers, to the kitchen.

"Don't!" I cried when Maram reached for the tajine.

She raised an eyebrow. "Is it a bomb?"

"It's hot," I said and picked up a towel. "But only food, see?"

"Is that fruit?"

"Yes, Your Highness."

Feeling exacerbated with Maram was new. I was used to frustration, rage, a great deal of hate. But right then it felt as though a child had entered my kitchen, determined to cause some mayhem.

"Well," she said, taking a seat. "Don't stop on my account. I've never seen a villager cook."

I imagined she'd never seen anyone cook, but I kept the thought to myself. The bread was all there was left to make, and the easiest part of the meal. I'd planned on making a single loaf, but if Maram decided to stay, I thought she would balk at having to share with me. With two loaves in the oven, I set water to boil and pulled out glasses, a teapot, and plates for the food.

"Do you mean to feed me?" Maram said, balancing her chin on her fist.

"If you like," I said, hoping my voice was noncommittal.

She hummed. "I've never had meat with fruit before."

"The Vathek idea of good food is unseasoned and dry, Your Highness."

She grinned.

When the kettle whistled, I gestured to the glasses I'd set out. "Tea?"

She shrugged.

"Tea, then."

"I never thanked you," she said when we'd moved to the courtyard.

I paused, one plate half in front of Maram. "Thanked me?"

"For your performance with Galene, and at the council meeting," she explained. I set the plate down. "My father was quite pleased. Thanks to you he believes perhaps I'm more suited to the throne than he previously thought. In fact, he's decided that it should be me and not one of the city magistrates who will give the speech to open up a new library."

I raised my eyebrows. "Walili is getting a new library?"

"Is that so surprising?"

"I didn't think the Vath valued that sort of thing," I said.

"What?"

"Reading," I answered dryly.

"I do like your sharp tongue, girl," she said with a grin.

"Are they replacing the Fihri library?" I asked.

"The what?"

"The two-hundred-thousand-year-old library they sacked," I said flatly. "And burned to the ground."

"I don't know," she said, strangely somber. "I've never done this sort of thing before."

At my look of confusion she clarified. "I don't go among Andalaans outside the Ziyaana. Ever. I . . . worry . . . I'm not up to the task. Of facing the people who have made it abundantly clear they hate me. Who have no ulterior motives to pretend to like me."

My eyebrows continued to rise in surprise.

"Oh, you needn't look so put out," Maram snapped. "It's me they hate, not you."

"I just find it hard to believe."

"Why? You hate me."

"I don't!" The words tumbled out of me louder than I meant, and surprisingly true.

Maram began to laugh. "You've gotten quite good at lying."

"I'm not lying," I insisted. "I mean. I did. It's very difficult to like someone who has you mauled by a bird."

"But now that I'm not having you beaten half to death you find me charming?"

I winced. Put like that it sounded beyond absurd. "It's just— you have no need of me liking you. But in general I've found that when you are not cruel to people, they have a chance to like you."

"I'm not a child," she replied. A cross of affection and amusement filled her face. "You've been here months now and you're still soft."

"You enjoy being hated then?"

"Fear and hatred are good deterrents against murderers."

It was my turn to snort. The sound made Maram grin, wide toothed like a shark.

"Oh, do share."

"Far be it from a village girl to advise Her Royal Highness."

"I can't tell if you've always had such a sharp tongue," she replied. "Or if you've picked that up here. I'm asking, village girl."

"You will find it difficult—as difficult as your father does now—to rule over those taught to despise you. In my experience, fear and hatred are great motivators for great evils."

She was watching me closely, her amusement nearly gone. "And what experience does a village girl have with statecraft and the motives of men?"

I shrugged. "Very little. But I do know that I hear your grandmother spoken of with a great deal of love and admiration. And the only time the Vath come up in commoner conversation is when they're being cursed."

She was playing with her ring, though her eyes had not left my face. "You can't be suggesting that my grandmother's rule of this planet was peaceful. I know she went to war with her brother."

"Her brother went to war with her," I replied. More and more I felt the ridiculousness of such a conversation. As though I could change her here and now. As if I could undo all she'd done. "And when it was over, the Dowager helped those who suffered under the war rebuild. The years that followed the war were not filled with rebels and dissidents. They wanted her to rule over them."

"Yes," Maram drawled. "Let's let goat herders and farmers decide who should rule over them."

Yes, I almost replied, but kept my mouth shut. I had said

enough. And even as sarcastic as she was, I could see her thinking it over. I did not expect change, not immediately. Likely, I
would see no change at all. But if there was hope, if she would
listen, I wanted to try.

To my surprise, Maram cleared her plate and finished her loaf
of bread. I had hoped to have some left over to share with Tala,
but it seemed I'd have to cook again. When the table was cleared
and the food put away, Maram rose to her feet, then paused.

"Yes?" I said when she remained silent.

"You'll help me. With the speech. Won't you?"

I fought back a smile. Asking was not in Maram's nature. "Of
course, Your Highness. I have nothing to do now, if you'd like to
start."

29

"Hopefully the rabble is quiet today," Maram said grimly, on the morning I was meant to give the speech at the unveiling of the library.

She appeared to be making a joke, but she did not smile. It was curious to look at her—was she imagining me dead? Was she imagining herself? I wondered what it would mean for Maram if I died for the whole star system to see. Would it be difficult for her to watch me die, or would she see only herself?

"Be safe," she added, looking at me. This time, there was warmth in her eyes.

I left Maram and made my way to the departure bay. Her words echoed in my head as Idris handed me into the closed coach and climbed in behind me. I didn't like having to wonder about

Maram—about what it was like for her to know she could not leave the Ziyaana today for fear of death. That half her heritage adamantly despised her as a symbol of their oppression. That she had bid me goodbye knowing that whatever I faced out there was meant for her. Did she feel it—was a war being fought in her blood every time she looked at me?

I watched through the tinted windows as the courtyard disappeared, and the coach turned to the enormous gates of the northern wall and into the wide, main boulevard that would lead into the rest of the city. As always, Idris had his hand over mine, his chin balanced on his right hand's fist.

If Maram were in the northern territories of Andaala, I imagined it wouldn't matter as much. They were safer, the anti-Vathek sentiment nearly nonexistent. They had few resources, and their integration into Vathek society had been quick and sure. But the capital city of Walili had been a royalist city. Its people, the poor and the wealthy alike, loved Queen Najat. She had been an idol, young and beautiful and fierce.

To them, Maram constituted the height of violation. She was their blood corrupted. I imagined, more than anything, this was why Mathis enjoyed parading her around when he did. If he couldn't have a pure-blooded Vathek child rule over us, then he would remind everyone of the cost of occupation.

Idris looked sadder than I had ever seen him, a flat approximation of the man I knew. "Idris?"

"My family—what's left of it—is based out of Al Hoceima." He'd looked away again.

I shook my head. "I don't understand."

"The Vath call it the Eastern Reach." My hand tightened around his. "Ah. Now you understand."

"I took Maram's place in the council meeting," I said. We'd

shifted closer, so that I could feel the warmth of him through the folds of my qaftan. It had only occurred to me peripherally that Idris's family was based there, and I hadn't thought of how it might impact him. A pang of guilt went through me again as I remembered the part I'd played.

Idris drew a hand over his face. It seemed that now that he'd told me, the worry and fear had amplified. "I don't understand why anyone there would risk a second purge. It wasn't so long ago that they might not remember. I know no one has forgotten."

Better death than slavery. Husnain had said it once in a fit of fury at Aziz—it had been a point of contention between all of us, but between Aziz and Husnain most of all. I'd thought then such a declaration was a product of youth and its bravado, that a few more years would temper Husnain's fire. But—there were people who believed that. Who would rather die than suffer under our occupation. People who would rather risk their lives in the hopes that their children might live to see a better to-morrow.

I'd become one of them.

"It's no problem of yours," he said suddenly. "It will turn out as it turns out."

"Of course it's a problem of mine," I said. I turned his face so that our eyes would meet again. "Friends care about one another."

He grinned. "Friends?" he said quietly.

"More than friends," I said as he kissed my palm. "Why not visit them? It would help, wouldn't it?"

My hands closed over where he'd kissed. It felt as if ages had passed since I last saw him, and I hated how restricted we were. Whether I saw him or not relied on where Maram or Nadine sent me and whether or not he would be there. I wished I could see him more, but I'd known from the very beginning that it would be this way. I spoke softly, lest the guards outside the carriage hear us—another constraint.

"I . . . I hadn't thought of that," he said. "It would help with morale, at least. It's my aunt's one hundred and sixth birthday soon—Maram wouldn't deny me leave for that."

"Would she go?" I asked, careful to keep my voice even.

"I don't know," he replied with a frown. "I imagine you know how she feels about her Andalaan family."

I nodded. "Still—it will be good for you and for them." I squeezed his hand. "Your presence would reassure them. And you'll be safe in Al Hoceima—they're concentrating further on the coast."

He brushed his fingers over my cheek then leaned forward and kissed my forehead. For a few moments the only sound in our carriage was the tide of noise from the city itself. There was some struggle on his face, as if he couldn't marshal his emotions.

"What is it?"

"You—" he began. "You are a great comfort, Amani."

I struggled not to laugh. "A comfort? Is that all?"

He opened his mouth and I shook my head.

"I was only joking. You don't have to say more."

"Come with me," he said suddenly.

"What?"

"To Al Hoceima," he said. "Please."

I opened my mouth to tell him why it was a terrible idea, then shut it. It wasn't a terrible idea. We had so little time together and this—it would be wonderful. And perhaps I would be able to get away and hand off the information to one of Arinaas's agents in the Eastern Reach.

"Alright," I said at last. "I'll try."

The speech—my address to the people of Walili—was to take place in a declining part of the city. According to the map Tala had shown me, at one point it was the merchant sector, prosperous and booming. But business had moved elsewhere, into majority Vathek hands, and while many of the merchants could get by, it was a far cry from what it had once been. The library wouldn't help.

El Maktabatil Fihri had stood for two hundred thousand years and served as an archive for the literature of the world. It had held the largest collection of Kushaila poetry before the Vath had bombed it out of the city. Its replacement was nowhere near its original site, and would hold census data and histories of the occupation.

Idris and I stood just off the elevated platform, the crowd below. Everyone in this quarter was required to attend, and they'd lined up in their somber clothes, silent and filled with resentment. I could feel the buzz in the air, recognized it from my own time in these mandatory assemblies. On either side of the thoroughfare where Andalaans were assembled were elevated seats, as if the Vathek who sat there were prepared for a spectacle.

Looming over the platform was an enormous statue of Massinia. I took an involuntary step forward. There were many ways of depicting her—in ecstasy, with an open book in her lap, her eyes heavenward, and so on. But I had never seen her depicted thus, her hands raised up toward heaven, a veil pulled forward over her head, and draped over her body down to her feet. It was the Book at her feet that made me sure it was meant to be Massinia.

The statue was beautiful, made of carved stone, and yet eerie to look at, too. I felt that at any moment she might lift the veil and walk among us. It was untraditional and unusual, and instead of eliciting the joy I normally felt when seeing her, it made me feel uneasy. Perhaps that was why the Vath had allowed it to remain standing.

I took a deep breath, and gripped Idris's hand.

"Easy," he said into my ear. "You'll be fine. I'm here with you."

I nodded, took a deep breath, and climbed the stairs to the platform with Idris close behind me.

"Fellow Andalaans," an Andalaan official said, leaning over the podium. "It is a great honor to welcome Her Royal Highness, Maram Vak Mathis, into our midst. We are grateful beyond imagining for our protector's constant benevolence and generosity."

The Andalaan crowd was unmoved and silent. What little applause there was came from Vathek spectators and Andalaan makhzen on either side of them. I watched, my face devoid of emotion, as the official completed his introduction, then beckoned me up to the podium.

The murmuring grew as I climbed the steps, and eased into an eerie silence as I tapped the holoreader before me, bringing my notes to the screen.

"Today marks an auspicious occasion," I began. "The first of many such auspicious occasions—the opening of the first Walili library in over a decade. A mark of the prize that is knowledge and our ability to move forward, united as one in the face of adversity."

It was Maram's voice that came out of me, but my sentiment had shaped the speech. I'd avoided mention of the Vath and hoped that in hearing Maram, in seeing her—me—wearing the old Andalaan seal, those who witnessed the consecration of the ground would leave with hope. Would think of our endurance and our survival. More than that, I hoped that Maram would think back on the words she'd helped me craft, and envision a world without the cruelties of her father's reign.

It was a small hope, I thought, looking out over the crowd. But an important one—if Maram could be the ruler that her father had failed to be, that her mother had wanted to be, then there was hope for us—for all of us.

Wasn't there?

I had to believe it.

⊰ 30 ⊱

Today seemed to be passing slower than most. Tala had checked on me in the morning, but when she'd seen the faraway look in my eyes, had left me with a pot of tea. I'd all but given up beating the shatranj AI when the royal bell rang, announcing a member of the royal household.

"Your Highness," I said, when Maram appeared, and rose to my feet. "How can I be of service?"

I was surprised when she lowered her eyes, as if embarrassed about what she was about to ask me. "I can't ask the kitchen staff to cook for me—not. I don't even know what to call it."

I bit back a smile. "Ah. You're hungry?"

She tossed back her head, daring me to laugh. "Yes."

"The same dish?"

"Surprise me," she said.

I made harira and miloui—they were easy, fast, and would hopefully not raise notice with the kitchen staff. Maram sat in the same chair and watched me as I brought the soup to a simmer, then turned my attention to the bread.

"You should let me help," she said, then made an impatient noise. "You needn't look so shocked. Fine, I rescind my offer."

"No," I said, struggling not to laugh. "Please. Come, you can flip the bread."

"I can do more than flip bread."

She sounded peevish and young, but I didn't trust her with anything else.

"Let's try the bread first."

Having Maram in the kitchen made me increasingly sympathetic to my mother. Maram shied away from the skillet's heat, waited too long to flip it, and more than one of the flatbreads ended up on the floor.

"Here," I said at last, and handed her a clean cloth. "If you fear the fire so much, use this."

She stared at it for a long moment. "How will that protect my fingers?"

"It won't," I said. "But it may fool you. Besides, my mother used to say you never learn unless you're burned at least once."

"She sounds charming."

"No more so than any other village mother," I said with a smile.

She turned her attention back to the bread after that. Still, I noticed a number of strange things. She was silent, and when she wasn't biting at the edges of her thumb, she was pulling her bottom lip into her mouth. Maram had always shown an extraordinary ability to showcase either complete apathy or rage; nervousness was not an emotion I'd ever seen from her.

"Is . . . is everything alright?"

Her eyes widened. "What? Of course it is."

"Your thumb is still in your mouth."

She snatched it out and hid her hand in the folds of her skirt. For a moment she said nothing, just glared angrily at me. "You know I'm to accompany Idris to the Eastern Reach?"

"This is the first I'm hearing of it," I lied. "Is there a reason you go with Idris?"

She looked away from me and fiddled with the ring on her finger. "My—my mother had a stipulation in her will. They— their families were close. Or so I'd guess. She wanted me to visit."

"Ah," was all I could think to say.

"They all hate me. A very. Great. Deal."

It may have been stupid of me to be shocked. And yet. "Why?"

Maram seemed to agree with my estimation, and leveled a look at me that would have made me cringe a few months ago. "There's the little issue of my father." She rolled her eyes. "You must learn to stop being so shocked all the time. Everyone hates me. I'm used to it."

"But—they're your mother's people, too," I said without thinking.

"I don't think anyone sees it like that."

I had a hard time believing it for some reason. I knew exactly what Maram was like. I had experienced her cruelty firsthand. But as I'd seen with the Dowager, many of Maram's Andalaan family mourned her loss. It was a cruel person that judged a child by their parent's legacy. And while Maram had proven herself a worthy inheritor of Mathis's regime, a person who knew the circumstances—how she'd been treated by everyone on Luna-Vaxor, by her own half sister—would not hate her for it. Would they?

"You are lucky," she said.

"Me?"

"You know exactly where you belong. You have your family, and your traditions, and no one is . . . is screaming at you to be something else. All my Vathek family can see is my lesser blood. And all my Andalaan family can see are their conquerors. I am treated like a bad omen of a horrible future no matter where I go."

It was a strange thing to feel such a strong swell of pity for her. But we'd come far, she and I. I touched her arm without asking and waited for her to look up at me.

"You can choose who you want to be," I said. "You can choose what you are."

She scoffed. "Everyone has already decided what I am not— I am not Vathek and I am not Andalaan."

I squeezed her arm. "You are the trueborn daughter of the last queen of Andala. They can't choose what you are."

I was surprised when she raised a ringed hand to cover mine, though she wouldn't meet my gaze. "I know it's unfair of me to say, but . . . I'm glad you're here. I'm glad you're you. I don't think anyone else in the world would be kind to me after what I've done."

I had nothing to say to that. I couldn't tell her why I was so kind, what I saw. She would resent me for my pity and my worry.

"Why don't I go for you?" I suggested.

I'd become quite good at controlling my expression and tone and it served me well with Maram. I needed to be the one in the Eastern Reach to deliver my information to Arinaas's agent. And I wanted the time with Idris. But more than that, to my surprise, I wanted to help her. Despite all she'd done to me, all I could see now was a scared girl who didn't want to face the disapproval of her relatives, or worse: their rejection.

"Really?" She sounded small and young—younger even than me.

"Really," I said, and bumped my shoulder against hers.

"What's that smell?" she asked a moment later.

I sighed. "You've burned the bread."

The meal wasn't ruined. The soup finished cooking, so we took the remaining unspoiled pieces of bread into the courtyard, along with tea and bowls for the soup. We sat in companionable silence. For the first time there was no undercurrent of tension, no fear. It was a strange feeling, but one I liked.

She toyed with a pendant I'd never seen her wear before, swinging the gold piece lazily up and down the chain between her fingers.

"I wanted to ask you something," she said. She'd caught the pendant in her hand and closed her fingers around it.

"Of course."

I watched as she lifted the chain from around her neck and held it out to me, the gold charm swinging lazily to and fro.

"Can you—do you know what this is?"

My eyebrows raised as I got my first clear look at it. "Probably no better than you . . ." My voice trailed off when I flipped it over.

"What? What is it?"

"Nothing," I said with a laugh. "It's a royal seal. If you'd been born before the occupation, you would have had the same design inked on your back."

Maram rolled her eyes. "Thank you for that clever deduction. I gathered that much from the roc on the front."

"It's not a roc. It's a tesleet bird."

"A what?"

"Tesleet," I repeated. "The bird of the Banu Ziyad is the tesleet. And on the back is your name and this line: I was marked before my husband. I shall be marked after."

"What in the world does that mean?"

"It's a quote attributed to Massinia—she had a scar with gold twisted into it on her back. Many took the scar as a sign from Dihya, that she'd been chosen by Him to be a prophetess before her husband's death. Historians like to argue that his death was the making of her—it wasn't."

She leaned forward. "And why is that strange?"

"The seals are like daan. They are meant to denote family, ancestry, faith—all the things prized by the Kushaila. Whoever made this seal meant for you to prize this above all else."

"Wonderful," she drawled, taking the seal back. "My mother wanted me to remember she hated my father."

I tried not to laugh. "That is not what the quotation means."

"Enlighten me."

"Massinia loved her husband very much. Many sources say she was of a higher class than him, and she was Tazalghit. She married him in secret anyway. That is unheard of, even today."

"So . . . ?"

"It means she—you are not defined by the men in your life, no matter how powerful. You lived before them and you shall live after them. You can't let them determine your path."

She stared down at the seal, thoughtful. "She disappeared in the end, didn't she?" she said.

I nodded. "She was seen once after, but the popular opinion is her mother's people took her back and after that it would have been impossible to track her."

She smirked. "What's the unpopular opinion?"

"That the tesleet bird she carried with her revealed itself as a spirit and offered her entry to its kingdom in the sky."

The smirk turned into a genuine, wistful smile. The seal was worn, rubbed thin and smooth in some places. It was clear she kept it close to her whenever she could. Her mother had likely had it made and then given it to her herself. Parents designed their children's daan, and I imagined among the nobility their children's khitaam.

"I like the second one better," she said.

"Your grandmother may know more about the seal," I said instead of answering. "What I know is from history books. Your grandmother is royalty; she would have designed your mother's seal."

She said nothing, but stared hard at the pendant. I wanted to ask her what she was thinking, but I imagined asking me to explain the seal had been hard enough for her. Her mother had left her something precious and invaluable; I didn't want to distract her from that. And maybe it would serve as a bridge, however tenuous, to her grandmother.

Eventually, she looked up, her gaze unfocused and a little lost, and shook her head. I said nothing, but gestured to her bowl. At last, she rehung the pendant around her neck and returned to her food.

After Maram left, I cleaned our dishes, packed away the food, then retired to my room.

I hated this place, I hated Nadine, I hated what had been done to me. I'd been transformed, reforged into a girl my family wouldn't recognize. But I'd found—I'd found so much and I didn't know if I would exchange one for the other. The girl I was for everything else. If—when—the rebellion succeeded, there would be no going back to my old life. What would I do? Where would I go? Where would Maram go?

And did the rebellion have to sacrifice Maram in the name of freedom? She could be a powerful ally—a figurehead no one would reject.

I pulled my own charm out of my gown and slid the communication tab behind my ear. It warmed quickly, and a moment later I heard a beep.

"Yes?"

"It's me," I said. "I have news."

"Has there been a change?" Arinaas said. "Or have you missed me?"

I laughed. "There's been a change," I said. "Maram is joining the convoy to the Eastern Reach."

"She's not a target at present."

"Nor should she be," I said sharply. "But I am to go in her place."

I could almost hear the gears turning in her head. "And you can bring the plans you smuggled out of the council meeting?"

"Yes."

She drew in a sharp breath. "Amani. Carrying something like that out of the Ziyaana . . . you'll be taking a great risk."

"It's all a great risk, isn't it?"

"We'll arrange a handoff," Arinaas said finally. "Keep safe in the following days, hm?"

"You too, Arinaas."

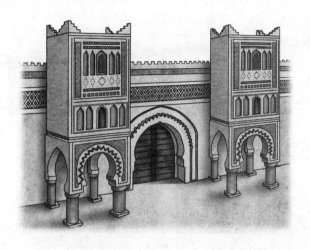

al hoceima,
andala

⚡ 31 ⚡

Several days later I boarded a cruiser with Idris and a small reti-
nue and traveled east to Al Hoceima. Though Idris's real intent
was to check in on the state of his family and his home, he had
timed the visit to his great-aunt's birthday. Three years had passed
since his last visit and I could see the nervousness in him as the
cruiser landed in the city with a soft hiss.

While most of the Salihi clan was extinguished, some of
Idris's aunts and uncles had survived. A clan that had numbered
in the thousands now numbered a little over a hundred, most
of them either very old or very young. He knew the young better
than he knew the old—the Vath had allowed him to keep in
contact with his cousins, but not anyone who might have retained
their loyalist leanings.

His aunt had lived to one hundred and five years and was now celebrating her hundred and sixth. It amazed me that anyone managed to live so long. Most of the elderly in my village didn't make it past sixty. Poverty and war did not encourage long life.

The guest of honor, Naimah, sat at the front of the gathering hall, flanked by sisters and nieces. She was a small woman, more like a bird, with sharp eyes and a sharper nose. Her shoulders were stooped and her mouth curled. The daan on her face were a faded green, having never been retouched. The room was filled with women—I imagined all the women left to the Banu Salih, old and young alike. Only the very old among them, like Naimah, bore daan. They, like their great matriarch, flitted around the room in brightly colored garb, whispering and giggling with one another. The men, as they normally did when faced with so many women, had gathered in the back and monopolized the tea.

For my part, I stood by a window, my back turned to most of them.

From the window I could see the run-down city of Al Hoceima. In antiquity and before the occupation, it had been one of the greatest cities on the planet. The Lions of Al Hoceima had ruled from the northern coast all the way to the south of the continent. And when they'd married into the Ziyadis, they formed the largest army the world had ever seen. They'd marched across the planet, conquering everything in sight until nothing was left. Now, there was more dust than people. No one could afford to fix the roads or the houses. The filtration system that purified the poisoned water had nearly broken the city with its cost.

In the distance I could see the red of fire painted across the horizon, smeared by smoke. All day there had been a steady trickle of refugees who'd escaped the coast with all they could carry, hoping to find safety further in the reach. Away from rebels and fire.

So far the Vath's bombing campaign had been confined to the two cities: Sidi Walid and Tairout. But the rebels hadn't taken it lying down and even without my information had fired back. The rebel flag still hung in the center of Ghazlan from its bright white tower, or so what little news I'd gotten said. And I understood the Vath a little better now—rather than feel relief, anxiety gnawed at my mind. They would respond like cornered beasts and lash out at the rest of the region if the rebels' luck held. The information I had was all that stood between the rebels and certain death. Arinaas knew it as well as I did, and had arranged a handoff for the middle of the night.

Just below in the courtyard was Idris. He'd escaped the festivities as soon as possible, to entertain a gaggle of cousins around him vying for his attention. I'd never seen him as he was now. Some of his fear had washed away the moment we touched down in his city, and now, surrounded by loved ones, he nearly glowed. And they glowed in return. I'd watched him stop to talk to uncles and cousins and aunts, and each of them had shone a little brighter, smiled a little easier, in his wake.

He helped a younger boy onto a horse. Though I couldn't hear what he said, it was clear he was teaching him how to keep his seat. He loved them, no matter how long he'd been apart from them.

I wondered uneasily what he would say if he knew of my rebel ties. From his upset at the cause of the bombing campaign, I knew he had no love for what the rebels' campaign might do, or what retaliation it might provoke. But they—*we*—were necessary if any of the people on Andala were going to survive the century.

"She looks just like Najat," a voice murmured to my left.

I stiffened, but didn't turn around. Maram didn't speak Kushaila—she might have, once, but time with the Vath had taken it from her as it had taken it from most of those fostered away from their Kushaila families.

"It doesn't matter," a second voice said. "She can look like her mother all she wants. She's still an outsider."

Given everything Maram had said, I'd expected those words to be spoken with venom. Instead, all I heard was pity. They would have mourned her, I knew. Filial ties were important to us, and to have her taken away from family so young and then never returned would have pained them. And now, much like the Dowager, they didn't know how to reach her or what to do with her. Maram didn't help matters. I was beginning to suspect she didn't hate Andalaans so much as she hated remembering what her father had done to them.

I was pulled from my thoughts when something—someone—tugged on my skirts. The girl couldn't have been more than eight or nine. She looked up at me with wide eyes, as if torn between fear and fascination.

"Yes?" I said in Vathekaar.

"Khaltou Naimah has summoned you," she replied. When I looked to the platform where the aunt sat, I saw her watching me.

"Well," I said. "Let's go then."

I didn't know if I was meant to kneel or kiss her cheeks or bow. Naimah and I regarded each other, I a bit warily, and she hawk-like. In the end, she said nothing, but gestured to a cushion beside the little girl. I sat. I had no intention of drawing the attention of the rest of the room or the group of aunts around her.

A pregnant aunt, who'd managed to walk her way to the platform, sighed. "What are we meant to do with her?" she said in Kushaila.

Naimah clucked. "Do with her?" she said. "If you all had not been such bumbling fools when she returned five years ago, she might know us. Like us. Now look at her. Vathek to her core."

The aunt sighed again. "You can cry over the past, khaltou. But there is nothing to be done now."

A third aunt nodded wearily. "Idris will marry her and that is that. We may as well resign ourselves."

"To what?" Naimah asked.

If I could have, I would have warned the sisters not to answer. I recognized the tone—Maram had it, my mother had it. The question was not meant to be answered.

But the third aunt looked startled, as if she'd never heard such a tone in her life. "The rule of the Vath," she said, as though it were obvious.

Naimah snorted. "This is why you've only ever born sons, Nusaiba. You are a weak-minded fool." She flapped her hands. "Go. All of you. Out of my sight."

I expected to be left alone after that, but instead Naimah returned her gaze to me. I couldn't pretend I hadn't been watching. She waited for the aunts and nieces to clear, murmuring among themselves. And then she gestured me up beside her. I flinched when she took hold of my chin. Her fingers were thin, and I had the impression of being held by claws.

"You must eat more," she said in heavily accented Vathekaar. "If you are to be any good at bearing daughters."

"Why daughters?"

"Only your daughters will have the stomach for the future," she said. "It is why your mother had you."

"I want to," I said softly. "Have the stomach for it."

Naimah stilled and her grip on my chin tightened just a little. I wasn't overstepping—I knew Maram now, knew how she felt. She wanted to be able to do the right thing, she wanted her mother's family to love her. She was only afraid.

I knew if Maram had a chance, if she gave her mother's family a chance, they would love her. And their love and her hope *might* shape her into a queen the Andalaans didn't have to fear or hate.

"Change takes bravery, yabnati," she said, quietly enough that those around us couldn't hear. "You are brave. Like your mother. I can see that. Visit more often."

I nodded in response to her request and at last she let me go. I returned to my seat, heart pounding, but could feel her eyes on me for the rest of the evening. When I looked up there was a strange turn to her gaze—fixed and nearly hopeful, as if she were looking at someone altogether different. As if she were seeing Najat instead of Maram, and it gave her hope.

The party seemed to last an eternity. Khaltou Naimah kept me on the platform with her, and when she got tired of speaking in Vathekaar, enlisted the younger girl beside me to translate Kushaila. It was strange to pretend I didn't understand while I was being spoken to. I caught myself at least once, mouth open, before she'd finished speaking and had to bite my tongue. By the time I was free to return to the suites I shared with Idris, I felt as though I'd been wrung dry.

Idris stood in front of the large window in the sitting area, outlined by the glow of the setting sun.

"Where did you get off to?" I asked, closing the door behind me. "Your aunt kept a close watch on me the whole party."

He laughed a little. "Sorry," he said. "I didn't mean to abandon you to her."

"You didn't answer my question," I teased, and laid a hand on his arm.

"Oh," he said, and I frowned.

"Are you alright?"

"I went to the mausoleum," he said after a moment. "My parents and siblings are buried there."

I paused. He'd never spoken of his siblings—all I knew about them I'd heard from Tala when she'd told me about the night of the Purge. "Idris—"

At last he looked at me and gave me a faint smile. "It was easier this year," he said. His hand came to rest on mine. "It's never easy, but—it was easier this year. With you here."

I smiled. "How are your cousins?"

"As well as they can be." He let go of my hand. "The younger ones keep asking when I'll stay for good."

There was nothing I could say to that. Not that perhaps one day he might be able to, to be certain. I imagined for Idris such a future didn't exist. Instead, I kissed his cheek, then went to take off my jewelry and change into something more comfortable. When I returned, Idris had shed his jacket and shoes, and was sitting in an alcove by the window. There was a slender folio volume beside him.

"I found this," he said when I sat next to him. "Ever since you corrected my horrible translation I've been thinking of this. I want you to have it."

I stared blankly at the volume he held out to me. I could see it was in Kushaila from the writing on the spine, and that it was very old, too. Nearly as old as the folio Husnain had given me so many months ago.

"It was my mother's," Idris added.

My eyes jerked up to meet his. "What?"

I couldn't take it. He knew I couldn't keep something that belonged to his mother. No matter how much I wanted it, no matter how much it meant to him or the both of us. Idris didn't know about the folio Husnain gave me on my majority night; he couldn't guess how much I would cherish a second volume of poetry.

"What is it?" I found myself asking.

He grinned. "A collection of Kushaila poetry. She and my father loved to read it to one another."

"Idris," I breathed, and reached out for it. I couldn't. I shouldn't. It was dangerous to have, tangible proof of what Idris and I felt for one another.

"Furat said that you must love the old poetry if you knew it, that it's . . . it's hard to come by now."

I tore my eyes away from the cover and looked at him. He was grinning, and he watched me as if seeing how much I wanted the folio gave him joy. As if my happiness made him happy.

"You can't give me this," I tried again.

"It's a gift," he replied and folded my hands over it. "It would be rude to refuse."

I kissed him, furtive and quick, then pulled the book against my chest. His grin widened and he bent his head to mine and pressed a firmer kiss against my mouth.

"Thank you," I whispered.

"May it bring you much joy, Amani."

The next morning we went down to the stables where two horses were waiting for us. I ignored his look of surprise when I pulled myself up into the saddle, bypassing his outstretched hand.

"You're full of surprises," he told me, getting on his own horse.

"Hardly," I replied, and smiled. "How do you think I got around before the Ziyaana?"

There were no guards, though I'd seen him pack a phaser. He led us through the city, and then past its limits into the desert.

I'd never seen pictures of Al Hoceima before the occupation, so I had nothing to compare it against, but I could imagine its splendor. The high walls of the city still stood with its four gates, though they were run-down and covered in desert sand. In the center of the city was not the Salihi stronghold, but the Dihyan temple and its zaouia. The streets were narrow and tight, and I couldn't imagine trying to get a carriage through them. Wherever I looked was evidence that the city had stood for at least a thousand years and meant to stand for a thousand more. Faded mosaic tiles inlaid in entryways, empty fountains engraved with desert flowers in the style of antiquity, and so on.

Despite the end of summer, the air was still hot and dry, and there was no water anywhere to make it less so. The desert seemed to stretch out in front of us for miles, an unchanging sea of orange and gold.

"Are you sure we're safe without guards?"

"There's no one around the city," he promised. "Not for miles. The water supply is halved—they go elsewhere now."

We continued on, mostly silent. It wasn't a long trek. Before the hour was up I could see palm trees outlined against the horizon, and a small shepherd's hut leaning just a little. There was a decaying post we tied our horses to, and beneath the shade of the trees, I could see the oasis's pool, half dried up.

"My eldest brother, Ishaq, used to bring me here," he said, taking my hand. "My parents wanted to hire an instructor to teach me to swim and ride. Ishaq refused—our father had taught him and he would teach me."

"He was so much older?"

"Twelve years. Herders would come through and see the prince of Al Hoceima teaching his younger brother." He smiled. "They liked him for that, little good it did him in the end."

I squeezed his hand and lay my head on his arm. "He sounds very kind."

"He was. I worshiped him, trailed behind him whenever I could get away with it. He would make room on his chair during council meetings and share his plate with me." He shut his eyes. "They took him first, when they came."

This, then, was the legacy of the Vath. I'd never thought much about how the makhzen had survived their regime—I think few of us had time to spare to those above us. But the grief on Idris's face was as real as the grief I saw in my parents when they thought of their siblings.

"Thank you for coming with me," he said at last. I didn't smile, but pressed a kiss against his shoulder.

"Of course."

We journeyed back to the stronghold soon after. Everyone had retired to nap through the heat and so the palace was hushed and quiet. We returned to our chambers and Idris moved around the room easily, closing shutters to keep out the sun.

I stretched out on one of the couches, and a moment later he joined me with a carafe of water and cups. The water was set on a table, while Idris rested his head in my lap, eyes closed. I could not rest—what he'd said, and how he lay now, made me restless. I could imagine him young, a small boy on a large horse, with full faith that his brother would catch him if he fell. I didn't want to think what it was like for him, having that taken away in front of him.

His gift lay beside the water carafe, taunting me. There was an inscription on the opening page:

From Itimad—may this fill you with unrelenting thoughts of me.

I frowned as I began to flip through the book. Itimad was his mother, not his father. It was a collection of romantic poetry, some from antiquity, some more recent. Nearly all of it made me flush. I'd never read such words, nor could I imagine gifting a collection like this to anyone. But I couldn't put the book down. Much of the poetry was written in the classical style, and over-flowed with passion.

A part of me felt like a child, suddenly confronted with the reality of what women thought. How young I felt, thinking of my kiss with Idris. How young were my clumsy attempts at articulating what I'd felt. I couldn't imagine myself penning such words, or sending them to anyone as many of these women had done. But the rest of me, the part aware of Idris's head resting in my lap, the part that needed reminding to not touch him as if he belonged to me—that part could not close the slender volume.

When night falls, come and visit me,
For I have seen night keeps secrets best.

And another:

I urge you to come on feet faster than the wind,
Come and rise over my breast and take root in me and plough me.
And no matter what befalls you while we're entwined,
Don't let me go until you've flushed me thrice.

I hissed in surprise when Idris hooked his hand around the back of my neck. I dropped the book, and stared at him wide eyed as he drew my face down to his. He swiped a thumb over my cheek, slow and deliberate, and smiled.

"You're blushing," he said.

"The heat," I said. I felt—I had felt like this before. Flushed skin so hot it felt too tight, my heart beating quicker, a strange and thrilling twist behind my ribs. I could feel breath coming too fast, as if I'd run to get here. But I'd never had such words or phrases to apply to it. I was all too aware that even if Idris had no idea what I'd read, he would recognize what I was feeling.

"Amani," he murmured and sat up.

"It wasn't—your father didn't give this to your mother," I said, looking away. "She gave it to him."

When I looked up again, he was grinning. With his hair in disarray from sleep, he looked more boyish than I'd ever seen him, as though he were itching for trouble.

"Is that why you're flushing?"

"No," I said, too quickly. "Yes."

"Oh?" He'd leaned in again. "What's in the book?"

"Nothing."

"Amani," he said, this time in a cajoling tone.

"Poetry," I said at last.

His expression went from confused to comprehending in a moment. "Ah," he said, and leaned his forehead against mine.

"We shouldn't—" I started.

"We haven't done anything," he said. "You won't read any to me? Not even in Kushaila? Poetry is meant to be read out loud."

"Not even if your life depended on it," I replied.

I could feel his laugh, vibrating under my palm in his chest, and puffing over my cheeks. One of his hands had come to rest against my ribs, and the thumb swept small arcs. He hadn't moved, and when I blinked my lashes brushed his cheeks.

The verses echoed in my head, inescapable, on the tip of my tongue. I'd never been filled with such sharp want, tantalizing the palms of my hands. I should not have—my hands rose from his

chest to his cheeks, and the wooden frame of the couch dug into
my back. He was over me, blocking out the world, his face an-
gled in such a way—

"Amani."

His hand tightened against my ribs. The look in his eyes made
my toes curl, the flush deepen, the twisting thrill sharpen against
my breastbone. I wanted it to end, wanted the poetry forgotten
or consumed with something else.

"Tell me," he said. "Tell me what you want."

I shook my head, unable to speak. I had never felt the stran-
glehold of my want so strongly. I wanted—Dihya, I wanted everything, as I always did. My skin, the palms of my hands, my
mouth—all of it was pricked with want, with the need to press
as close to Idris as I could, to pull desire from him as he would
pull it from me.

He sat up and came to lay beside me.

The difference between every touch before and every touch
today was the leisurely way it seemed to unfold. I'd not forgotten
the sharp twist of desire in my blood, nor had it faded away. But
it had the time now to figure out the best way to heat, and where
best to entrench itself inside me. When Idris drew me down to
his side I felt a soft tremor and a deepening flush everywhere.
Idris was unchanged, but I was aware of more of him; aware of
the lazy thumb tracing shapes on my arm, of his broad shoulders.
And I could see him watching me, noticing where my eyes wandered before looking away.

"My father used to recite poetry whenever my mother was upset with him," he said. He'd leaned back just a little so that there
was space between us. "My mother used to say to him that if he
used it more sparingly, it would be more effective."

"She was upset with him often?"

Likely not, if Idris's smile was anything to go by.

"No," he replied. "Or at least, not as often as he would recite the verses he liked best."

I didn't expect Idris to recite them himself. My hand pressed just over his heart as the words tumbled out, rough and beautiful.

"I thought you couldn't speak Kushaila."

"It was my mother tongue until I was ten, Amani," he replied, looking up at me. "I have forgotten how to speak it. Most days, I've forgotten how to hear it, too. But I remember those lines. I just can't remember what they mean."

"*She sways and pearls dance at her throat, she steps and anklets cut her delicate skin,*" I began softly. "*The sun nursed her beauty, though she walked veiled and hidden from its light. And her cheek seemed a talisman, a mirror to heaven, beautiful and shining.*"

"Now, how did you translate that so quickly?"

I lowered my gaze. "It's a popular love poem. That's only a piece of it."

He sat up just enough that our eyes were level with one another. He could not read Kushaila, of that I was certain, not enough to understand the poetry in his mother's collection. He didn't need to, I thought. He only needed to see what it had wrought on my face, to lean forward and let the slow-burning fire spread. His kiss was gentle, questioning, as though I might pull away at any moment. My hands didn't move, and when he pulled away I thought he might stop.

And when I am with you . . .

I drew him to me with a sigh, my hands on his shoulders, fingers bunched up in his shirt. I didn't need words. A hundred women had already spoken for me.

Would that the sun never rise nor the moon set...

A frisson of shock went through me. We'd never given in, I realized, not truly. Every step, every touch, every breath had been watched and measured and reined in. I'd never let my hands roam over his shoulders and arms, nor had I pushed back or demanded anything from him. Here, now, I did and I did and he gave as much as he took.

Had Itimad seduced her husband thus? Had she filled his blood with the words of bygone women and claimed him when she knew he would be unable to resist? Had she waited for the air to thin in his lungs, for the world to seem strange, for every touch to set fire to his skin as Idris did to mine?

Would that the stars remain fixed in heaven...

I wanted Idris, and the feeling of featherlight touch trailing over my throat and his hands on my waist. I wanted the stars to keep this secret, as they had kept the poetesses', to protect us against those who wanted us apart. I pulled him down with me and watched the sunlight play in his hair, saw the broken-up reflection of a girl flushed to the brim in his eyes.

This was not a half life, I thought when he kissed me again. I belonged to him and he belonged to me—we had made the choice. Nothing had felt as real as this since I'd come to the Ziyaana. All choices had been taken from us, and still we'd found a way to forge paths independent of what our masters wanted.

He pressed his forehead against mine and breathed. My eyes closed, and my hands looped around his neck. Outside the world continued, but for now there was only the two of us and what we felt for one another.

"Amani."

I hummed in response.

"I can't marry Maram," he said.

My eyes flew open in shock and I scrambled to sit up. "What?"

"I love you," he said.

Joy surged through me, overwhelming my shock. "What?" I said again.

He smiled and covered my hands with his. "I love you," he repeated. I didn't realize how fiercely I grinned until he leaned forward to kiss me again and I felt the shape of my mouth try to change and fail.

"I want to be yours," he said against my mouth. "And no one else's."

I cradled his face, afraid to believe him. "Really?"

"Yes. Really." I felt like a different person when I kissed him again, as if my joy and desire had twined around one another and transformed me. I wanted, and not just Idris, but everything. Everything those words promised, everything he wanted to give me. A life outside of what we were trapped in. I didn't know how, and in that moment it didn't matter. We had promised ourselves to each other, and there was no one who could unmake that promise.

"Do you love me?" he asked, pressing me into the cushions.

"Yes," I murmured, echoing his promise from the beginning. "Yes."

32

The palace was silent in the middle of the night. The noises I'd expected—desert creatures, a large family settling into sleep, were largely absent. There was the whistle of wind, the crackle of fire in the sitting room, and the soft whisper of fabric as I dressed. I drew the gray mantle over my shoulders and the hood over my hair. The data packet was safely hidden in the folds of my qaftan. I covered my face and froze when I caught my reflection in the mirror. I hardly recognized the girl looking out from under the shadow of her hood. A rebel. A spy. The farmer's daughter from a backwater moon and the body double couldn't have been more different.

I paused in front of Idris's door. The giddiness from this afternoon hadn't passed. I pressed a hand against my ribs as another flutter of joy washed over me. What would he think if he knew where I was going tonight? Would he be angry? Would he understand?

It was, I told myself, a problem for another time.

The halls were just as quiet as the rest of the palace, and the light sconces were turned down to half light. I moved as quietly and quickly as I could, and kept my eyes turned to the ground. Arinaas's agent dared not breach the walls of the palace, especially when it was believed Maram was in residence. I would have to make my way through to the lowest levels of the palace and out through the tunnels that led to drinking wells. Arinaas's agent would be waiting at the very end of the westernmost tunnel.

The tunnels were less quiet than the palace proper, filled with the sound of rushing water and the hollow knock-knock as water buckets bumped against one another in the wind.

The moon was full tonight and the sky clear. Its light cut a clear path, illuminating the tunnel's entrance, and framed the waiting agent. He cut a stark figure, dressed all in black, his turban and face veil covered in a thin layer of desert sand.

"You will return, oh mourner," he said in Kushaila.

"Set your feet toward the citadel," I replied.

The tight lines of his shoulders relaxed and he drew down his veil. Dihya, he was young. Too young to have received his daan, too young to have started to grow a beard. Fourteen. Maybe fifteen. But his face was hard and lean—he'd suffered. Suffered enough to take the risk of becoming a rebel before reaching his majority. Suffered enough that no one had stopped him.

"Well," he said, "your face. Let's see it."

The words were fast and harsh—regional. He was from the Eastern Reach.

I stepped out of the shadow of the tunnel and pulled down my veil. His face whitened and his mouth thinned in shock.

"I thought she was joking," he said hoarsely. "Dihya. You're the spitting image."

I didn't smile when I said, "That's the point." My fingers folded over the small data packet and pulled it out of my gown. "This is what you came for. It's a list of all the Vathek munition depots in the Eastern Reach, as well as base locations and strike units."

His eyebrows rose in surprise. "And no one knows you've taken this?"

"I'm good at being her," I said. "So, no. No one knows."

I dropped the data packet into his open palm. It was such a small thing, but meant so much, would do so much, to defend the rebels and civilians here. More than Idris's presence, more than anything any of us could do in the present moment. The war wouldn't be won by thwarting a single bombing campaign, but lives would be saved and hope secured. It was a step, and one we desperately needed.

"Siha, yakhoya," I said as he folded his hands over the packet. Health, brother.

"Baraka, yakhti," he replied. Blessings, sister.

the ziyaana,
andala

⊰ 33 ⊱

"So," Maram said, "was I right?"

I looked up from fiddling with my skirts. I'd returned to the Ziyaana nearly a week ago and Maram had wasted no time summoning me to her chambers.

While I'd been gone, Mathis had at last named her sole Imperial Inheritor of the Ouamalich System and its ancillaries. She seemed happy—she'd gotten what she wanted. But there were moments when I caught her looking less so, as if the responsibility weighed too heavily on her mind, her gaze distant, her fingers twisted in the chain of her mother's pendant. Perhaps I gave her too much credit, but part of me wondered if the flippancy with which she addressed her ascension to the throne was borne out of something deeper than what she showed the world. If she truly was more her mother's daughter than her father's, but couldn't afford to show it.

The confirmation ceremony was tomorrow—sped up, I suspected, because the king wanted to distract from the progress the rebels had made in the Eastern Reach, where the Vath's munitions depots were being raided and destroyed. Maram had come to my chambers with three chests full of gowns ostensibly to help her choose one for the ceremony. "Right about what?" I asked.

"About the Banu Salih?"

"It will shock you when I say no, Your Highness, you were wrong."

She laughed. "Do tell."

"Some of them are frightened of you—the ones your age. But the elders . . . they all mourn you."

"I had not realized I was dead," she said, raising an eyebrow.

"You—" I began, and then stopped. Too often I forgot that there were lines I could not cross. Too often I fell into the trap of imagining Maram and I as equals.

"I love it when you realize you are about to be incredibly presumptuous," she drawled. "Few people have such a skill. Please, go on."

"You look like your mother. I think they're sad that you don't value them. Family is important, especially to a dying tribe like theirs."

She wasn't looking at me. "They might have thought of that before trying to usurp me when I was a child." Despite her harsh tone, her fingers were now white knuckled around the charm.

I wanted to tell her no one held her responsible for the occupation, or the Purge, or any of her father's evils. No one saw Mathis when they looked at her—until she acted like him. But there was no way to do it, no way to be sure. And likely, above all, she would not take the word of a village girl from an isolated moon. Even one that was her double.

Maram was watching me with interest and some confusion.

"You make me think I might have liked a twin sister," she said as she pulled her hair into a tie. "A real sister; a friend instead of a competitor."

I felt myself smile a little at the thought. "You would have done better with an elder sister, I think."

She raised an eyebrow. "What makes you say so?"

"Elder siblings protect their younger siblings. Or the good ones do, at least."

I expected Maram to scoff, but she just stared at our reflection, wondering.

"Maybe," she said at last.

The pendant came out, clasped against her palm. "Sometimes . . . sometimes I think about my mother. I know people think—well, I don't know what they think. But I loved her, and her dying . . . I never forgave her for it. There are days where I think—" She closed her eyes. "There are days where I think she won't forgive me for what I've done. For what I've watched other people do."

She opened her eyes again, and shook her head as if coming out of a dream.

"I don't know why I'm telling you this."

I gave her a weak smile. "Nor do I."

She stared at me as though there were a secret she might divine just by looking. "Tell me what to do," she whispered.

My jaw went slack. "What?"

"Tell me," she said, her eyes wide, "how do I . . . how can I . . . ? How do I rule over people who hate me? How—how can I be the queen my father wants when I know it turns my mother in her grave when I consider it?"

"We are not responsible for what cruel masters enact in our name."

"I'm a little responsible."

"But what can you do about it now?"

She looked away from me, her jaw tense with grief and rage. I hesitated before taking her hand in mine. "You must think of the days and years to come as a shatranj board. If you wish to help—it will not happen any other way."

She nodded. "I'm sorry," she said.

"Sorry?"

"For . . . for the beginning. Nothing I do will change what I did. But—"

"Sisters fight, sometimes."

She coughed out a laugh. "Sisters do not have one another mauled half to death by hunting birds."

"You have not read enough Kushaila folktales if you believe that."

A weak but real smile emerged on her face.

"Do you . . . really see me that way? As your sister?"

She wasn't looking at me, and instead focused on her hand clenching and unclenching around her mother's pendant.

"I am the youngest of my siblings," I said at last. "My elder brothers always watched over me. And now—now I will try to watch over you."

Her eyes widened just a little. She leaned in and pressed her lips against my cheeks, furtive and quick, before she pulled her hood over her hair and secured the veil over her face.

I watched her go, wondering, all too aware the next time I saw her she would be that much closer to being queen.

I spent the rest of the evening deep in thought, curled up by my window. I'd been right about Maram, about what she wanted and was afraid of. She wanted to be a good queen, but the Vath had done their work, and she was too frightened to take the right steps. She only needed help.

The communicator pressed against my charm gave one sharp beep, blisteringly loud in the quiet of my room. I startled, confused for a moment before realizing the noise came from my charm. My fingers shook as I peeled the communicator gel and put it against the spot behind my ear. We had a rule—only I ever reached out, never the other way around. If I beeped randomly I would be quickly found out.

"Yes?" I said hoarsely.

A sharp breath, almost like relief, sounded through the communicator. "Thank Dihya," Arinaas said. "I was worried we wouldn't get to you in time."

Unease pricked at my neck. "In time for what?"

"We've sent an agent to Walili, to attend the inheritance ceremony," she said. "He's our best shooter and his job is to kill Maram. Mathis is likely to be present and he's been instructed to kill him first, of course, if he has the chance."

Unease turned into panic. My fingers numbed and my breath went short. Kill Maram? No—not when it seemed, at last, that she could be persuaded into being a truly Andalaan queen. Not when we could save lives and avoid bloodshed.

"You can't!"

"This is war, Amani," she said, voice hard. "We can and we will."

"No," I said, thinking quickly. "It won't be Maram at the ceremony tomorrow. It will be me."

Arinaas sucked in a breath. "Get out of it, Amani. Do you understand?"

"Call the assassin off!"

"You are not a princess to command me," she snapped. "And I may not be able to. He is traveling from the Eastern Reach. The message may not reach him in time."

"Please, Arinaas," I said softly.

I heard her take in a breath. "Dihya help us all."

34

I greeted the next morning with a single thought—I couldn't live with myself if Maram's blood were on my hands. She was a cruel girl who had been raised among crueler relatives, but she wanted to do the right thing. She was capable of it, more so than any of the Vath. And if the rebels succeeded in killing her—even if they killed Mathis as well—they would have to contend with Galene, a girl who did hate Andalaans as baselessly as Mathis did.

I dressed quickly, thoughts racing, desperate to find a way around this. The only way, I knew, was to do as I'd told Arinaas I would do. I'd been bluffing, but the possibility that Arinaas wouldn't be able to call the assassin off ate at me. I would have to take Maram's place and hope I could get a signal to the assassin in time. And I could only do that by convincing Maram to let me. I summoned a droid to take me to her.

Maram was alone in her room, standing in her wardrobe and examining herself. Her hands twitched over the folds of her skirt nervously, then flattened as if she were willing herself to be still. When she saw my reflection in the mirror her eyes widened in surprise.

"What are you doing here?"

I forced myself to smile. "You aren't the only person who gets bored," I said. "And I thought you might want help getting dressed."

She looked relieved at the idea. "Yes, please," she said. "I can't decide between three gowns."

We fell into our ritual quickly. She, sprawled over the divan, and I pulling one then another gown from the wardrobe and modeling it against myself. She calmed, but only a little. Despite her stillness on the couch, her frantic energy, her nervousness, bled through.

"Your Highness?"

"What?"

"Would you prefer I go in your place?"

Her eyes jerked up from the jewelry box she was sifting through. "What?"

"I could go in your place," I repeated.

She shook her head. "No. It has to be me this time. It's my inheritance ceremony."

I didn't sit beside her like I wanted to. Instead I inclined my head. "You just seem nervous. And I am here for a reason."

She let out a disbelieving laugh. "Are you offering to enter the crossfire for me again?"

I was, I marveled. How quickly our relationship had changed in the span of a few months. This time I did sit beside her. "Older sisters protect their younger siblings," I said. "Remember?"

She bit the corner of her thumb, worried and deliberating. "Alright," she said softly, then lay a hand over mine. "Thank you, Amani. I— Thank you."

I inclined my head again and breathed a sigh of relief. One problem solved. Now I only had to figure out how to communicate to the assassin not to kill me.

I was used to the heavy weight of Maram's gowns and jewelry, but this was the first time I'd ever worn her crown. I eyed it on the velvet cushion. What I was expected to wear today in front of hundreds, if not thousands, of Andalaans on the edge of riot was the old Andalaan crown, last worn by Maram's mother, Najat.

It was beautiful—a golden tesleet with outspread wings looped around in a wide circle, its chest an enormous green jewel. It looked impossibly heavy. Most people now assumed the bird on the royal crown was the Vathek hunting bird, the roc. But the tesleet had been on the Ziyadi royal seal centuries before the Vath came to our world.

Maram said nothing to me. The two of us stood there quietly, the crown between us. I was silent as I knelt and waited for her to settle the crown on my head.

Dihya protect me, I thought.

Nadine led me to the north end of the palace. The air felt heavy, as though someone had lit too much incense to mask something far worse. There was a growing murmur the farther north we went, and I was reminded of the stories my mother had told me about the Ziyaana. Everyone spoke of it as if it were a living, hungry thing, waiting to devour those who passed beneath its shadow. In the old days, it must not have been so hungry for blood. But now it squeezed out every drop, ground down every bone. When the large double doors to the wings parted, the Ziyaana's murmur transformed into a roar.

I didn't know if this section of the Ziyaana predated our Vathek rulers. It was a wall of balconies, made so that we might look out at Walili, and so that they might look up at us. It was full to the brim, every courtier and servant milling around, pressed up against the railings. A hot, stifling wind blew in.

Thousands had gathered outside the Ziyaana. They were pressed up against the walls, fit into alleys, hanging off of roofs. Brought here by royal decree, they were restless, waiting for the ceremony to start, waiting to be freed to go home. A pair of over-wrought thrones sat waiting for Mathis and Maram; they were made of dark wood and veined with black metal. The back of each was carved in the ornate Vathek style, baroque and floral, gilded and gleaming in the sunlight. A clarion call went out, as though they'd been waiting for us, and pulled my eyes away from the throne. The king was already seated, flanked by a pair of hovering droids. In the sunlight I could see the glimmer of the shield they'd erected around him. He'd survived in his court of vipers by being prepared, I supposed. I imagined it would serve him well here.

Did he care so little for Maram that I had none of the same protections—or did her body double not require them? I knew the sort of man Mathis was, and yet still I was shocked at his care-lessness, his ruthlessness, with his own child and the people around her.

He met my eyes and didn't smile. I wasn't sure that I wanted him to smile at me—I remembered being on the receiving end of his approval in the council meeting and repressed a shudder. There seemed to be no pride in his daughter's success or her ascendancy to the throne. Did Mathis not love Maram? Did he love any of his children, I wondered.

Hovering in the air were several screens, so that everyone would be sure to see the proceedings. A droid handed me a great, sheathed sword. It had belonged to Mathis's father before he killed him, and was the symbol of his empire. I bore it aloft, its hilt in one hand, the flat of its sheathed blade balanced on the other.

"By the Will of Vathek House of Lords," a minister recited in Vathekaar, his voice booming. I began to walk. "And the Rightful Will of the King, Lord Mathis, Conqueror of Stars . . ."

A shiver went up my spine. The ceremony would be broadcast not just around Andala but through all parts of the Vathek empire. The eyes of the whole world were on me, Andalaan and Vathek alike. And if Arinaas hadn't been successful in reaching her agent, a pair of those eyes were an assassin's eyes.

"In accordance with our High Laws, we hereby declare Maram vak Mathis Inheritor of the Realm, Sole Heir to the Ouamalich System and its ancillaries, future queen of Andala, Gibra, and Cadiz. Protector of Qilbir, Verdan, and Shelifa."

I knelt at Mathis's feet, the Vathek sword still held aloft, and cast my eyes down. The minister removed the Andalaan crown from my head. A moment later another crown, Vathek and made of excelsior, dotted with a hundred gems mined from Shelifa, settled on my hair.

"Kneel," the minister called out. "In the name of the queen."

The sound of a hundred thousand people kneeling at once echoed through the air.

"In the name of the queen!"

The ceremony was over. All that was left was for me to rise to my feet and sit on the throne at Mathis's side. If the assassin was going to strike, it would be now, while I was in full view of the

Andalaan public. My hands were surprisingly still despite my fear as I rose to my feet and turned to face the crowd.

Then there was a scream.

I flinched at the sound, though I could not tell from where it came, and watched the crowd shift like a roiling sea. There was another scream, and the crowd surged forward, toward the balcony—toward me.

Though I'd known this moment was coming, I froze in fear as they swarmed in all directions, knocking over the barricades that separated them from their Vathek spectators, and the ropes meant to keep them in line.

One of the Garda moved forward and slammed his baton into the face of a terrified Andalaan man. And then another, and another—chaos erupted, and yells sounded over the pounding of fleeing feet.

One of the Garda collapsed in front of me. I stared at him for a moment, uncomprehending, and watched a red stain spread across his chest. When I looked up I saw a boy, several feet in front of me, pointing a shaking blaster at me. His face was clear of any daan, his eyes bright and fierce as they looked at me.

Dihya, I thought. It was the boy from the Reach.

I threw myself to the ground as he fired twice, and something exploded behind me. He'd hit the throne where I was meant to sit. Where there had been a gold curlicue of design there was now a crater. The king had already been ushered away by Garda and droids.

I looked up at the boy advancing toward me. I hadn't even learned his name. Our words had all been business. He was a rebel forged in fire—what in the worlds would make him stop?

"Siha, yakhoya," I said, just loud enough for him to hear.

Health, brother.

He froze, his eyes widening in surprise, his gun still aimed at my chest. He was close enough to touch me. It was all the time the Garda needed. A squadron swept in and slammed him into the ground.

No, I thought, but it was too late. I'd stopped him, but now—

"We need to go," Nadine said, appearing behind me, and I turned to see her racing up the stairway. "Now." She jerked me away from the shooter and I tried to remember why I was doing this: for Maram. To save her life and mine. I couldn't throw it all away right now, but I was not just her body double; it wasn't even the thing I cared about the most. I was a rebel, and I'd condemned one of my own to prison or worse. A third shot rang out, and rock and dust sprayed down around us as a corner of Maram's throne blew apart. I flinched away and into Nadine's grip and at last allowed her to lead me away.

I turned at the sound of a scream just behind me, animal and in pain. The Garda were dragging the gunman up onto the platform against his will. He struggled, kicking his legs out and twisting his body this way and that.

He could not have been more than fourteen. He reminded me too much of the boys in my village, of my brothers when we were young, face dirt-smudged, cheeks hollowed from hunger. He didn't even have his daan, I thought again. If it had been Maram, would he have gotten away and back to his family? Did it matter? I'd had a choice between him and Maram. His life or hers, and I'd chosen hers.

I'd chosen her.

"Maram," Nadine said, and urged me toward the steps, but I resisted.

The Garda forced the boy to his knees, and I realized what they meant to do. His hands were behind his back, his face hard as he stared at the ground. The Garda pulled out a sidearm and aimed for the back of his head. I'd known and I'd done this and still alarm roared through me, as loud as the gunfire still ringing in my ears. I twisted in Nadine's arms before I could think better of it, my heart beating so hard I could feel the blood drumming in my veins, and came between the boy and the Garda.

I knew no one saw me, whoever I was now, they saw Maram. And they couldn't harm her. She'd been named inheritor of the realm, future queen. They'd all kneeled and witnessed it.

"Your—Your Highness," the Garda stammered. "What are you doing?"

"You can't kill him," I said.

"But Your Highness—"

"Are you trying to start a riot?" I asked. My voice didn't shake, and I managed, somehow, to channel the strongest part of Maram inside me. Aloof and haughty, with a lifted chin and a calm demeanor. I remembered all too clearly the cost of interfering with the Vath and their business. But I was one of them, today. I ruled over them. "He's just a boy. Think of what will happen if you kill him here."

He hesitated, but then to my relief he tucked away his firearm and gestured to two of the other Garda.

"Take him in," he said just as Nadine caught me by the arm and pulled me off the stage. The last thing I saw was Maram's future throne, shattered to pieces, its beauty riddled by holes standing a strange sort of witness as the Garda shoved the boy toward a prison transport.

35

A droid brought me to the glass-domed aviary where I had taken some of my first lessons in the Ziyaana. Roosting in the trees above was the roc, feathers fluffed up, warbling to itself softly. I was led beyond the places I was familiar with, to an alcove thick with vegetation. There Maram stood, alone, cloaked in a severe black qaftan, without ornament except for the royal seal she'd asked me to decipher hanging from her neck.

She didn't look up when I arrived, nor when I sank to my knees. For long moments, we remained still, master and servant, future queen and current subject.

"Tell me," she said at last, her voice even, "that it was simply bad luck on your part that had you standing in for me today. Tell me you had no prior knowledge of the attempt on my life."

I lifted my eyes from the floor just as she looked away from the fountain. I knew what she would see in my face—grief, loss, but most importantly, the truth. I could deny it all I wanted, but Maram wouldn't believe me. She'd lived her life in fear of her sister usurping her and now I had done—or seemed to do—just the same.

I rose to my feet slowly. "I never meant . . ." I began.

"To hurt me?" She scoffed. "Don't lie. It's beneath you. It's all anyone has ever done, my whole life. Lied to me, used me for their own aims. Until . . ." She stopped and looked at me, furious at herself for letting the word slip. Her hands shook, bunched up in the folds of her gown, white knuckled with rage.

She was not angry that someone had tried to kill her, I realized with a start. She was angry that I'd known, that I hadn't confided in her, that I'd manipulated her. She was angry at everything it implied. I had secured her trust, I had befriended her and joked with her and cooked for her. I had offered to take her place in engagements and advice when she was sad and confused.

But it was all a lie. In her eyes, I was a serpent who'd stolen into her heart and then attacked when her defenses were lowest.

"I—" she began, her voice breaking on the word. She shook her head and stiffened her jaw, as if that would rid her of her hesitance.

"Please, let me explain," I tried again.

"Nothing you say will fix this," she said. "Nothing. You have shown yourself to be like everyone else around me."

I flinched as she spoke. I'd plotted against her in the beginning, knowing that any success I had—the rebels had—would end in her failure. Our aim from the beginning had been to disinherit her, to dismantle the Vath, to run them out of our system. Did it matter if my opinions had changed, even if only about

Maram? That I truly cared for her, that I saw her as a sister? That I'd risked my life for hers? Would any of that matter to her?

It had to. Didn't it?

I reached out to her, and watched her flinch from me as I had from her.

"Whatever you might think," I said at last, "I was sincere."

"A viper is never sincere," she spat.

Anguish caught fire in me, and I stepped back, nearly a perfect mirror of her, my hands fisted in my skirt.

"Please, Maram," I tried again. "I took your place and risked my life for you. You know that."

I watched her turn that over in her mind. She knew I was right—that whatever else she might think of me, that whatever had come before it, I had protected her today as sisters did. I was her friend and I knew she wanted that to be true. She didn't want to go back to the way things were any more than I did, and if I could just make her see—

"I told you not to converse with her without a guard present, Your Highness," Nadine said, sweeping into the garden. She laid a pale, ringed hand on Maram's shoulder. "She saved a rebel, a person hired to kill you. Andalaans—and this one in particular—are untrustworthy to the core—what might have happened if she attacked you?"

I knew it was my fatigue and lingering horror that made it seem as though the hand on Maram's shoulder were threatening, as if at any moment she might wrap her fingers around Maram's throat. Maram looked up at the stewardess, her eyes wide, nearly pleading.

Please, I thought, understand who the viper is.

The hesitation disappeared bit by bit from her face, the wide-eyed shock and horror was shuttered away. Nadine's smile spread just a little, became just a bit sharper. I watched as Maram methodically closed her heart, as her face smoothed and turned to stone. When she looked at me, the girl I'd come to know and care for was gone. In her place was the Imperial Heir I'd met months ago, rigid, furious, and isolated.

"She behaved in a manner I never would have," Maram said, not looking at me as she spoke.

I held my breath, terrified of what she would say next. So far, Nadine knew only what she'd seen at the coronation. Would Maram reveal what else she knew to Nadine? Would she tell her I was a rebel?

"Confine her to her quarters. She is not to leave that wing. Ever," she said, turning away from me. "And punish her as you see fit."

Nadine inclined her head. "I serve at the will and pleasure of Your Highness."

"Maram!" I cried out, but she was already walking away.

Nadine's smile bloomed into something fouler as she signaled to her droids. I was forced back down to my knees, with my hands behind my back. Maram had disappeared into the greenery of the aviary. I had neglected my duty to the rebels to *save her*—how could she not see that? Whatever other loyalties I had, I'd protected her.

"Please," I tried a second time. "Maram!"

But my cries were swallowed up by the foliage and cut short by the angry shriek of the roc as it launched itself into flight.

Back in my rooms, I wore myself out pacing, waiting for Nadine to return and enact whatever punishment she *saw fit*. Fear at what would slow her approach preyed on my mind. Would she bring the roc into the courtyard again? Or was I to suffer some new Vathek form of punishment I hadn't imagined? I had survived the fires of my first week in the Ziyaana. I knew I had the strength to survive nearly anything. And yet, I was afraid and could do nothing to quell that fear. I found the poetry Husnain had gifted to me on my majority night, but even its evocations of peace and endurance could not calm my heart. Every platitude sounded hollow.

How had I failed so thoroughly? I'd condemned a rebel to death. I'd lost Maram's trust. I had likely doomed the rebellion.

Eventually I took a seat, where I fell asleep. The sitting room was dark when I jerked awake, and found Nadine standing over me. She looked like a phantom, with her silver hair gleaming in the dark, and her black gown melting into the shadow. She was as impassive as I'd ever seen her, and I could not fight the wave of fear that swept through me, hot and nauseating.

"Get up, girl," she said. Her voice cracked through the air like a whip. "What was the single command I gave you when you first arrived?"

"To be Maram," I said, my throat tight.

"Is there something in your breeding that makes all you Andalaans so stupid?" she hissed at me.

I couldn't stop myself from shrinking from her.

"You will look at me when I speak to you," she said.

When I looked up at her, her face was twisted into a sneer. But it was her eyes that terrified me, flinty and calculating, as hard as they'd been the night we met. I'd gotten used to seeing her approval, not the undiscriminating hate practiced by the Vath. She made a noise in her throat, as if disgusted, and threw a cloak at me.

I had experienced Nadine's hatred, which to me seemed a far

worse thing. My kidnapping had been her doing. All her actions were borne not out of the circumstances of her birth and how she had been raised, like Maram, but simply because she believed she was better than me. She had no reason to hate me—I had done nothing to her. And yet, as I put the cloak on with shaking hands, I could feel her revulsion radiating off her in waves.

"Put that on and follow me."

The halls were empty so late at night, lit by flickering sconces. Every shadow seemed to hide a ghost, and more than once I imagined an eerie, pale face disappearing around a corner just ahead of us. Nadine never reacted, but I clutched my cloak tighter around me, and my breath quickened behind my veil. The droids who lined the halls like so many corpses jerked awake at our footsteps. Their eyes spun, widening to take in the little light we provided, and their heads moved, following us as we passed them by.

We descended into the underground rotunda together and then emerged into a dark, empty room with an enormous screen at the far end. For a moment, I couldn't believe my eyes. My mother looked out at me, her face blown up over a holoscreen, larger than life—but they were the same eyes, the same wrinkles, the hard mouth. I hadn't seen her face in months, and the sight of her nearly made me burst into tears.

My heart jumped, and I walked forward, one hand out-stretched.

"This," Nadine said, "is a live feed."

And then the image pulled out.

My mother and father and two brothers.

Husnain, I thought. Alive and unharmed from the night in the kasbah. My joy died as quickly as it came.

All four of them were on their knees, with the Imperial Garda behind them. Both of my brothers had taken beatings to their faces—Aziz with a split lip, and Husnain with a cut over his brow and an eye that was swollen shut.

My throat closed up. I'd wondered what new form of punishment Nadine would devise for me. But there was no need to devise a new method when a tried one would do just as well. Take the family of a dissident and hurt them until the dissident broke or the family died. Whichever came first. I couldn't move from where I stood.

"I am loathe to strike you. I fear I would not stop and then your injuries would be beyond repair." Nadine said from behind me. "But I have no need of a family from a backwater moon that can barely farm enough to keep themselves alive. A family that you, however, love and cherish."

I couldn't look away from the image on the screen. I'd dreamt of them, prayed for them—but I'd never imagined that this would be how I saw them again.

There was a beat of silence, then Nadine said, "The woman."

One of the Garda moved on screen, and slammed the butt of his gun against the back of her head. My mother was silent, though her face contorted into a grimace. I cried out, and rushed forward, one hand outstretched, as though I could catch her.

"The younger boy," Nadine said.

I had forgotten the most important lesson I'd learned in the Ziyaana: there was no end to fear. You could not become hard enough to escape it. Terror swept through me as one of the Garda pulled out a knife. The ground seemed to tilt underneath me. It was an image straight from my nightmares, so much worse than anything that had come before. Husnain.

"Please!" I said.

I hated myself in that moment. Hated my voice, hated my

shaking, hated that I could still be victim to Nadine's cruelty, even after everything I'd survived. "Whatever you want—"

Her lip curled. "You know what I want, girl."

The knife pressed against my brother's throat.

"I will never do anything like that again," I said, frantic as the knife pressed and a drop of blood welled up. "I know—I know the cost. Never. I swear it."

The knife continued to press and my heart beat frantically, choking up my lungs. "Please! I swear on my brother's life."

"Release him," she said derisively, and the knife left my brother's throat.

I collapsed to my knees, breathing hard. My brother couldn't see me. None of my family could. But my mother made a choked sound when the Garda moved away, a sound I echoed. I reached out for the screen. My hands were shaking.

Nadine walked around me, and caught me by the chin.

"Remember," she said, voice harsh, "what it is I hold over you. You have many family members and there are many, many ways to inflict pain. Understand?"

"Yes," I choked out. "Yes, my lady."

She released me with a snarl of disgust.

"You may remain here until I feel like looking at you again," she said.

After a moment, I heard the door groan shut.

There was no window in the room, nowhere to look but at the screen before me. Just as I grew used to the horror of that last frozen image of my family, it all started again—they'd recorded it, I realized. They were playing it back for me to watch, again and again. I measured the time by the start of the recording— my family, sitting down to dinner. The door being kicked down. Aziz and then my mother being hit. I could not forget the sounds.

I could not breathe through the sounds. Over and over, there was the sound of flesh being struck and then a voice crying out. It all blurred together.

At the end, they were alive. At the end, the Garda marched out, and my mother rose, swaying, to her feet, and cried out.

"*Where is she?*" she said, and took hold of a Garda's arm. "Where is my daughter?"

She was struck a final time, so hard she fell sideways and her shoulder hit the floor with a resounding *crack*. My family was left to nurse their wounds with more questions unanswered and new fears to entertain in the dark.

Every family lived under constant threat of the Vath. But now my parents and brothers would fear the Vath and what the Vath was doing to me. What new thing had I done to incur their wrath? What horrible things did I suffer, or how badly had I angered them that now they suffered alongside me? My mother had searched for her siblings for years before realizing they were dead—and now she would wonder every night if I were alive or dead. Or if I was suffering something much worse.

I shook myself to exhaustion at the thought of my family living under such terror.

It could have been worse, I told myself.

For whatever reason, Maram had kept my secret. Nadine still believed I was useful, that I was still necessary to ensure Maram's safety. But there was nothing stopping Maram from revealing my secret, from sentencing me and my family to death or worse. And the Vath could always do worse.

My family would always be in danger now. Because I had dared to dream of a world without the Vath. Because I'd dared to put that dream into action.

And the danger would never fade.

36

I sat in the center of my bed, knees pulled to my chest as the light orbs murmured back at me. I spoke so little here that I forgot how they picked up sounds and parroted them back to their listeners. But now they whispered back at me, hushed, tight breathing and hiccupping sobs.

I tried, too, not to think of what would happen to Maram now that Nadine had gotten to her. She trusted so few people to begin with, and now—the fragile bond I'd formed with her was broken beyond all repair, and all things I'd hoped for gone. The softening of her heart toward Andalaans would reverse. She would flinch back from it, convinced that I was proof of a base, traitorous nature in our race.

The small and great tragedies weighed equally on my heart,

and at last I fell into an uneasy slumber, pulled down into half dreams by the weight of what I'd done.

I don't know how long I slept, but when my eyes opened again the room was still dark. For a moment, I stared into the gloom, confused. The orbs pulsed softly back into light, illuminating Tala's form curved over me, a hand outstretched to my shoulder.

"Tala?" I croaked. "What are you doing here?"

And then the world came rushing back and I sat up, heart beating painfully in my chest.

"What's happened?"

"Amani," Tala repeated. "Idris is here."

I jerked around. "What?" I pushed myself away from her and tried to stand. I was shaking, I realized, as I tried to digest what she'd told me.

How could Idris be here? This wing was sealed off from the rest of the Ziyaana, and to try to breach it—to be here. Dihya, it was such a risk to take. I felt as if I were hallucinating as his shape resolved in the courtyard.

He crossed the space between us then and I let out a soft cry, heartbroken and heavy with grief. My heart gave a painful thud as he leaned down and kissed me. We stood like that, wrapped around one another, for long moments.

At last he raised his head, and laid his forehead against mine. His thumb swept over my cheeks, wiping away tears I hadn't realized were falling.

"What . . . what are you doing here? How did you even know how to find me?"

He smiled just a little. "I took a risk and asked Tala," he said softly. "Then she took a risk and helped me."

I looked over my shoulder at Tala—she hovered in the doorway to my chamber, eyes cast down, fingers twisted in the folds of her skirt.

"You shouldn't have—" I began and cut myself off. The danger now more than ever was beyond imagining—and he knew that. If Nadine or one of her droids came in, if Maram stormed in still furious, it would be not our lives, but the lives of our families.

"I've been so afraid, Amani," he continued. "I knew it was you the moment you stood up for that boy."

I let out a sound, half sob, half laughter, and he smiled.

"I've never known anyone so brave."

"Not brave," I whispered. "Foolish. Filled to the brim with stupidity."

He pressed a kiss to my forehead and combed his fingers through my hair. "What did they do to you, Amani?"

I pressed my face against his shoulder, unwilling to speak. I would begin to cry if I told him, and I wanted this memory untouched. I wanted to be able to hold this close to my heart—his arms around me, his chin in my hair, the steady beat of his heart beneath my ear.

"I'm fine," I said at last. "But Maram is furious."

"Yes," he laughed. "Of course she is."

"No," I said, and pulled away. "She found my family, Idris. My mother and father. My brothers—"

He hushed me softly and pulled me back.

"It was all my fault," I whispered. "I don't know what to do."

There was nothing to do—for either of us. I laid my head against his shoulder and listened to him breathe, hoping it would calm my mind.

"I wish," he said finally, settling his hands on my waist. "I wish we'd been born in a different time."

I smiled. Such a statement seemed almost too fanciful for Idris. "Me too," I replied. "Or that the Vath had never come."

"Would we have met?"

I rested my head on his shoulder and sighed. "Sometimes . . . sometimes Dihya means for two people to love one another, no matter the circumstances."

He chuckled. "But He doesn't engineer it so they will spend their lives together."

I tried to smile. "Trial and tribulation is how poems are penned."

He laughed. "Being with you," he started, and I shut my eyes again. "Amani . . . being with you is like being home. I haven't felt this way since . . . since before."

I'd never felt about anyone how I felt about Idris. When I was with him it seemed that the entire galaxy was open to possibility, that we could do anything, achieve anything, if only we tried.

"Run away with me," he said softly.

I gripped the lapels of his jacket. I wanted to. Dihya only knew how much. But I couldn't—my parents, my brothers. They would always been in danger now. Anything I did the Vath would take out on them. I had to be here. I had to remain here. I had to obey.

My fingers tightened their grip, trying to come to terms with what I knew I had to do.

"You know as well as I do," I said, "that the risk is too great, now. My family—"

"Amani—"

"Please," I said, my voice cracking. "They don't even know why they were beaten—" I wanted to shut my eyes so that I didn't have to see my grief mirrored in his gaze. He looked alone, as alone as I felt standing in front of him. I could see the future unfolding, forlorn and bleak. Idris had become one half of me, and now I had to cut that half away.

"Can you turn your heart away from mine, Amani? Can you cut me away so easily?"

"Never," I said fiercely, and drew his face back to mine. "Never."

"Then run away with me," he whispered. "We'll go anywhere you like. I beg you, Amani—"

"Could you do it?" I asked. "Truly? Abandon your family to the mercy of the Vath?"

He closed his eyes. When he opened them again I knew his answer.

"No," he said hoarsely. "No more than you could abandon yours."

"We wouldn't be who we are if we could run away," I said, pulling his hands into mine. "We wouldn't love each other if we'd been those people."

For a moment, I pictured it. Not running away—but a world without the Vath. A world where I might have crossed paths with Idris, where I could seek patronage in a magistrates salon, where I could write poetry without fear of reprisal, where we might have loved one another freely and happily, without worry or censure.

I drew him down for a kiss, hoping he might taste the dream on my lips, hoping I could keep this memory. His mouth against mine, his hands cradling my head, his broad chest pressed against me.

I pulled away at last and drew in a breath. "We . . . can't take a risk like this again," I made myself say. "We can't risk—I can't risk what will happen to my family. We can't . . . be together . . . anymore."

"Amani—"

"We knew from the beginning," I said softly, looking up at him. "We knew this would happen."

"Is it foolish that I began to hope?" he asked.

"Then we were fools together," I said. "I don't even know how to say goodbye."

"Don't," he said. "We're apart. But nothing will change that I love you."

I kissed him again, then said, "Lamma bada yatathana, hubi jamalah fatanna . . . man li raheem shakwati . . . fil hubi min la'watee."

He laughed. "What . . . ?"

"It's the song I sang," I said, feeling an answering smile on my mouth. "That day in Ouzdad."

"What does it mean?"

"When he first approached me, his beauty seduced my heart," I whispered, pressing my forehead against his. "Who will soothe my complaints, born of suffering a love unfulfilled."

"Amani . . ."

I didn't want to cry again. I didn't want the last time I would let myself touch him as *mine* to be tainted by it, to remember this moment always broken up by my tears.

"I love you," I said, pressing my face against his chest. "I love you."

Walking away from him, it felt as though my feet were weighed by stones. Every step took all my willpower, and it seemed to take an eternity for me to reach the door to my chambers. Don't look back, I told myself even as I turned my head. He stood where I'd left him, his hands at his sides, flanked by pulsing orbs. Dawn's first light was peeking in through the roof, and it haloed him against the doorway.

I forced myself to turn away.

Tala was waiting for me in my chambers. She said nothing as she eased me down onto the bed.

When she laid a hand on my head, I broke. I curled up as

though hunching over my heart might save its pieces from flying out, and I wept. I would likely never see Idris again, and if I did it would be at public functions where we were watched. I would never again know him in private, and the hazy future I'd hoped for had disappeared.

Tala said nothing, but gathered me up in her arms and rocked me slowly. There was nothing she could say to ease what I felt; there was no solace to be had.

This was life under the rule of the Vath.

37

I could hear the bells.

They had rung so loudly and for so long only once before in
my lifetime—on the morning of Maram's birth. Now they rang
five times at the top of every hour, reminding the citizens to re-
joice. Our princess had at long last secured her inheritance. And
though the public was barred from this ceremony, the truth was
still the same: she was now the Imperial Heir.

I sat in my window seat, joyless and without direction. The
gate had not opened in a week, and I had been visited by no one.
No droid or human passed through the courtyard except for Tala.
Even Nadine had not come to gloat over her accomplishment. For
the millionth time I fought against my tears. I slipped between
grieving Idris, Maram, and the boy from the Reach, whose fate
was unknown to me.

I should have tried harder to convince Maram. I should have pleaded more, demanded she listen to me. I should have been able to convince her how much I cared, that I'd willingly risked my life for her. That I'd wanted to secure her inheritance, not steal it. But now—I would never get the chance. Nadine would ensure it. Under her sway and with the crown finally in her grasp, Maram would revert to the girl she'd been when we met. Cruel, thoughtless, hateful.

You are not responsible for the cruelty of your masters.

And yet, in this, I felt I was. If I'd been more careful, more diligent, Maram would have grown, not regressed.

The bells continued to ring.

What ambitious plans I'd had. To mold a queen, to shape her as I'd reshaped myself. Foolishness. I had anticipated none of my enemies, none of hers. And so I'd lost the game before it ever began.

I tried to choke down a sob, unsure what had elicited it. There were mornings I woke up trying to grasp the fading sound of Idris's loutar in vain. Mornings where my chest felt tight, as if there weren't enough room in my lungs for grief and air both. Mornings where I couldn't stop berating myself for loving him, for caring about Maram, for the suffering I'd brought onto my family.

My only triumph was the rebels' success, and even that was marred by the fate of the boy the Garda had captured. How did one go on under the weight of such grief? How had my mother and father?

I tried to breathe.

You do not kneel or bend, I told myself. To anyone. You continue.

I raised my head from the window a moment later. Something had broken through the sound of bells, a sharp, discordant cry.

There was nothing living here, nothing but myself. I prepared to settle back into my seat, but it came again, louder and sharper than before, in the half second between bell peals. This time it was followed by a wing beat, heavy as a thunderclap.

I couldn't be bothered to pull my mantle up my arms and over my shoulders. It whispered as it trailed behind me in the grass, and the orbs echoed the sound, hush-hushing as I made my way through them. The cry came a third time, muffled by the door to the queen's garden. No one had sealed that section away from me, because there was nowhere to go from there. There was the garden, a chamber, and no other way out.

The air inside the garden was cool. The end of summer was upon Walili, and so the cool nights would turn cold, and the days mild. I breathed, and the orbs illuminated a faint puff of steam in the air. Tonight there was no moon, and the black sky that pushed through the cracked dome was oppressive, without stars or light.

A soft warble pulled my eyes from the sky and further into the garden, toward the tree.

"Dihya," I breathed.

Nesting on a branch high in the tree was a tesleet. Its body was black, different from the sky, streaked with darker jewel tones of purple and green. Its crown was white; it sprouted from its head and curved over its body. The tips of it brushed its tail, and looked as if it had dragged it through a pool of liquid gold. It was enormous—nearly as tall as I was—and I couldn't begin to imagine its wingspan.

And from His first creatures He made stars, glowing hot with their fire and warmth.

The air around it seemed to shimmer as if that space were not of this world. As if I were looking through a glass to another realm. It spread its wings, twice as long as its body, and pumped itself off the branch.

I stared, my mouth slack with shock, as it made its way down from the tree with a soft cry, and landed on a bench at its base. It examined me, tilting its head this way and that, its dark eyes intelligent and discerning. My hand trembled as I reached out to it. Its beak was cool to the touch, its feathers glossy and warm. Real, I thought.

I wasn't hallucinating.

It spread its wings again and gave another cry, sharp and piercing, and launched itself into the air.

All may see the stars, but few will see their forebears. And to those whose eyes see golden fire We say heed Us and listen.

It winged its way around the dome, its crown streaming behind it like a banner, and then disappeared through the crack in the dome.

For long moments I stared at the space it disappeared through, mesmerized and in awe.

It had left no feather behind, but then, a feather was not needed.

For We have sent unto you a Sign. See it and take heed.

I could not give up hope. I had been commanded to hold to it, to find a solution to my impossible problem.

No matter what it took, no matter the cost, I could not waver and I could not give in.

Hope might have set fire to all things, but out of those ashes the resistance to the Vath would rise. I would make sure of it.

ACKNOWLEDGMENTS

It truly takes a village, though some days it felt like a small town.

Eternal thanks to my sister Ruqayyah, who insisted I needed to write this book. I wouldn't have taken the leap otherwise. Thank you to my mother, who believed from the time I was small that I would one day be published. To my mother again, and my aunt Naima, both of whom spent many hours on the phone with me lending me their knowledge of the Arabic poetry canon and their aid in walking me through the translations present in this book. To my youngest sister, Tasneem, who gave me unending emotional support and belief. And to my nieces, India, Haniyyah, and Hajr, who have been fans since day one.

This book would not have come together if it weren't for #teamMirage! Endless thank-yous to Annie Stone, who trusted me with this book; Joelle Hobeika and Sara Shandler, who helped ferry it into a complete draft; and Josh Bank, who was always present with a plot solution. Sarah Barley, my dream editor and the best champion an author could ever wish for, I don't know where this book would be without you. Everyone at Flatiron Books: Patricia Cave, Nancy Trypuc, Molly Fonseca, Jordan Forney, Amy Einhorn, Liz Keenan, Keith Hayes, Erin Fitzsimmons, Bill Elis, Anna Gorovoy, Lena Shekhter, Emily Walters, Lauren Hougen, and Liana Krissoff. Thank you so much for loving Amani and Idris as much as I do; I couldn't have asked for a better home for *Mirage*. And of course, team New Leaf: I don't know where I would be without agent extraordinaire Joanna Volpe and Devin Ross.

There is an endless string of people who kept my head straight during this process. Much love and gratitude to the Snek Pit: Anna Prendella, Ronan Sadler, and Isabel Kaufman, thank you for yelling with me daily. To Karen Chau and Alex Cauley, thank you for griping with me about translation and being awesome. To the Salt Mates, Ashley M. and Catherine B., y'all know what you did. To Amanda Shah and Pauline Heejin Kim, who listened to my fears patiently even when I began to repeat myself. To Nur, your biting sarcasm and mathematic wit powered me through so much of the last year. To all my Demons: Aja, Sassy, Meg, Max, Gray, Zach, Noelle, Annie, Tropie, Rawles, Anna, Lys, Rachna, Nicole, Shruthi, Carrie, Jordan, Zara, Michele, Ari, and Riley, thank you for listening and bearing through my all-caps yelling as I worked through this book.

To Veronica Roth and Courtney Summers I owe a special debt of gratitude. The best N7s a friend could ever ask for, and who bore me through post-drafting and read *Mirage* hot off the presses. To Sarah Enni, who's been there from the start: your friendship and support has meant so much. To Tahereh Mafi, whose sage advice has guided me through many a career hurdle. To the Hags: Kody Keplinger, Laurie Devore, Samantha Mabry, Stephanie Kuehn, Stephanie Sinkhorn, Alexis Bass, Debra Driza, Kaitlin Ward, Kara Thomas, Kate Hart, Kristin Halbrook, Lindsey Culli, Amy Lukavics, Maurene Goo, and Michelle Krys, thank you seems like not enough.

And last, but certainly not least, to my dissertation committee: Jesse Oak Taylor, Charles LaPorte, and Juliet Shields. I am eternally indebted to you for your support as I went through exams and drafting, then revising, a novel, and for the intellectual challenges that enriched this book. To Jesse in particular: thank you for saying it's okay to press pause on one thing so that I might pursue another.